1.1.99

The HOLLOW CROWN

THE KINGFOUNTAIN SERIES

BOOKS BY JEFF WHEELER

The Kingfountain Series

The Maid's War (prequel)

The Queen's Poisoner

The Thief's Daughter

The King's Traitor

The Hollow Crown

The Covenant of Muirwood Trilogy

The Banished of Muirwood

The Ciphers of Muirwood

The Void of Muirwood

The Lost Abbey (novella)

The Legends of Muirwood Trilogy

The Wretched of Muirwood

The Blight of Muirwood

The Scourge of Muirwood

Whispers from Mirrowen Trilogy

Fireblood

Dryad-Born

Poisonwell

Landmoor Series

Landmoor

Silverkin

The HOLLOW CROWN

THE KINGFOUNTAIN SERIES

JEFF WHEELER

47NORTH

Text copyright © 2017 by Jeff Wheeler

Published by 47North, Seattle

www.apub.com

Amazon, the Amazon logo, and 47North are trademarks of Amazon.com, Inc., or its affiliates.

ISBN-13: 9781503943964
ISBN-10: 1503943968

Cover design by Shasti O'Leary Soudant

Printed in the United States of America

To Kenzie

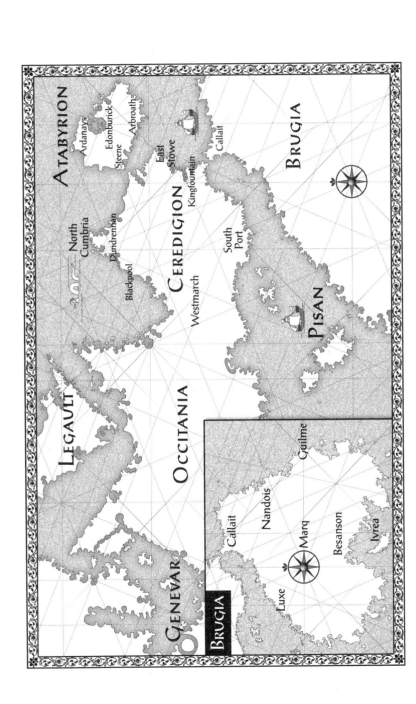

CHARACTERS

MONARCHIES

Ceredigion: Drew (House of Argentine): The young ruler of Ceredigion has been on the throne for eight years since the Fountain chose him to lead his kingdom. With the guidance of his capable counselors, including the Wizr Myrddin and Lord Protector Owen Kiskaddon, he has increased the dominion and influence of the court of Kingfountain.

Brythonica and Westmarch: Owen and Sinia (Houses of Kiskaddon and Montfort): This couple rules two duchies, which combine to be the largest of the realm. They rule from Ploemeur and have one child, a daughter named Tryneowy Kiskaddon, who goes by the nickname Trynne. After experiencing the anguish of a stillborn child, they are expecting another baby.

North Cumbria and Atabyrion: Iago IV (House of Llewellyn): Atabyrion continues to be the chief ally of Ceredigion. Iago pays homage to King Drew for the rights of North Cumbria and has played a strong military role in all of the larger kingdom's conflicts. Iago and Evie have four children, the eldest being their daughter Genevieve, whom many expect to be the future queen of Ceredigion. Their second oldest, Iago Fallon, is the heir apparent and was sent to Ploemeur under wardship to be trained by Lord Owen.

Occitania: Chatriyon IX (House of Vertus): Occitania is now a tributary duchy of Ceredigion, ruled by the boy duke Chatriyon under the guidance of his mother, Queen Dowager Elyse. The treaty of peace signed two years previously has brought a much-needed cessation to hostilities between the opposing realms, allowing both realms to unite under the banner of the Argentines.

Brugia: Maxwell (House of Asturias): Through an alliance with Legault, Duke Maxwell has fomented intrigue after intrigue in an attempt to discredit and undermine Ceredigion. His realm is the last of the regions once held by King Andrew, the ancient ruler of Kingfountain, that has not sworn fealty to King Drew. His attempts to assassinate the young king have all been prevented. The Espion has reported that Brugia is gathering together an army of mercenaries. A reckoning between the two rulers seems inevitable. Maxwell has a single heir, the young boy Elwis.

LORDS OF CEREDIGION

Owen Kiskaddon: Duke of Westmarch and Brythonica, Lord Protector of Ceredigion

Iago Llewellyn: Duke of North Cumbria

Halldur Ramey: Duke of East Stowe

FitzHugh Lovel: Duke of Southport

Lord Kevan Amrein: Lord Chancellor of Ceredigion, master of the Espion

Severn Argentine: Duke of Glosstyr

PROLOGUE

The Fall of Callait

Trynne stared fixedly at the Wizr board, sensing her father was about to defeat her but unsure of how. She glanced up from the beautiful pieces and saw his smug smile, which made her even more determined to prevent it. Her hand was poised over a knight, her favorite piece, but wouldn't Father expect her to use her favorite? The Wizr set was a gift he had received from the old king Severn when her father was a child hostage at Kingfountain. Owen had been trained in the game by Ankarette Tryneowy, Trynne's namesake and the woman who had saved her father's life when he was a child. She loved hearing stories about her father's past. She never grew tired of it.

She *hated* losing Wizr.

"I swear, Trynne," Fallon said with an exaggerated yawn, "if it takes you any longer to move, the pieces will actually grow moss." He was only three years older than her, but he acted as if he were a man grown. "Just move there and get it over with," he added, pointing to one of the squares.

"Did I ask for your counsel, Fallon?" she said in frustration. She began grinding her teeth. "You can't beat Father either."

"But it's taking so *long*." Fallon sighed melodramatically. "Let's go down to the city for a pie."

"You just ate," Trynne said, turning her gaze to him. The boy had inherited a full dose of his parents' impetuosity, a roguish grin, and a twinkle in his gray-green eyes that she found fascinating—not that she would ever say so out loud. Their families had been friends for longer than she could remember. Her father and his mother had once intended to marry, but circumstances had thwarted their union. They remained close friends. Fallon had been sent to live with the Kiskaddons for several years so he could learn the skills of leadership and the ways of other lands—knowledge he would need before inheriting his titles.

"The sooner you move, the sooner Lord Owen will *beat* you. Then we can go somewhere more interesting," he quipped.

"I'm not done with the game yet," she said stubbornly. She enjoyed roaming Ploemeur with Fallon, but she also hated letting her father win Wizr without working for it. "Go fetch a pie, then. I don't care."

Fallon sighed and raked his fingers through his thick dark hair. He blew out his cheeks and started pacing again, giving her one of his impatient looks that said *Hurry up, Trynne.* Well, let him fuss. She didn't want to be rushed. At seven years old, she could defeat almost everyone in the palace at Wizr except her own parents and the Wizr master they had hired to teach her. She pressed herself every day to get better, secretly hoping not just to defeat her father, but also to feel evidence that she was Fountain-blessed herself. Both of her parents had the gift, after all. Her father was a knight in service to King Drew, and her mother was one of two Wizrs who also served King Drew. Trynne hungered to follow in her father's footsteps.

Of all the pieces on the Wizr board, it was the knight that intrigued her the most. Even though it was not the most powerful piece, it was the most capable of defeating the Wizr piece. Its hooklike pattern of movement allowed it to get places other pieces could not, and it could be used in sneak attacks. She loved the look of the piece so much that she would have preferred a horse's head sigil to her father's badge, the heads of three antlered bucks, or her mother's, the Raven.

Suddenly, everything snapped into place in her mind, and Trynne recognized the move her father was about to make. She blinked in surprise. Why hadn't she seen it before? She suddenly moved her hand away from the knight and then countered his upcoming move with her deconeus. Her eyes flashed with triumph as she looked up at him.

"Well done, Trynne," he said approvingly. He was very patient with her, even though he was an inordinately busy man. His duties often called him away to Kingfountain or other portions of the expanding realm. He was the king's most trusted emissary, and Trynne admired him for the way he honored that trust.

"That means this is going to take even longer, doesn't it?" Fallon said, depressed.

"I'm afraid so," Owen replied with an honest chuckle. "Unless you want to forfeit now?"

"Never," Trynne said obstinately. "Go on and get your pie, Fallon. We'll probably be done by the time you get back to the castle."

He wore a dagger on his belt—he was ten after all—and closed his fist around it. "Do you want me to bring you one, Trynne?"

"Blueberry," she answered, not taking her eyes off the board. She was calculating all the possible moves her father might make.

"I don't like blueberries," he said with a sniff.

"Get whatever berry you want, then," she chided, watching eagerly to see what her father would do next.

"I like apples," he said.

"They have apple tarts at Madame Fisk's," she said absently.

"Where is that?"

"Two streets past Grenuin," she answered. She could walk Ploemeur blindfolded without losing her way.

"You wanted raspberry, right?"

"Fallon!" Trynne sighed with exasperation.

"He's just goading you," Owen said with a laugh. They could both hear Fallon chuckle as he sauntered away. Her father's next move countered her threat with one of his own. She was about to respond quickly, but she paused again, tapping her finger on her lips, trying to see if there was another way. Her father was always adept at finding solutions no one else would consider—a quality she wished to share.

Not long afterward, Trynne's mother, Sinia, came into the solar with a guest. Trynne glanced up and recognized the newcomer as Lord Amrein, master of the Espion. The game was halted immediately. Trynne's eyes shot to the little white patch amidst her father's dark hair, which she adored. It was the mark he had earned when Ankarette saved his life all those years ago.

"That you are even here does not bode well, Kevan," Owen said simply as he rose from the stuffed chair opposite Trynne. His frown deepened the wrinkles around his eyes; he expected bad news. "I take it that Brugia has besieged Callait at long last."

The master of the Espion smiled and shook his head. "It never ceases to amaze me how you know things before you've been told. Am I to assume that Lady Sinia had a vision?" He glanced at Trynne's mother expectantly.

Sinia nodded, her gaze guarded and thoughtful. "The king sent you to bring Owen to Kingfountain."

"Indeed, my lady. The matter is most urgent. King Maxwell has hit Callait with his largest force and blockaded the city with his fleet."

"That's bold of him," Owen said flatly. He sounded neither surprised nor worried. Trynne knew that no man could best her father in battle. There was no doubt of what the outcome would be.

"Bold, stupid, call it what you will," the Espion master said with a shrug. "The king would like you to advise him. I came by boat, which is the fastest transportation *I* can muster, but with your lady's help, you can be at Kingfountain this evening."

Owen glanced at his wife a moment. Her hand covered her swollen belly protectively. The two exchanged a glance that was private and serious. Trynne didn't understand it, but she was excited by the prospect of war. Her father had managed to subdue all of King Drew's enemies through his tactics and cleverness. Now, it would seem that it was King Maxwell's turn to fall into line.

"Can I come with you, Father?" Trynne pleaded. She loved visiting Kingfountain.

He glanced down at her, his raised eyebrows showing he was surprised by her question, and perhaps a little annoyed. "No, Trynne. You're only seven. You need to stay in Ploemeur."

She understood why she had to stay, but it frustrated her. There was an ancient magic that held the Deep Fathoms at bay and kept them from sweeping over the duchy of Brythonica. The invocations needed to be renewed regularly, and by someone from Trynne's lineage. Since Sinia and Owen didn't know how long they'd be away, Trynne would have to stay behind to manage the defenses of the borders of Brythonica. It was an important job, but she chafed at the thought of being trapped in Ploemeur.

Trynne hungered to see the rest of the world, which she had only learned about by stories from her father. She wanted to see the giant waterfalls of Dundrennan. She longed to visit Fallon's homeland, Atabyrion, and visit Wizr Falls. She'd been to Pree when the treaty was signed, but she could remember only snatches of the journey. Her mother's magic as a Wizr made it possible to cross great distances. But that same magic bound her to Ploemeur so she could keep the boundaries that had been set by ancient Wizrs long dead and gone.

The adults were talking again, not including her, and Trynne wished she had gone with Fallon to fetch treats from the city. But while she wouldn't be able to finish the game anyway, at least she'd be able to see her parents off. Within the hour, she followed them to the bubbling fountain inside the chapel of the palace. From that fountain, Sinia could transport them to any of the major fountains along the linked paths binding the kingdoms' cities together. She listened in on their adult conversation for a while, grew bored, and then walked around the edge of the fountain, running her hand along the smooth stone. There were flecks of wetness from the constant splashes of the waters. Her father had donned his hauberk and war tunic. He'd strapped his sword over both, and she noticed the raven-marked scabbard that was so special to him. A relic of the Fountain, it healed the wearer, and her father claimed it had saved his life more than once. She was relieved to see him wearing it. Her parents clasped hands and gestured for her to come.

"Try not to argue too much with Fallon," Sinia said gently.

"I'll try, but he really can be difficult sometimes," she said sincerely, making both of her parents laugh for reasons she couldn't understand.

Her father ran his fingers through her dark, curly hair. Trynne liked her hair color, even though its mouse-brown tint wasn't as fashionable as her mother's golden locks. She rarely fussed over her hair as girls were supposed to, but she privately enjoyed the way it linked her to the Kiskaddons. For while the people of Ploemeur doted on her, which she enjoyed, it was her father's approval she sought most. He teased some of her curls, then knelt down and kissed her cheek. She kissed his cheek in return, the stubble tickling her lips.

"I'll miss you, Papa," she said, squeezing him tightly. Her mother bent more awkwardly with her swollen abdomen, and pressed a kiss into her hair.

"Will you stay long, Maman?" Trynne asked, hugging her in return.

"I don't think so. You will be in charge while we are gone."

Trynne beamed. It was disappointing they were leaving without her, but it was heartening to know they trusted her. A mist rose up from the water, and when it receded, they both were gone.

Trynne went back to the solar to search for Fallon, but he wasn't back yet. Lord Amrein had taken a seat at the table and was savoring a meal one of the servants had brought him in her absence. She studied the Wizr board for a while, thought about a move that would counter her father's, and then shifted the piece. They'd have to wait until he returned to continue the game.

Feeling restless, she went back to her room to read while awaiting word of Fallon's return. The corridor was empty and had a strange, lonely feel to it, like the loss of candles in a dimly lit room. It was because her parents were both gone. She brushed her hand along the wainscoting, trying to decide on which book she wanted to read. It was nearly sunset and the servants were starting to light the torches set in the wall sconces.

She opened the handle to her room and walked inside. Her enormous bed with the large wooden posts draped with silky cream-colored curtains greeted her. There was a fire in the hearth, and she savored its warmth as she walked to the balcony ledge and stared down at Ploemeur, wondering where Fallon was at that moment.

A strange, queer feeling bubbled up inside her chest. Wind from outside tousled her hair, bringing in the beautiful scent of flowers from the planter box beneath her window. It was a long way down the cliffside. A shudder went through her. Something felt . . . wrong.

Trynne listened carefully, trying to understand what she was feeling. The dread made her want to move away from the window, and so she did. There was a shuddering feeling in her heart, a pulsing, agitated sensation that made her fretful and worried. What was this feeling? She stared at the room and saw the thickening shadows of evening. She was alone, but it didn't *feel* like she was alone. Trynne took a few steps toward the door, searching one way and then another. Was someone hiding in there?

With both of her parents gone, a slice of fear ran down her stomach to her toes. Her parents had gone to Kingfountain together before. Yes, it did feel awkward and strange when they left without her, but it had never felt like this before. It was probably her imagination, but she couldn't shake the sensation that she was in danger.

Trynne decided to go back to the solar, feeling a little silly and foolish, but walking helped calm her heart. She was acting, moving. Was this sensation what the Fountain magic felt like?

That was the last thought she had before pain exploded blindingly on her face.

♦   ♦   ♦

When Trynne awoke, there were faces hovering over her. She was lying on her bed, head propped up with pillows, and her nose and her upper lip were throbbing and swollen. After blinking a few times, she could see better.

There was Lord Amrein, looking sick with worry, and Fallon, watching her with scrunched-up eyebrows and his mouth twisted into a wince. The palace surgeon was waving something sharp-scented under her nose. She jerked her head, and her nose ached even more. Trynne's maid, Yvette, was wringing her hands.

"Tryneowy?" the surgeon asked. "Can you hear me?"

"Of course I can," Trynne said, but her voice sounded wrong in her ears. Her nose was so swollen and puffy, but when she reached to touch her face, the surgeon caught her hand. "What happened?"

"We were hoping you would tell us," Lord Amrein said gravely. "Who did this to you? Did you fall?"

Trynne blinked. "I don't . . . remember," she said, feeling suddenly nervous. "Are my parents still gone?"

The surgeon nodded. "Yes. They left earlier this evening. Your mother may not be back until morning. You say you can't . . . remember?"

"No," Trynne said, growing more worried by the moment. "It hurts."

"I'm sure it does," he said. "I can give you some herbs for the pain."

Trynne nodded, but the motion made her head hurt even worse. "Did you bring me the pie?" she asked Fallon, smiling broadly. Her mouth felt distorted. "I should have gone with you."

The look on Fallon's face startled her. His eyes were wide with . . . was that fright?

"What's wrong, Fallon?" she asked.

The boy looked at the doctor in obvious confusion. "What's wrong with her?"

"I don't know, lad," the surgeon said.

"What do you mean? It hurts, but I'll be all right," Trynne said. She tried to sit up, but the doctor pushed her back down.

Fallon was still staring at her worriedly. "Your mouth isn't moving. On that side," he said, pointing at the left side of her face.

Her left eye also hurt a lot, and she realized that she hadn't blinked once since awakening.

"Her smile . . . it's gone," Fallon whispered, still pointing.

In that moment, Tryneowy Kiskaddon realized that something truly terrible had happened to her.

♦ ♦ ♦

Life teaches us through contradictions. If you don't get what you want, you whine; if you get what you don't want, you suffer; even when you do indeed get what you want, you grieve because you cannot hold on to it. The mind wants to be free of change, free of pain, free of the obligations of life and of death. But change is law and no amount of pretending will alter that reality. Change is the great teacher. Pethets refuse to be taught.

Myrddin

♦ ♦ ♦

PART I

Wizr

CHAPTER ONE

The Royal Wedding

Trynne stared at herself in the mirror, tortured by what she saw there. No amount of healing, no amount of magic, not even her father's prized scabbard had been able to restore the smile she had lost. In the six years that had passed since that night in Ploemeur, her smile had never fully returned. And she had never felt the loss so keenly as she did on the day of Genevieve Llewellyn's wedding, standing in the dressing room of the beautiful woman who was to become the Queen of Ceredigion that very afternoon.

She did not often gaze at her own reflection. There were no mirrors in her room because she didn't wish for the constant reminder. Staring at herself now, she tried to focus on her other features—the blue-green eyes that were more her mother's, and the chestnut curls that favored her father. Still, there was no denying that at thirteen, she was short, thin as a rail, and decidedly unbeautiful. At least that was how she saw herself.

"Trynne?" Genevieve asked, snapping her attention back to the moment. The queen-to-be's mother, Queen Elysabeth *Victoria* Mortimer Llewellyn—called Lady Evie by the Kiskaddon family—was also standing behind the princess's chair, scrunching up her face at the handful of hair she was working into intricate braids. That critical function would not be trusted to servants, not on such an occasion.

"Yes, my lady?" Trynne asked.

Genevieve smiled prettily at her. "Don't be so formal. We've known each other far too long. You must still call me Genny, even after the coronation." She reached over her shoulder to clasp Trynne's hand. "Your mother isn't coming to the wedding, correct?"

Trynne nodded. "My little brother is still rather sickly," Trynne said, thinking of the coughing six-year-old she'd left behind several days ago. "She didn't want to leave him with our grandparents. If he rests and starts to feel better, she will try to come for the ceremony at Our Lady."

Genevieve smiled again. "I'll not forget the first time I went to Our Lady," she said with a sigh. "I fell in the river and Lord Owen saved my life. I still shudder to think of it." There was a slight tremor at her words, and Trynne could not resist the urge to smile. It was such a natural thing, so normal for most people. Her eyes darted to the mirror again, and she saw the right side of her lips had quirked up, revealing her teeth. But the left side was flat, unresponsive, giving her a mischievous look. Her heart throbbed with anguish at what had been stolen from her.

The Queen of Atabyrion's hands were working feverishly at the braids, but she had glanced up and seen the darkness fall on Trynne's countenance. "I understand from Owen that they never discovered for certain who attacked you," she said with compassion in her voice.

Trynne shook her head. "Everyone believes it was a thief named Dragan. Lord Amrein found a note that had been tucked into his luggage after he'd arrived in Ploemeur. 'A daughter for a daughter' was all it said." She smoothed the beautiful fabric of Genevieve's dress, feeling the ripples of tiny seed pearls and the smooth, elegant brocade. Dragan's own daughter, Etayne, had been the king's poisoner years before. Trynne didn't know all the details, only that the woman had died saving Owen's life.

"And he's your father's sworn enemy," Lady Evie said with a serious tone. "I know the Espion have been hunting him for years. It's difficult finding a man who can become invisible."

"Indeed it is," Trynne said. "We don't know for certain, of course. I never saw anyone, but I felt something was wrong. The Espion and I are good friends now," Trynne said with another half smile.

The queen's eyebrows lifted in curiosity.

"She's accompanied by them day and night," Genevieve explained. "Who is your favorite? I love Clark the best. He's quiet and unassuming, but he's quite funny."

"Funny?" the queen said with a short laugh. "He hardly says two words together."

"Only because you never stop talking, Mother," Genevieve teased.

"Don't be impudent, dearest," said Lady Evie with a laugh. "Even though you will outrank me after today, it doesn't give you liberty to be rude to your mother."

"I would never dream of it," Genevieve said with a laugh.

A question bubbled out of Trynne's mouth before she could stop it. "Do you love him, Genny?"

The princess's smile shone with a radiance too great for words, and her eyes sparkled with warmth and excitement. There was no doubt in the world how the girl felt. Oh, to smile . . .

"I do, Trynne," Genevieve said with a sigh. "And not just because he's a king."

"The most powerful king in all the lands," Lady Evie added wryly.

"He is that *too*," Genevieve said, laughing. "We've known each other since we were children, Trynne. I was half in love with him when I was practically a baby. We didn't rush things, and some people gossiped that he was biding his time for a political match. With Atabyrion already as an ally, he could have looked farther afield. Some whispered that perhaps the Brugian king would sire a daughter, or that Drew could marry another lady from that kingdom."

"Do you know how it happened that he chose you?" Lady Evie asked. "Did you know of Myrddin's role?"

"No," Genevieve said. "That man completely fascinates me. Doesn't he fascinate you as well, Trynne? What did he say, Mother? Tell me if you please."

"If you please, there we go. Much better than a command from Your Highness." Having finished the braiding, the older woman set her hands on her daughter's shoulders. "I heard this from Trynne's father, of course. When the king was almost eighteen, he asked his Wizr and Lord Owen for advice on whom he should marry. He said he knew his heart, but would be guided by their counsel. Not many a young man would take such a risk. But he trusted Lord Owen's knowledge of the foreign courts and the impact his marriage would have. And he knew Myrddin was very wise. He's traveled to other worlds, you know. There are distant realms where water comes gushing from stones. Places where men can fly by only taking a breath. Myrddin has traveled far and has many tales."

"But what did he tell Drew?" Genevieve pressed.

"I was getting to it. Be patient." She smoothed the fabric along her daughter's shoulders. "Myrddin said"—and she changed her voice to match the Wizr's interesting accent—"'Well lad, if you are asking for my advice, I will tell you. You should—'"

Another voice broke in at just that moment, a young man's voice that was also mimicking Myrddin's tone. It was Fallon. "'—marry Tryneowy Kiskaddon, that strange pethet from Brythonica. Bah, you can even call her "my queen" so you won't have to pronounce her awful name! I hate speaking this language. It makes my tongue all itchy.'"

Everyone was shocked by his sudden arrival through one of the Espion doors. He was three years older than Trynne, and it showed. He had sprouted into a man since their younger days, and when she'd first seen him on arriving at Kingfountain, she had almost mistaken him for one of the palace knights. His dark hair and mocking eyes appeared from the doorway, and he was grinning in his dangerous way.

"Iago Fallon Llewellyn!" Lady Evie scolded. "If you are not the rudest child a mother could ask for. How long have you been skulking behind that spy hole?"

He sauntered up to his mother, gripped her shoulders, and then stooped to plant a noisy kiss on her cheek. "Mother, all this fussing and primping is taking ages! Poor Drew is pacing at the sanctuary of Our Lady right now, wondering if his bride will ever show up. Sister, you look uncomfortable in that gown. How hard did they yank on the corset?" He bent down with an exaggerated flourish and kissed Genny on the cheek as well.

Trynne bared her teeth angrily at Fallon as he lifted up and gave her a sly wink. It did nothing to hide the fact that she'd blushed six degrees of scarlet.

"What, no kiss for you, Cousin Trynne?" he said mockingly.

Being with Fallon made her stomach feel akin to a rag being wrung out. He was probably the handsomest man in Atabyrion, a willful flirt, and tended to trample on other people's feelings without care. He deliberately *teased* her about her affliction, even though she'd told him how much it hurt.

"I am *not* your cousin, Fallon," she said.

"Well, it *feels* like it," he said, beginning to wander the room, touching and poking at everything he saw. He lifted a bottle of his sister's perfume, smelled it with an appreciative nod, and then set it down and folded his arms imperiously.

"Sister, you're the ugliest wench I've ever seen," he said with a sad shake of his head. "I don't know what Drew sees in you. But alas, his blindness is your blessing. Can we all come along now? The poor chancellor is fidgeting outside, debating with himself about whether or not he should intrude. They were going to send for Father, but I volunteered.

You should have named me *Farrel* instead of Fallon, Mother. I am rather brave." He puffed out his chest and made a dashing pose.

"They should have named you *Feckless*," Trynne countered, arching one eyebrow.

He gave her a wry look. "It was either Fallon, which means *ruler*, or Fionan, which means—"

"Dung shovel?" Trynne asked, fluttering her lashes.

"You two," Lady Evie said with exasperation. "Why can't there be some civility between you? Not so long ago, you were thick as thieves. Fallon, tell them she's almost done. Trynne, if you'd fetch the crown? I want to make sure it will fit well on this heap of braids."

Trynne went to obey, but Fallon darted impishly to the chest first, which made her anger flash to life. No doubt he planned to hold it over her head or something childish like that. She rushed over to the chest, her mind already conjuring a strategy to outwit him.

As their hands collided over the crown, Trynne stamped on his boot, distracting him with pain, and pulled out the crown first, watching as a look of wounded amusement spread across her adversary's face.

"Trynne," he complained. "I was just going to fetch it for you."

"I'll believe that when pigs fly, Fallon," she countered. Then she handed the crown to Genevieve's mother, who set it gently down on her daughter's head. They all stared at the soon-to-be queen's reflection in the mirror. Instead of opulent jewels, she had chosen a single gold-threaded necklace fixed with seven turquoise gems that Drew had given her for their engagement. The gems were symbolic of the Fountain and had been made by master craftsmen from Genevar.

The crown fit perfectly and Genevieve looked so happy and beautiful it made Trynne's heart ache. She was exactly the sort of woman that a husband would want. She was kind but also quick to laugh; moreover, she invited confidences and made others feel comfortable. While Fallon had inherited a double portion of his parents' impulsiveness, Genevieve's experiences as a child hostage at Kingfountain had marked her differently. She was more sober-minded, much like her husband-to-be.

Fallon gave Trynne a curt look, still limping slightly, and then wrinkled his nose disapprovingly. "It'll do, I suppose," he drawled. "It's probably too late to send for something better."

"Thank you, Fallon. That's the closest you'll come to a compliment," Genny replied with sisterly affection.

He clasped his hands behind his back. "Old king Severn was Fountain-blessed, they say, though he had a sarcastic mind and a barbed tongue. I treasure the thought that it will be *my* gift as well when the Fountain chooses me. It's best to practice early."

His mother sighed and shook her head. A tap landed on the door.

"Come in, we are ready at long last," their mother said. Her eyes suddenly filled with tears and she bent over her daughter and kissed her fiercely.

"The siege has been broken!" Fallon said. He went to the door and opened it with a gallant bow.

It was a strange coincidence that Morwenna Argentine stood there, dressed in black and silver.

Trynne felt a shiver of worry go down her back. Had the girl overheard Fallon's jibe about her father? Morwenna and Trynne were of the same age, both born within the same year, but they didn't know each other and had never spoken. Morwenna was the only child born of the marriage of Severn and Lady Kathryn, King Drew's mother. It made her a possible rival to her brother's throne. She had the looks and coloring of the old king, paired with her mother's beauty. Her hair was black and wavy and lusciously thick, and it was said that her smile could turn a boy's head—if she ever flashed it. She was staring at Genevieve with a look that was difficult to describe. Could it be envy?

"My mother sent me," Morwenna said with a bob of a curtsy. "The rest of the company has assembled in the courtyard of the palace for the escort to Our Lady. Shall I tell them you are ready, my lady?"

Trynne shot a quick glance at Fallon to see how he had reacted to the intrusion, but he was fiddling with flowers in a vase, not deigning to look at the girl at all.

"Yes, please," Genevieve said, some of the brightness fading from her eyes. Morwenna was like a winter's chill. Despite her beauty, coldness seemed to radiate from her eyes and skin like a blizzard. The effect rattled Trynne, who felt the icy tendrils try to wrap around her. The prickle of gooseflesh crept across Genevieve's arms, and the soon-to-be queen unconsciously stroked them.

Trynne felt her own magic prickle in response. Just as she'd hoped as a young girl, Trynne had inherited her parents' magic. The gifts of other Fountain-blessed could not affect her, or those near her, if she repulsed them. But the constraints were the same for her as for everyone with the power. Her reservoirs of magic had to be earned and stored, and she had found playing Wizr to be especially helpful in that regard. That and discussing politics with her father. As she stared at the other girl, Trynne exerted her influence on the room and suddenly the coldness sloughed away. The warmth from the braziers could be felt once again. The strange whispering feeling was silenced.

Morwenna's eyebrows lifted just slightly and her gray eyes settled on Trynne. A small, curious smile stretched on her mouth.

"Thank you for fetching us, Morwenna," Fallon said, starting to march toward the door. "Come along; you're shamefully late, my sister. Come along, *Cousin* Trynne. Mother, can I take your arm and escort you? If I don't, you're likely to prattle on with half the castle staff." He wagged his finger at her.

"You are incorrigible," his mother said affectionately.

"Incorrigible, incomprehensible, infallible, impassible, and incontrovertible as well," he added. "I'm sure you regret making me study so hard instead of spending all my time in the practice yard."

"You forgot *unintelligible*," Trynne muttered.

"Only because I ran out of breath," he shot back. "Really, Trynne. You can be so childish sometimes. But then again, you are only twelve."

His mistake was another deliberate insult, for he *knew* she was thirteen. She wanted to stomp on his foot again, but Genevieve caught her arm and interlocked it with hers. "Ignoring Fallon is difficult, Trynne, but it's the only thing that truly works." She gave her brother a sidelong look.

"Unignorable!" Fallon said with a disarming grin.

"That's not a real word, dear," Lady Evie said as they all proceeded to the door. "And it sounds too much like ignoble." She gave Trynne a look. "I almost named him Iago Farren, which means 'adventurous.' Or Fane, which means 'good-natured.' Those are all Atabyrion names I thought might suit him. We realized soon enough that calling him by his middle name prevented much confusion. Besides, it fits his personality almost *too* well." Then she shook her head. "But he's his father's heir, the future king of Atabyrion or duke of the North. I don't think he's decided yet which one he wants. To be a king or a duke."

"Neither actually," Fallon said, coming up alongside Trynne. "I just want to be a knight and serve my sister and brother-in-law. Being a ruler is boring. Have you seen the table that Myrddin conjured in the great hall?"

Trynne shook her head, wrinkling her brow.

"You won't believe it," he said with an excited laugh. When they reached the doorway, no one acknowledged Morwenna. Trynne met the girl's gaze and saw an unreadable look there. The girl was quiet and cold, but there was a spark in her eyes.

"Inscrutable" was the word that popped into her mind.

The girl was also Fountain-blessed. Like her father.

CHAPTER TWO

Coronation

It was a part of the coronation wedding tradition for the daughters of the high nobles of Ceredigion to hold the train of the new queen as she approached the fountain for the rite. It was a solemn and momentous occasion that had not been performed since Severn's first wife, Lady Nanette, had become queen following his usurpation of the throne, and the shadow of that event hung over the gathering. Trynne felt the tension in the hall as she carried Genevieve's gauzy veil with the other girls.

All the lords of the realm had gathered at Kingfountain for the coronation, including the previous king. Severn's black hair was well silvered, and he looked haggard and in ill health. Lady Kathryn stood by his side, their arms interlinked. For a moment, his stern gaze seemed to narrow on Trynne, and she felt a tremor of fear at having been singled out, only to realize that he was looking past her to his daughter, Morwenna. As they passed the nobles dressed in their finely cut doublets and vests, displaying for all to see the growing wealth and dominion of Ceredigion, Trynne realized her gown was a bit on the simple side. Her father, who smiled at her as they passed, was also simply dressed, though he wore the double badge of his two duchies, the Aurum.

Grand Duke Maxwell of Brugia, who stood near her father, had a sardonic look that rivaled Severn's. It was clear he was not happy being a vassal of Ceredigion—the consequence of a lengthy, arduous war instigated by his ill-conceived siege of Callait, back when Trynne had been injured. The armies of Ceredigion had waged a full-scale assault on Brugia's domain, breaking city after city, disrupting trade with blockades, and grinding down Maxwell's army month after bitter month. Eventually there was nowhere left for Maxwell to run, though he had successfully dragged on the negotiations for his surrender for nearly a year to ensure that his son, Prince Elwis, would rule after him and not be supplanted by one of King Drew's favorites.

Because the procession of the queen was slow and ponderous, Trynne flicked her eyes to the prince. Elwis was a tall and slender young man of eighteen with a very fair complexion and hair so blond it was nearly white. He wore the Brugian style of doublet, very opulent with frilly lace at his wrists and a wide neck ruff that looked silly at Kingfountain but was considered the height of fashion in his realm. It made him look like a strutting peacock, and any semblance of handsomeness he may have possessed was further marred by his discontented frown.

So many of King Drew's nobles are disaffected, Trynne thought sadly. Her father had tamed all of the men instead of destroying them. But they resented him for it. She could feel that seething emotion bubbling beneath their veneer of goodwill at the gathering.

The procession stopped as the hymn the chapel choir was singing reached its culmination. She had stopped on a black tile on the checkered floor, and that felt unlucky, so she shuffled her steps until her slippers were touching a white one. Then she turned her eyes to friendlier faces. Iago and his wife were beaming with love and joy for their daughter, who would become the most powerful woman in all the realms. Standing in the same line, Fallon was looking at her. He winked and then made an exaggeratedly grotesque face—his attempt to make her break countenance. That boy could never be serious, even during such a solemn occasion! She gave him an icy look before shifting her gaze back to the assembled lords. There was Duke Ramey with his balding pate, stifling a yawn on his clenched glove. She also saw Lord Amrein, the king's chancellor and master of the Espion, his eyes darting to the various spies planted throughout the hall acting as guests and bodyguards. He looked very worried, as if he were expecting an archer to suddenly appear.

Trynne felt her father's magic joining the turbulent waters of the fountain. She sensed it like an ever-present feeling of comfort. Her father was one of the most powerful Fountain-blessed in all the kingdoms. The only ones who were stronger in the Fountain were possibly Trynne's mother and the Wizr Myrddin himself.

She caught sight of the Wizr as they began ascending the steps to the fountain. He was a dumpy-looking fellow that looked more like a wandering pilgrim than an all-powerful Wizr. He wore sandals that were chafed and broken and exposed some hairy ankles. His middle was girded with a leather belt, and his dark hair was silvered at the ears and thick and wavy. Myrddin had a prominent nose and a jaw lined with slight stubble. She'd always been fascinated by his crooked walking staff that looked as if it was a massive root that had been wrung and twisted. The top had a mushroom-shaped end. A sword hung from the massive belt spanning his hips. The pommel had the design of an eight-pointed star on it, and the metal was beaten and battered.

Trynne's attention was jarred from the Wizr when the procession came to a stop again. At that time, they were to leave Genevieve. If it had been left up to Trynne, they would have just dropped the train in a heap, but the ladies of court were particularly attuned to such details, so she helped the others neatly arrange the gauzy fabric. Morwenna caught her eye and offered a private smile before leaving the steps and joining her parents amidst the crowd.

With everything in order, Trynne joined her father's side and reached for his hand. Against her best intentions, she glanced at Fallon, who was wagging his eyebrows at her and giving her a mocking smile. It made her want to stomp on his *other* foot.

The anthem finished with a swell of voices, instruments, and pitch that made the vaulted ceiling ring. Trynne tried not to fidget, but she was ready for the ceremony to be finished. She was eager to get back to the palace to see the new table in the throne room.

As the music calmed, the deconeus began to speak in a sonorous voice that made Trynne want to writhe in frustration. But then she caught sight of Myrddin again, and it put her in mind of how well Fallon had mimicked the Wizr's voice. Myrddin did have an odd manner of speech; his Ceredigic was heavily accented, and he often spouted off words and phrases that no one else understood. She'd asked her father if he was Genevese because he was so fat. Owen had told her many stories about Dominic Mancini, and she'd come to associate Myrddin with the wily spy in her imagination. Her father had laughed at that and said that Myrddin was from another world. In that other world, he was called a Wayfarer, not a Wizr. He'd also whispered to her that despite his ill-looking aspect, he was more than capable with his twisted staff and sword. Anyone who could handle weapons earned Trynne's respect. She knew that he was, miraculously, the same Wizr who'd served the original King Andrew, the ruler who had brought all the kingdoms together. His return had helped Drew achieve the same accomplishment.

Growing increasingly bored with the ceremony, Trynne glanced across the various faces again, deliberately avoiding Fallon. Her eyes settled on Morwenna. What was the other girl thinking at that moment? Did she crave the crown for herself? Trynne imagined that her life had not been easy. Her father, who had been king, was relegated to the office of duke. No one willingly gave up power, but the girl could have no memory of her father's previous glory. Morwenna had not been raised at court and had seldom traveled outside of Glosstyr. Despite Morwenna's renowned beauty, which stirred Trynne's jealousy, Trynne had heard her name mentioned before in a teasing way. Some claimed she'd been born out of Lady Kathryn's pity for the crushed king. Others argued Severn had used his twisted power with the Fountain to persuade Morwenna's mother to love him—and the girl would never have existed if he hadn't committed that grave wrong. Having been teased herself because of her face, Trynne felt some sympathy for Morwenna.

A sudden shout of acclaim startled Trynne, and she realized she had daydreamed her way through most of the ceremony. Finally, it was over, and the city of Kingfountain would be celebrating for days. The streets had been decorated, and the people were anxious to rejoice in their new queen. Genevieve was popular, and little girls often sighed over the romantic elements of her match with King Drew. It was a story for the ages, a repetition of the legends of the past. Trynne's father had often said that time came around over and over, like a waterwheel dipping into a river. There were roles people were destined to play. In some cases, as in Drew's and Genevieve's, even the names were the same.

"How did you like it, Trynne?" her father asked, bending lower so she could hear him over the tumult.

Trynne watched as King Drew kissed his bride and then held up her hand to display the glittering coronation ring. The king was a handsome man but not arrogant. His tunic bore the crest of his Argentine ancestors, the Sun and Rose, the standard of his grandfather, the beloved King Eredur. Drew's hair was a golden color, having darkened with age to the color of wheat. The legendary sword Firebos was belted to his waist, showing he bore the authority of the kings of the past.

"I'm glad it's over," Trynne said as an aside. "We were standing here so long my feet hurt."

Owen laughed and squeezed her hand. "To be honest, I'll be grateful when this is over as well. I wish your mother were here to transport us back home instantly."

"Fallon said that Myrddin conjured something in the throne room?"

"It's a table," Owen replied. They would need to start the procession back to the palace soon. "Unlike any you've ever seen."

"Tell me!" she insisted.

"You'll see it soon enough. Patience, Tryneowy."

She liked it when he used her full name. It reminded her of another question she'd been bursting to ask—one that had only gone half answered earlier. "Why did King Drew choose Genevieve? If he'd married one of the ladies of Brugia, it would have stopped the war earlier."

Her father's mouth quirked with amusement. "You *love* discussing politics, Daughter. Probably too much."

"I *am* your daughter, Father," she replied sweetly. "He's truly in love with her, isn't he? I know she loves him."

Owen nodded simply. He was staring at the couple, a strange look coming over his face. "When he asked Myrddin and me for advice on whom to marry, do you know what that shrewd old Wizr said?"

Trynne shook her head no, but gave him an eager look. At last she would hear the end of the story Fallon had interrupted.

"He said, 'Well, that depends, lad.'" Owen didn't mimic the Wizr's voice like others had. He had great respect for the eccentric wanderer. They were often in counsel together for hours, just the two of them. "'There are many wealthy, prosperous lasses you could marry who would bring you certain advantages.' Trynne, I've never forgotten what he said next. 'It will be no greater miracle that brings us into another world to live forever with our dearest friends than that which has brought us into this one to live a lifetime with them.'" Trynne felt a shiver go down her spine at the words. Her father's voice was low and earnest and hopeful. He smiled at her. "Can you feel the Fountain shuddering at his words? I can." He smiled and then stroked her locks. "So then Myrddin asked the king if there was a girl who was already his dearest friend." Owen's eyes glimmered. "And the king said yes, it was Genevieve Llewellyn of Atabyrion. Then Myrddin answered with a shrug, 'It seems to me that you've chosen well on your own.' Then he asked after Liona's honeycakes!"

Trynne laughed out loud. "He did? I *love* Liona's honeycakes, ever since you first took me to the palace kitchen at Kingfountain!"

Owen proffered his arm. "I'm sure we'll find some at the palace. And you'll get to see the new table."

"I'm excited to see it," she said, practically bouncing on her feet in excitement. "Can I stay at Kingfountain while you're here? I don't want to go back to Ploemeur yet. I love it here."

Owen pursed his lips. "I'll discuss that with your mother."

"Please, Father? There is so much happening at court right now. Grand Duke Maxwell looks as if he's bitten into a lemon. Elvis looks like he's drunk vinegar. Duke Severn isn't very happy with you either."

"These are *my* concerns, Trynne," he said, patting her arm. "And there are even more you *don't* know about yet."

"Like what?"

"Now is not the time. Lord Amrein told me that some Genevese ships returned recently from the East. There's a civil war going on in Chandigarl."

"I've not even heard of that place," Trynne said, scrunching up her nose in embarrassment.

"It's one of the massive eastern kingdoms far from our borders. They invented the game of Wizr over there. Something to keep an eye on." Together they started down the steps to join the procession.

There was a tug on Trynne's arm, and suddenly Fallon was at her other side. He was easily as tall as her father, which she detested because she was short, like her mother.

"What do you want?" she said scornfully. She shot a glance at her father. "He tried to get me to laugh by making faces at me."

"No, I was trying to make you *smile*," Fallon said. He put one arm around her shoulders in a sideways sort of hug. "You looked so serious."

"And smiling would have helped?" she asked with growing anger. She still hadn't forgiven him for his rude remarks from earlier.

"I like your smile, *Cousin*!" he said, and then he made an exaggeratedly serious look that was mocking her on another level.

"Fallon, you are—!" she started, nearly grinding her teeth with fury, but he barked out a laugh and interrupted.

"Actually, I came to *apologize* for my rudeness earlier. I'm a jack and I know it. I can't help myself. You just take yourself too seriously, Trynne. I consider it my duty to make you stop. See you at the palace." He patted her on the back in a brotherly way and then skipped down the steps to join his parents.

Trynne kept walking down the steps to the front of the sanctuary, but her mind was busy unraveling her feelings about Fallon. In many ways he *was* like an older brother or a cousin. He had been sent in wardship to Owen and Sinia for several years during their youth to learn how to be a man. After his fourteenth birthday, he'd returned to Atabyrion. It was there he'd sprouted like a beanstalk. She wondered whether her parents—and his—had intended them for each other. Her mother could see the future, but she rarely spoke of events until after they happened. When Trynne tried to pry for secrets, her mother would look at her seriously and then say nothing. It was infuriating.

Trynne sighed and then sidled closer to her father, resting her head on his arm while holding his hand with both of hers.

"Father, did you know Morwenna is Fountain-blessed?" she asked him softly.

"Yes," he answered. "She started showing the signs about the same time you did."

"I think she's lonely," Trynne said.

Her father grunted. "Yes, I suppose she must be. She chooses to spend so much time in Glosstyr with her father." There was another layer of meaning to his words, and Trynne wondered what it could be.

Her father was so wise and cunning. She wasn't at all surprised that he knew about Morwenna's ability.

"Do you know what her gift is?" she asked him.

He shook his head. "Not yet. It's early still."

Just as they were about to leave the sanctuary and enter the tumultuous street, a voice called out from behind them. "Lord Owen?"

They turned around to face Lord Amrein. Father asked, "What is it?"

"Your wife just appeared in the sanctuary alcove with your son. I thought you'd want to know." The spymaster wrinkled his brow in confusion as his attention shifted to Trynne. "You have some crepe or something on your dress . . ." He reached behind her and pulled off a strand of crinkled crepe that was not part of her outfit at all. Her mind flashed back to the memory of Fallon slipping his hand around her shoulders.

"He *didn't*!" she seethed, and snatched it from Lord Amrein. She glowered, trying to find him in the crowd, but he was already with his family. Raw fury boiled inside her. She wished she were a poisoner and could get her revenge in any number of interesting ways.

But Trynne's rage vanished when she saw her mother approaching them swiftly, tears streaming down her cheeks.

CHAPTER THREE

The Ring Table

Trynne had never seen her mother so distraught, and it was worrying because she knew that Sinia could see the future. The worry was a tangible thing that writhed inside her, and it only made it worse when her father told her in a curt command to take her brother to the palace and wait for them there. Gripping her little brother's hand, she escorted Jorganon away from the sanctuary of Our Lady.

"Are you feeling better?" she asked her brother, but he looked miserable and pale. He shook his head and wiped his nose on his sleeve.

The walk to Kingfountain passed in a blur as Trynne's mind whirled through the many possibilities. There was no way she could guess at the news, which only made her discomfort worse. Gannon, as she sometimes called him, was too young to be hounded for information. Although he was still sick, he was curious about everything and started tugging on her hand, eager to approach a vendor with a string of sausages. She reined him back and continued her hurried pace toward the palace.

"Is everything well, my lady?" asked a voice at her shoulder. It was Davyn Staeli, her Espion bodyguard. He wore no badge or insignia marking him as the duke's man. His brown hair was balding on top and his beard was trimmed. Two swords were belted to his waist, a long sword and a shorter one, and he used both with equal proficiency. The buckles on his leather tunic front were cinched and proper. He was a meticulous man, her own personal shadow. Though he usually kept a discreet distance, he must have sensed her grave mood, her hurry.

"I don't think so, Captain Staeli," she murmured, casting him a worried look. "Father wouldn't tell me." He frowned at her words, his dark eyes brooding, and then dropped back a few paces. Still, he followed her more closely, a hand on the hilt of his short sword. She saw him make a few surreptitious nods, which indicated the presence of other unseen Espion.

Her parents had insisted that she have a personal guard after the attack. Sometimes it bothered her that she was watched night and day, but at such a vulnerable moment, she was grateful for Captain Staeli's reassuring presence.

When she and Gannon reached the palace, there was much noise and celebratory commotion in the king's hall. Gannon shrank a little from the tumult and started to cough. The corridors were thick with servants bustling through with trays of meats and a variety of cheeses. Pitchers of wine and mead were also brought forth in a constant flood, giving the air a sour smell amidst the scent of the crushed pine needles strewn about.

While the festering worry would not allow her any peace, Trynne still felt a thrill of excitement as she entered the king's hall. There was no mistaking its transformation. She had come to Kingfountain many times throughout her childhood, but this was a massive change. The dais and throne were gone, and an enormous table stood in their place. Gannon tugged on her hand, wanting to get closer, eyeing it with great interest, and she let the lad drag her over to it.

As Trynne approached the gleaming polished wood, she realized that she was staring at the round of a massive tree. The circumference was not a perfect circle because of the irregular bends caused by the natural growth of the tree over time. It defied her imagination that a tree of such width could exist in nature. Three grown men could have lain on the table, end to end, and there still would have been room for a child at the farthest point. How tall must the tree have originally been? The visitors of the palace were all gathered around it, mesmerized by the sight. Twelve straight-backed chairs were arrayed around the table.

"Trynnee, can I climb on that chair?" Gannon asked, reverting to a pet name he used to call her when he was younger. He tried to yank his hand free of hers, but she kept a firm grip.

"Not now, Gannon. Shhh! Wait until Father arrives." She knelt down by him and put her arm around his shoulder.

"Trynnee?" ghosted a voice over her shoulder. She glanced back, only to see Fallon's sardonic smile.

In no mood to banter with him, she straightened and then punched his arm as hard as she could. "Stay away from me, *crepe master*," she said with a snarl and then tugged Gannon's hand and walked around to the far side of the table. She was furious and worried at the same time and felt ready to snap like a dog if anyone came near her. She tried to distract herself by tending to her brother.

"It's cut from a tree," she explained to him, bending low to speak into his ear over the commotion. "See this dark ring? It's the bark. Then there's a lighter ring. I don't know what it's called, but it's part of the growth layer. Each ring in the wood marks a year of growth." She reached out with her finger and touched the glossy surface of the table. It had been varnished and stained and sanded to a marble shine. There were splits and cracks in the inner rings, but there were so very many of them—perhaps more than a thousand. She rested her palm on the smooth, cool wood, allowing herself to feel the wonder of the thing.

The table was at least a foot thick and held up by stump-like struts. It would have taken fifty men to carry it, and only magic could have brought it into the throne room.

The twelve chairs surrounding the table could only be the work of master craftsmen. Each chair had its own personality, and to her eyes, they almost looked like wooden Wizr pieces.

Her lips parted with admiration and wonder. It was the original Ring Table from the legends of King Andrew. It had to be. Myrddin had brought it back. She'd never imagined that it was carved from a living tree or that a tree could grow so big.

"But they *do*," said Myrddin in his strange accent. "Trees, that is." With all the commotion, she hadn't noticed him sidle up next to her and Gannon. He gripped his gnarled staff, resting both of his hands on it. He had tufts of hair growing from his nose that she could see all too well as she stared up at him. She hated being so short.

"Where did you hide this table for so long, Myrddin?" she asked him politely.

"Pfah, far, far away, sister. It's been in an abandoned castle in the mountains that no one knows of and no one can get to. It was never from this world, child. Do you know why the king will sit here instead of a throne? What do you think, little sister?"

It was amusing that he always called her "sister" despite being centuries older than her parents, but she'd grown accustomed to Myrddin's ways. "Because he will be equal with the others," she answered, looking up at him again. Sometimes his breath smelled very bad, but it wasn't offensive this time. He was thousands of years old, according to her father, so perhaps he couldn't help it.

"True, true," he said, clucking his tongue and gazing across the table. There was a strange look in his eye, a sadness. "How like men to elbow their way to glory, eh, little sister? Most men are *pethets*." He pursed his lips and frowned. "Always seeking to grab something that isn't theirs simply because they want it." He reached into a pouch at his waist and withdrew an apple that was a curious color. She was used to juicy red apples, but this one had streaks of gold and pink in it.

Myrddin handed the apple to her brother, and Gannon's eyes lit up as he crunched into it.

"Mmmmm!" the boy mumbled around a mouthful of fruit. Trynne smiled and tousled his hair. The thought that Fallon might be watching her from across the room, ready to mock her, flashed through her head, and the smile faded.

"My mother is here, Myrddin," she said, looking up at him. "She just arrived."

"I know," he answered, nodding sagely. Then he winked at her and rocked on his sandaled feet. "I saw it on the Wizr board," he whispered.

The magic Wizr board was King Drew's most secret and powerful weapon. It was the means by which Trynne's father had defeated King Severn before she was born. The pieces on the set represented real people, each playing a role in a game of kingdoms that had been underway for centuries. The stakes of the game were terrible, for if a king forsook the ways of Virtus or was defeated without any heirs, their kingdom would be swallowed up by the Deep Fathoms as surely as Brythonica would be if the Montforts failed to renew the protection invocations. It had happened to ancient kingdoms like Atabyrion and Leoneyis. The point of the Wizr game wasn't to defeat and destroy enemies. It was to maintain a dynasty for as long as possible. The game was being played by the Argentine family and had been played for several hundred years. No one knew how the first Argentine king had acquired the board. Some said that his wife, the Queen of Occitania, had stolen it from her first husband and given it to him. There was no mention of the Wizr set in the histories. Yet its power controlled fate.

The wedding of King Drew and Queen Genevieve would mean that the game would be able to continue. But there were others who were determined to see it end.

Trynne had seen the Wizr board in its ancient chest—her parents had shown it to her—but she did not know where it was hidden.

"Do you know why my mother came?" she asked Myrddin.

"Aye, lass. I do."

"Will you tell me?" she pleaded.

"*Should* I tell you, little sister?" he answered, arching one of his shaggy eyebrows.

She frowned, conflicted. "I wish you would. Maybe I can help?"

The Wizr chuckled to himself. "Maybe indeed, little sister." He sighed. "Maybe indeed. It might be best to let things run their course. A lot has changed since I last walked these dusty roads. The faces are new, but they are the same. Like that one," he said, dipping the end of his staff forward. "The Prince of Brugia. Now *he* is a *pethet*." He shook his head. "Look at how he swaggers. Never satisfied." He sniffed. "He considers himself diminished because his father swore fealty to the king. He is still the heir of his father's lands, no? He still wears his *thallic* clothes, the preening sop."

Trynne's eyes found Elwis in the crowd. Arms folded, head cocked to the side, he bore the expression of a man who believed himself above his company.

"You can hear all of our thoughts, can't you?" she asked.

Myrddin's mouth quirked into a smile. "Aye, little sister. Though sometimes I wish I could plug my ears with wax and be done with this gift from the Fountain!" He shook his head. "He chafes and he bubbles and he stews. He deserves better than to swear homage to another man. Bah!" Leaning toward her, he pitched his voice for her ears alone. "But where would the king be now if Grand Duke Maxwell had won? Why, he would have been lashed to a boat and fed into the river to drown in the Deep Fathoms. What that lad considers an injustice is actually mercy." He shook his head. "Sadly, he cannot see the truth of things. That's why he's a *pethet*."

Trynne noticed Drew and Genevieve approaching them and felt a whir of excitement inside her. They were holding hands and looked so radiantly happy it made her a little envious.

King Drew cut a fine figure in his royal regalia. He wore the hollow crown, another relic infused with Fountain magic that tied the kingdom's weather to the ruler's moods and temperament. He must have been very happy about the wedding because the day could not have been nicer outside. He flashed Trynne a smile.

"I don't mean to intrude on your conversation, Myrddin," he said, putting his hand on the Wizr's stooped shoulder. "But I think everyone is here now. Hello, Trynne. Your parents just arrived. Over there." He nodded toward the door leading to the corridor closest to the chapel. Relief settled over her; her parents would explain what was happening and all would be well.

Trynne looked down and saw that her brother was crunching into the apple's core, eating even the seeds. "Gannon!" she said with a laugh and tugged his arm.

Myrddin touched her shoulder, startling her.

"I know you've wondered why the Fountain's magic hasn't fully healed you," he said in a low voice. "Just remember, little sister, that it *could* have. Sometimes the greatest blessings are those that are *withheld* from us."

That made absolutely no sense to her, but she tried to suppress a spasm of resentment. To avoid responding to him, she took her brother's hand and started to escort him toward her parents. His fingers were sticky from the apple he'd devoured.

"If you are ready, Your Highnesses?" Myrddin said with a bow and flourish, shifting his attention to the young couple.

"As ready as we can be," King Drew said. He winked at Trynne as she walked away and then turned to face the hall. It quieted instantly, as if a spell had been cast on it.

Trynne threw a worried look at her parents as she approached, hoping for a comforting nod or reassuring look. Her father's face was pale, his mouth tight with worry. Her mother's eyes were red from crying, and as soon as Trynne came within reach, her mother pulled her into *v* *r*ace and kissed her brow and her hair. Then Sinia reached

- pulled Gannon closer, as if she were clinging to both her

.o prevent herself from drowning in sorrow. Trynne glanced

r father, but he was looking worriedly at the king.

.ther?" she whispered in a pleading tone.

e shook his head.

I bid you welcome and greet you most warmly," King Drew said in

n, bold voice. "Today is a day of celebration." He lifted Genevieve's

.d, still entwined with his, and kissed her knuckles. "I have hearkened

the counsel of the wise Myrddin and chosen our queen. Finally, we

ave peace in Ceredigion." Trynne noticed Prince Elwis standing aloof,

iis eyes glittering with anger. "Peace is always a fragile thing," Drew

went on. "In the days of our ancestors, when King Andrew ruled from

this fortress, he had his Wizr create the Ring Table." At those words,

the king gestured with his free hand to the magnificent table before

them. He then rested his hand on one of the tall-backed carved chairs.

"A circle has no beginning or end. No one part of it is above or beneath

another. I am your king, chosen by the Fountain to draw the sword

Firebos from the waters. But I am not above you. I was once nobody,

and I remember what it was to feel powerless, afraid, and uncertain."

Trynne had always admired the king's way of speaking. He wasn't

proud or commanding. When he said he remembered a life before the

throne, he meant it.

"One does not need to be Fountain-blessed to gain a seat at this

table. One must only espouse the ways of Virtus—the courtly valor,

grace, and wisdom that I have come to admire in all the lands I have

visited. Those entrusted with a seat at the Ring Table will serve on my

high council. Each seat is uniquely carved. Each who serves will be just

as unique. My councilors will speak on my behalf and travel to the far-

thest points of this kingdom to dispense the king's justice in my name.

They will share in my authority and in my dominion. In a sense, they will be kings and queens themselves, sharing in our honor and in our grace." He lifted his bride's hand again.

"There will be one seat, however, that is different from the others," King Drew went on. "Not my seat, for I am the most ordinary of men. So it was in days of old. So it will be again. Myrddin?" he said, making a gesture of invitation.

The Wizr, gripping his gnarled staff, began to walk around the circumference of the Ring Table, his sandaled feet slapping on the marble tiles. Trynne saw the eyes upon him. As the king had spoken, she had seen the ambition lighting everyone's faces. She wondered if there was a single person in the king's hall who did *not* covet a seat at that table. Her mouth was dry as she felt the anticipation begin to churn inside her. All of her dread and panic suddenly subsided as she sensed the magic of the Fountain rippling through the stillness.

The Wizr stopped at a singular chair. He reached up and rubbed his chin, gazing thoughtfully at the assembled crowd. His eyes stopped when he reached Trynne and her family. "This seat," he said, his face stern and serious, "is different from the others. This seat is called the Siege Perilous."

As he said the words, Trynne heard a voice inside her mind mimicking them: *Siege Perilous.* A flash of light blinded her momentarily, and then a vision stole all her senses. It was of herself, wearing a knight's tunic with the symbol of a horse on it, sitting in that chair. When she surfaced, Myrddin was staring at her, his eyes riveted to hers.

"This chair," the Wizr said in a loud voice, "is the chair of the king's champion. His most trusted knight. The defender of his honor."

Trynne felt her father's hand on her shoulder, his fingers squeezing hard.

"Choose wisely," the Wizr said to the king, his voice becoming suddenly grave and full of warning. "For I foresee a day when another king will come with a vast and unlimited host to take your place at this table. If your champion fails or falls, this rival will hack this table into firewood and place his own lieutenants in control of your fractious dominion. If you lords and ladies do not stand firm and united, then this table will be shattered and broken forever. At great cost to us all."

The Wizr frowned solemnly. "Name your champion wisely," he said in an almost threatening tone.

King Drew looked shaken by the Wizr's pronouncement, but he answered him at once. "I name my champion Lord Owen Kiskaddon," he said firmly. "He will sit at the Siege Perilous."

You will sit there also, Tryneowy Kiskaddon, whispered the Fountain to her. *Tell no one.*

CHAPTER FOUR

The Vision

The prophecy of Myrddin had caused a ruckus. King Drew dismissed the assembly and the whispering visitors were ushered out of the chamber by the butlers and guards. The riotous noise was tamped down, though echoes of it could be heard throughout the palace until the massive wooden doors were shut and barred.

Only the Wizr, the king and his new queen, Trynne's family, Fallon's parents—though Fallon had balked at leaving—and Lord Amrein remained in the chamber. Trynne decided it would be presumptuous to assume she was invited too, so she took Gannon's hand and prepared to leave. Her father held up his hand, forestalling her.

The king's brow was furrowed as he paced the room, tapping his lip with a finger and glancing at the others with vexation. "You bring ill tidings on my wedding day, Myrddin," he said in a serious tone. The couples had all gathered around each other.

"I know, lad. I know," the Wizr said, puffing out his chest and sighing. "Something has changed. The Wizr board is beginning to move again. You can feel the pieces raking, stone upon stone, can you not?"

Trynne's father coughed into his hand, drawing their gazes.

"Lady Sinia," the king said, turning toward her. "Your presence at court was unexpected. At first, I thought you had managed to come celebrate with us, but I can see by your visage that you have had a vision—and that it troubles you."

"Aye, my lord," Trynne's mother answered. She was still clinging to Owen's hand.

"Tell us," Elysabeth said, her eyes shining with emotion. She sidled up near her husband, who also looked grave and concerned. They stood by one of the chairs at the massive table, his hand touching the back of it.

Trynne's parents exchanged a look, and then Owen looked back at the others. "I think we should tell them," he said softly.

Sinia quickly blinked away tears and brushed her hand across her eyes. "I did see a vision. I saw the horde that Myrddin spoke of. I have never seen an army of that size before. It was frightening in its power and immensity. A flood of men and shields and strange blades. I didn't recognize the land from the vision. It was . . . unfamiliar to me, not any place I have seen or visited. We were outnumbered. I saw you there, Your Highness. I saw many there." She looked at Iago and then at Lord Amrein. "I saw my husband leading our army." Her voice became thick. "The battle was terrible to behold. I saw myself at Kingfountain with the queen. Owen didn't come home after the battle. I saw grief and fear." She covered her face, but it could not mask her misery.

A stunned silence hung in the room. They were all looking at Sinia, even Trynne, her heart shuddering with violence. The premonition she had experienced during Myrddin's speech rang in her ears.

You will sit there also, Tryneowy Kiskaddon. Tell no one.

She stared at the chair called the Siege Perilous and a feeling of fear and misery struck her.

"These are ill tidings indeed," the king whispered hoarsely. Trynne knew he loved her father with all the devotion of a son. It was Owen's advice and counsel the king always sought first. Trynne's father's skill in diplomacy and war had expanded Ceredigion's dominion. The thought of another man defeating him in battle was absurd.

"Can nothing be done?" Elysabeth said with tears in her eyes and a catch in her voice. "Do all your visions surely come to pass, Sinia?"

She nodded miserably. "I have not seen all the future," she said. "But I saw myself alone, raising our son." Her hand reached down and stroked little Gannon's fair hair. The lad looked up at his mother, confused by the adults' conversation and the sudden ill wind that had swept the gathering.

The king began to pace. "Word of this cannot leave this room," he said firmly. He shot an agonized glance at Owen. "If we are to face such dangers, we need to muster our people's courage and not their fear. Your visions have all come to pass to our favor, my lady. While I grieve for myself, I cannot imagine the pain you feel. Thank you for coming straightaway. A king must often hear bad tidings. The taste may be bitter, but sometimes the cup we must drink is bitter."

King Drew shook his head, continuing to pace. "Myrddin, what counsel would you give me? What should we do to prepare for such an invasion?"

The Wizr glanced at his king, his eyebrows knitting together. "The gates of history swing on small hinges," he said. "I know of this tale. It has happened aforetime. But the past does not always repeat in the same way. Things were different then . . ." His words filled Trynne with confusion, but she'd learned that sometimes it was best to wait for Myrddin to explain himself. The Wizr started to walk around the circumference of the table and began tapping the chairs one by one with the knobbed end of his staff. "There is some time ere this vision is fulfilled," he finally said. "The Fountain is giving us time to prepare, if we will. You must raise a generation of warriors, my lord, if you know a fight will press on you. If a prophecy of a drought were to come, then storing food is what I would counsel." He smiled grimly. "Alack, many of our young men will see battle before they come of age." He looked shrewdly at Iago and Lady Evie, and Trynne felt her heart shudder with worry for Fallon. "The difference in the tide of battle may be shifted because of the efforts of *one* person."

As he said the words, he shot a knowing look at Trynne, and it kindled inside her heart a determination to thwart her father's destiny. A rebellious flame began to dance within her skin. She had always thought it unfair that women were not allowed to become knights of the realm. And yet one girl had—a young woman from the Occitanian village of Donremy. As Trynne thought on the legend of the Fountain-blessed girl, she felt a ripple of approval from the Fountain.

She made two decisions at that moment. Two decisions she wouldn't tell to a single soul.

Trynne would do everything within her power to *be* at that battle. And she was going to save her father's life.

♦   ♦   ♦

After the meeting was concluded, Lord Amrein was sent away to gather information from the Espion about the possible threats to the realm. The Espion was in charge of warning the kingdom in advance. Iago and Lady Evie left to find their older son and younger children, but they were commanded not to share with him what had been spoken. The king himself charged Trynne to keep the secret, even though it would be an awful burden on her. She promised that she would. Her parents offered some comfort to each other, but her mother wanted to return to Ploemeur at once. The legends were well known, and Sinia's people became anxious whenever she and her family were gone, even if it was only for a short while. Owen promised he would be ready to return home in two days' time, and they arranged to meet by one of the castle's fountains so she could transport them home. Two days was not enough time in Trynne's mind.

She found herself roaming the halls of Kingfountain, lost in thought, mulling over the decisions she had made. While the magic of the Fountain was powerful, it did not prevent all disasters from unfolding. If it was the Fountain's will to reclaim a person to the Deep Fathoms, no amount of magic could bring that person back. The stillborn birth of her sibling proved that. To go against the Fountain's will was to follow a path leading to destruction. The power of water was unpredictable at times. It had to be respected and handled with wisdom.

So, how could she save her father?

She heard the noise of boots clipping at a jog.

"What happened in the great hall?" Fallon huffed as he drew up beside her, out of breath from running. "My parents won't tell me! You were there, weren't you?"

She was not in the mood to deal with his playful banter, though she yearned to tell someone the secrets that burdened her. "The king commanded us to keep it secret," she said.

Fallon's eyes grew wide with wonder before his features tilted into a frown. "But that doesn't mean you can't *tell* me."

"That's exactly what it means," she said in exasperation.

"Very well, you can't say, but if I guess . . . you could give me a wink or something." He wagged his eyebrows at her. "This is literally torturing me. My parents always tell me what's happening. This is the first time they've refused."

"I suppose that means they are honorable and value their integrity. As do I, Iago Fallon Llewellyn. The king commanded it. I'm not going to tell."

"Trynne . . ." he said pleadingly.

"Enough, Fallon! I'm still angry at you for the crepe you put on my back."

"That was just a little fun," he said, waving off her glower.

"It would have been mortifying to go into the great hall with it clinging to me still. Which was exactly why you did it. Why do you delight in tormenting me?"

"Because it's so easy!" he said in feigned shock. "You take yourself so seriously—"

"And you aren't serious enough. Even when we were children, you could hardly sit still. You were always getting into trouble."

"Might I remind you that it was *your* idea to steal the treacle pot and hide it in the bushes?" he said. "How many insects did we eat before we realized that treacle isn't supposed to be so *crunchy?*"

"Stop!" Trynne said, waving her hands and shuddering in disgust. "I don't even like remembering that happened and you keep recollecting that silly—"

Abruptly Fallon grabbed her shoulder and stopped her from walking. His voice pitched lower. "If I had a secret like that, I would tell you, Tryneowy Kiskaddon, because I *trust* you. We've known each other since we were children. You would never betray me. And I would never betray you. Our parents are *old*. Their duty binds them. But surely you can see it's not fair for *you* to know something that I don't."

The weight of his hand on her shoulder sent a peculiar rush of warmth through her. He hated being left out of a joke or a jest. Yes, the secret was torturing him. But it wasn't torturing him nearly as much as it was tormenting her.

Her heart felt like bursting. "I can't, Fallon. And neither would you if the king commanded you not to. I know you well enough."

He let go of her shoulder and raked his fingers through his unruly dark hair. He was put out and the sour twist of his lips made him look like he'd bitten into a lemon rind. "It's not fair," he muttered.

"Life isn't *fair*," she shot back, pointing to her mouth. She was angry, and that feeling helped soothe the pain in her heart. When she started walking again, she hoped that he would follow her, that he'd say something to make her feel better about her slack cheek and unresponsive lip. That he still found her pretty, even though she'd seen herself in the mirror that morning and knew she wasn't.

He didn't follow her.

♦　♦　♦

The interior of Kingfountain's palace was a giant circle around a verdant interior garden with bubbling fountains in the exact center. Trynne had always loved to roam the main corridor, admiring the suits of armor, the polished floors, the rich legacy sewn into tapestries and other decorations, and the familiar smell of pine and pitch. The palace had been built centuries ago and she wondered how many daughters of Westmarch had walked the same aisles. She knew about the secret corridors honeycombing the walls and recognized which decorative panels led to them and which did not. At her insistence, her father had shown them to her when she was little. She'd wanted to visit every room, hallway, and tunnel that had been part of his life while he was the old king's hostage. Since she was not part of the Espion, she wasn't allowed to use the passageways, but she did remember where they were.

As she passed one of the arches leading to an upward stairwell, she heard whispered voices coming from the interior. She peered into the shadows and saw two people half hidden in the gloom.

Trynne slowed her steps, trying to place the familiar voices.

Suddenly the sound of bootfalls met her ears and Prince Elwis strode down the steps and appeared in the hall. He looked vicious, and his eyes flashed with rage when he saw her. "What are you standing there for, Kiskaddon?" he snarled.

Trynne was startled to see him and even more startled by the vehemence of their introduction. They had never spoken together before, yet he obviously knew who she was and hated her for it. Blood began to pound in her ears as her heart raced.

"I heard voices. I was just looking," she answered, feeling a little flush stain her cheeks.

"Or you were spying on me," he replied in a challenging voice. He was looking at her face, and his lips curled with revulsion. "It is true. You *are* ugly." Then he glanced behind her, probably at Captain Staeli, who was never far away, turned on his heel, and strode away quickly as shock and pain ripped open the old wounds inside her. She stood there mutely, her mind unable to develop a retort out of the shock of his deliberate insult.

Morwenna appeared in the arched stairway from which the prince had emerged. The girl was chafing her wrist and gazing down the corridor at the malcontent. She then turned to Trynne and said, "I'm glad you came when you did. Thank you."

Trynne felt like a fish yanked from the waters and passed from one fisherman to another. Why wouldn't her mouth work?

"I'm . . . I'm sorry," Trynne said haltingly, her cheeks still flaming. "It's just . . . I hadn't expected him to be so rude."

Morwenna smiled at that comment, a lovely smile that made Trynne ache with jealousy. She hooked arms with Trynne, and they started walking the other way by silent agreement. "He is ill-mannered." Morwenna glanced back at Elwis, who had nearly reached the end of the hall. "His father wants him to marry me. I think he's used to getting what he wants."

"To marry you?" Trynne said with disgust. "He's eighteen and we're only . . ."

"Exactly," Morwenna said with a nod. "A plight troth will do. But my blood-brother, the king, is too wise by far." She gave Trynne a kindly smile. "As is *your* father. It doesn't take a Wizr to foresee the trouble such a marriage would cause, now does it?" After a pause, she continued. "Yes, I'm grateful you arrived when you did. It was becoming more . . . unpleasant by the moment. Men tend to . . . overestimate their finer qualities. Especially rich, spoiled young men."

It made Trynne think of Fallon, and her mouth tugged into a smile of agreement. Self-conscious, she forced it to go flat.

"Can I ask you something, Tryneowy?" Morwenna asked.

Trynne looked up and noticed Captain Staeli leaning against the corridor wall, arms folded, his eyes following the fleeing prince. His face looked neutral, but Trynne knew him enough to recognize his subtle frown and the narrowing of his eyes. Morwenna glanced at him as they walked by.

"Of course you can," Trynne answered, patting the other girl's arm.

"What happened to you as a child?" Morwenna asked. "I've heard rumors you were attacked. Is that true?"

Trynne, who was tired of being the object of others' pity, sighed.

"This makes you uncomfortable," Morwenna apologized. "I'm sorry I asked. I'm not a gossip. It's just . . . I hear so little . . . from Glosstyr." She sighed herself.

"Why don't you come live at court, then?" Trynne asked.

Morwenna shook her head and laughed in a self-deprecating way. "That is rather complicated. I know I am welcome, of course. My mother insists as much every time I see her. She only lives in Glosstyr for certain seasons of the year. Some like to gossip that even *she* cannot stand my father, but that's not true. But he is so lonely when she is gone. And I will be leaving him soon. I wanted to spend as much time with him as possible. Before I go."

Trynne looked at her in surprise. "Are you going to stay in another household?"

Morwenna patted her arm. "It's not like that," she answered. She looked back at Captain Staeli and pitched her voice even lower. "How can you bear having the Espion crawling around you all the time? It would drive me *mad*." She leaned closer. "I will tell you. Your father already knows, but he may not have shared it. I'm going to Pisan." There was a gleam in her silver eyes. "I'm going there to train to become my brother's poisoner. The thought of being a lady of court has never interested me. I want to know how to fight. How to disable a man like Elwis with a twist of the wrist or a little potion. I'm not content to sit out my days in the parks and gardens or doing needlework. I belong in the shadows. I'll be gone from court for years. But I just wanted someone . . . someone to know where I was while I'm away."

"And my father *approved* of this?" Trynne asked. She was desperate to talk with him about it.

Morwenna nodded, flashing another lovely smile. "It was his idea."

◆ ◆ ◆

I have been an observer of humanity. Most men are petty, base, and cruel. Most women are fickle, proud, and cunning. Nearly all are shortsighted and tend to view happiness as a crumb worth hoarding. There are a few, however, who stick to a goal and pursue it regardless of obstacles. They are fired with ambition to achieve something at all costs. From the deepest desires often come the deadliest hate and the profoundest love.

Myrddin

◆ ◆ ◆

CHAPTER FIVE

Prince of Brugia

Although the day had felt as if it would stretch on forever, it ended like all days do. Trynne watched the final rays of sun disappear over the eastern hills as the shadows stretched in slices along the courtyard walls. From the window in the solar, she had a view of the gorgeous sunset, but her heart could find little beauty in it. Her father was going to die.

She listened to him speak to Lord Amrein in furtive tones and watched the spymaster's reflection on the glass of the window. The chancellor was crestfallen, his eyes burdened by the knowledge from that day. The castle had been noisy with the wedding and the news of the Ring Table and the looming threat. But only a handful knew about Sinia's vision. Already they were mourning. Trynne chewed on her lip, willing herself to find a way to overturn the calamity.

"Sinia returned earlier this afternoon," Owen said with a hollowness in his voice, sitting back in his chair. He was brooding. "I don't imagine what news you will find in just a few days, Kevan, but do your best. Send me word at Ploemeur."

"I will," the other man answered. Then he dropped his hand onto Owen's shoulder and the two friends locked eyes. What passed between them wasn't spoken aloud, but it was powerful. Trynne knew the story of how Lord Amrein had saved her father's life after Owen had committed treason against King Severn. There was trust between the men that had held fast over time.

Owen nodded and held up his hand. "We all must return to the Deep Fathoms some day, my friend. I think it's a blessing from the Fountain to know my fate early."

"You're bearing the news better than I," Lord Amrein said in a husky voice. He patted Owen's shoulder and then abandoned the solar, leaving Trynne alone with her father.

She was unwilling to accept her mother's vision as a blessing from the Fountain. No, she would fight her father's fate with everything she had. She turned and leaned back against the window, watching her father as he stared vacantly into the distance, as if trapped in some long-ago memory.

"Father?" she called after a moment of silence.

He slouched in his chair, stroking his bottom lip thoughtfully. His eyes shifted up to meet her gaze. His eyebrows lifted, as if that was all the strength he had for a reply.

"I spoke to Severn's daughter today," Trynne continued. She walked up and planted her hands on the table. "She told me she's going to Pisan."

"Did she?" Owen answered, looking back down at the table and sighing. "That was supposed to be a secret."

"I helped her out of an uncomfortable situation with Prince Elwis. Maybe she assumed I'd know because I'm your *daughter*." She emphasized the word.

"I hope that's the case." He looked up at her. "Your tone of voice implies you question the wisdom of such an action."

Trynne shrugged and stifled a smile. Her father knew her well. "It's just that she's . . . she's *Severn's* daughter."

Owen smiled and sat up higher in the chair, seemingly grateful for the change in the conversation. He likely didn't want to brood on his future any more than she did. "You remember the stories I told you about Dominic Mancini, don't you?"

She nodded, recalling several of the episodes concerning him.

"He once said—keep your friends close. Keep your enemies *closer*. Now, I'm not saying Morwenna is our enemy. But Severn is not exactly a friend. Glosstyr is a different duchy with him ruling it. They are more isolated from the rest of the realm. More insular. I'd wish it were otherwise, but it is what it is. Losing a throne is hard on a man. I know he still resents it . . . resents *me*." Owen rubbed his mouth. "We've tried to get Morwenna more involved at court, but she has no interest in fitting in here. And, to be honest, the other girls haven't treated her in a friendly way."

"I've tried," Trynne said. "We spent a good portion of the afternoon together walking around the palace. She's never had a friend."

Owen nodded at her and smiled approvingly. "Her father is her closest companion. She is fiercely loyal to him. Bear that in mind, Daughter. But I'm proud of you for trying. The idea to send her to Pisan came from her mother, actually, who suggested it to me. And based on what Lord Amrein has told me, Morwenna has an aptitude for spying and has, over the years, managed to root out the Espion we've planted in Glosstyr. Obviously we replaced them when their covers were compromised. Maybe her gift is intrigue?" he mused.

"She was more interested in talking about politics than dresses or fashion," Trynne said. "Actually, I enjoyed talking to her. I wish she weren't going now. Did you talk to Mother about her becoming a poisoner? Has she had any visions?"

Owen smoothed his hands across the polished wooden table. "Yes. Your mother saw her at the poisoner school and then working as an agent for her brother. It is a difficult life and a dangerous one." His eyes tightened with memories of the past. "But ultimately it was the king's decision." He glanced up at her. "It's spring and so the daylight has lingered, but it is getting late, Trynne. I have much work to do this evening still. I'd best get to it." He leaned forward and rose. The weight of the news had aged him, and it made her ache inside.

"Father?" she asked again as he was turning.

"Yes?"

She tried to keep her voice as casual as she could. "I don't think it's fair that only the boys get to use the training yard. May I have your permission to practice wooden swords with Captain Staeli tomorrow?"

He chuckled to himself. "That's how Evie felt as well," he said. He pursed his lips and then shrugged. "Just don't make a nuisance of yourself, Trynne. After Myrddin's warning today, the training yard was overcrowded with boys hoping to earn a seat at the Ring Table. That was one of Myrddin's hopes, actually. By creating a goal to strive for, the king will inspire a generation of boys into practicing hard."

"Thank you, Father." She kissed his cheek and left the solar. As she started down the hall, she spied Captain Staeli following her, faithful shadow that he was. She turned and gave him a serious look. "Tomorrow before dawn. Meet me at the training yard."

There was a wariness about him, but his only answer was a curt nod.

♦ ♦ ♦

Sweat dripped off the tip of Trynne's nose. Her body was trembling with the exertions of the morning. The torches they had used for light had nearly burned out, and the birds were chirping up a ruckus in the woods surrounding the Kingfountain palace. The sun had yet to show itself, but the world was pale and drowsy, and smoke lifted in puffs and plumes from the many chimneys. From her vantage point in the training yard, she could see the poisoner's tower—the windows dark. She leaned forward, hands on her knees, and panted.

"I thought we were . . . going to use"—she gasped, shaking her head—"the wooden ones!" Her hair was tied back with a strap of leather. She wore a page boy's clothes and was skinny enough to be mistaken for a boy. Her entire body was dripping and her muscles felt pushed past all endurance.

She had hoped to spend the morning drilling in the techniques of the sword with wooden blades. Instead, Captain Staeli had had her practice swinging iron pokers from the blacksmith forge. For a long while he had pushed her, walking around her in a circle, not exerting himself in the least. He'd had her repeat the same drills over and over again until her shoulders throbbed and her forearms hurt. She'd dropped the pokers noisily several times, earning a frown of disapproval from him whenever it happened.

Captain Staeli shook his head and stifled a yawn. "If you want me to teach you, then you will learn the way I did. If you don't quit before a fortnight is through, then maybe we'll get started with the wooden ones."

"Maybe?" Trynne gasped despondently.

"A wooden sword keeps you from cutting yourself, 'tis true," he said. "But they don't build up the muscles you need. That will take time. *A lot* of time. Again." He gestured for her to continue even though her arms were whimpering in relief over the brief rest. She had a feeling she wouldn't be able to brush her own hair later that afternoon.

She gave him a determined look. "I'm not going to quit, Captain. Count on that."

"We'll see," he said with an unconvinced sniff. "Girls are made of softer stuff than men."

His words sent a shock of outrage and anger, giving her a new burst of strength. But she realized almost as quickly that he had said it on purpose to goad her into working harder. After giving him a black look, she continued. She had been given two pokers, one for each arm. Captain Staeli had told her that most men were trained to favor one arm and use the other with a shield. He had been trained with two weapons equally and found advantages in being able to attack with two. It would give her an advantage that might compensate for her smaller size and frame.

And so she drilled with the heavy iron poles.

And she drilled.

Until she vomited.

Then, after pushing her that far, it was enough and the lesson was over. She wiped the spittle from her lips, sitting on her knees, shaking all over. Then she saw him smile. Just a small one.

♦ ♦ ♦

Trynne found Morwenna later that day and the two resumed their conversation as they walked through the palace together. The day before, they had been hesitant with each other, unsure of how much to share. But after talking with her father, Trynne felt better about developing a connection with Morwenna, who was despised because of her own father just as Trynne felt shamed because of her palsied face. As they spoke, they shared more and more about their life experiences and found in each other a sympathetic companion.

"What I don't understand," Morwenna said, shaking her head, "is your parents *both* are Fountain-blessed. Could not they heal you?"

"They tried to," Trynne said, feeling the familiar taste of bitterness once again. "Many things are possible with Fountain magic, but nothing they tried worked. Perhaps it was because they did not use their magic straightaway. Perhaps it was because it wasn't what the Fountain willed to happen."

Morwenna frowned at that. "You speak of the Fountain as if it were a person."

"I've—*my* father has heard it speak to him," Trynne said, catching herself in time. "The magic is benevolent. It is aware of us and our circumstances."

Morwenna smirked and shrugged. "It has its favorites, then," she said with a gleam in her eye.

"Those who serve it tend to be favored," Trynne pointed out. "But not all who do are Fountain-blessed. If one is capable of practicing the principles of the magic, it will respond to them, regardless of their motives."

Morwenna's eyes narrowed on her. "Like my father."

"I didn't mean that at all," Trynne said, shaking her head.

Morwenna shrugged. They continued to walk for a moment in silence, connected only by their clasped arms. Then the raven-haired girl spoke again. "Have you ever felt a sense that the Fountain knows your destiny?" She cast a sidelong look at Trynne.

Licking her lips, Trynne nodded. "Yes. I have."

Morwenna nodded. "So have I. I feel it bubbling inside me sometimes. A huge and powerful certainty. That I am *meant* to do something. To *be* something." She shook her head. "No one understands me. At least, no one did. Until now." She gave Trynne a furtive look.

Trynne nodded to her, feeling her own secret writhing inside of her. Long ago, when she was a child, her father had told her that her namesake, Ankarette Tryneowy, had explained that secrets were like butterflies trying to escape the cocoon. The Fountain had trusted her with a secret. She was determined to keep it, especially from her parents. Especially if it could somehow help her save her father.

From the corridor ahead, Trynne spied Fallon walking toward them. He had a cocksure look on his face and was wearing a padded leather doublet that was scuffed and battered, the kind that was used in the training yard. His prince's finery was gone.

"Be warned. He is very rude," Trynne said to her companion in a low voice.

"The excessively handsome can afford to be," Morwenna murmured back with a smirk.

"I was just on my way to the training yard," Fallon said proudly. "Would you two ladies care to join and watch my heroic exploits?"

"Will there be any, I wonder?" Trynne pondered, arching her eyebrows and sounding indifferent.

Morwenna gave her a startled look.

"Come and see for yourself. Lady Morwenna, I don't believe we've ever conversed. My name is—"

"Fastidious Llewellyn," Trynne supplied for him. "He goes by the nickname *Tedious*, though."

"Fallon, actually," he said, giving Trynne an annoyed look. "It means *featherbrained*. Doesn't it, *Cousin*?"

"It is nice to meet you, Prince Fallon," Morwenna said, bowing her head respectfully and curtsying. "We would be happy to join you." She glanced at Trynne. "Well, *I* would." A little blush came to her cheeks.

"By all means, come along." He offered his elbow to Morwenna, spurning Trynne, which made her growl inside with fury. They walked to the training yard, with Fallon talking the entire way about nothing important. Trynne realized that he was likely going back to Edonburick, and the thought of not seeing him for a while panged her. She regretted all the barbs that had passed between them since they'd been reunited.

Upon reaching the training yard, Trynne felt a flash of hotness come over her. Her forearms were still lethargic from the morning's activities and the once empty yard was bustling with young men. Trynne had never seen it so crowded. There were young people everywhere, and the sword masters were all leading groups of boys and young men through different drills and exercises. Small rings of adults were also cloistered together, the older men sparring with wooden blades, the younger ones sparring with steel swords that clanged and tolled like bells as they moved. Trynne and Morwenna were not the only ladies in the courtyard, however. It seemed half the maidens from the palace had assembled to gawk at and encourage the men. The smell of sweat brought back more memories of the morning, making Trynne feel light-headed.

As they wandered in a bit, Trynne spied Prince Elwis with a crowd of young men from Brugia around him. They were wearing training gear as well, though the gear was more black than brown and full of buckles. Elwis was scowling at the noisy crowd, and his scowl turned into a sneer when he saw them. Trynne's cheeks flushed.

"I don't like him," Trynne said under her breath.

"Who? Elwis?" Fallon said. "He's a fop. He doesn't know anything."

"He insulted Lady Tryneowy yesterday," Morwenna said softly, casting a wary glance at the stuck-up prince.

"How?" Fallon demanded, whirling and gazing at Trynne.

"It's no matter, Fallon," Trynne said, shaking her head. "Let it be."

His lips curled into a snarl. "Tell me," he demanded of Morwenna.

"He disparaged her looks in a manner not befitting a prince or any man," Morwenna said. "He said she was ugly, which is not only discourteous, it's also a lie."

A flush of anger spread over Fallon's cheeks as he looked from Morwenna to Trynne. Then he whirled and started right toward Elwis.

"Fallon, no!" Trynne gasped, reaching for him, but he was already well on his way. Morwenna's eyes were bulging with surprise as well.

Prince Elwis's mouth tipped into a smirk when he noticed Fallon's approach. His arms were folded across his chest and he looked as if he were about to start laughing.

"Hail Prince of Atabyrica," Elwis said disdainfully, offering a meager bow. "You've decided to join us at last—"

His last words were cut off when Fallon punched him in the face and sent him staggering back into his companions, who gaped with surprise.

Fallon jabbed a finger toward him. "If you ever utter another insult toward *any* woman, Elwis, then I swear by the Fountain—!"

There was blood dribbling from Elwis's nose and his lip was already turning puffy as he grazed it with his gloved hand. The look on his face turned from pain to surprise, then fierce anger. He dropped his hand to the wooden sword at his waist and pulled it out.

"Prince Fallon!" someone shouted and threw him a wooden sword.

Trynne clutched Morwenna's arm as the two young men flew at each other with the wooden sabers. The swords were made of sturdy pieces and clacked against each other like battle staves. Fallon ducked as one sweep came toward his head and then countered with his own. Trynne's heart nearly ruptured with fear as she watched the two young men collide, their size not that different, their aggression equally ferocious.

The fight lasted hardly a moment. Elwis trapped Fallon's hilt, then stepped in and clubbed Fallon in the groin with his fist. As his adversary doubled over in pain, the Brugian prince brought his elbow up to catch his nose. Fallon toppled backward, stunned and in obvious agony. Elwis sneered down at him and then slapped the flat of the blade down against his unprotected head, hard enough that it cut his ear on a snag of wood.

Staring down coldly, Elwis lifted his weapon again to continue beating the helpless man. Without thinking, Trynne let go of Morwenna to charge in and block the blow, but another beat her to it.

It was Captain Staeli, who caught the attack on his own short sword. The wooden sword split apart like wood from an axe. Trynne's protector stepped in and backhanded Elwis across the face with his fist, sending the prince to the cobbles.

Then he drew his other blade and faced the young men of Brugia with defiance in his eyes. "'Tis not the way of Virtus," Captain Staeli said in a low growl. "I mean that for both of you sorry cubs! Now get you gone 'fore I thrash you both!"

Looking mortified and repentant, Fallon obeyed. The Prince of Brugia's face was a mess of blood, but he didn't look injured, only angry.

Trynne saw that Fallon had just earned an enemy for the rest of his life.

CHAPTER SIX

The Gauntlet

Trynne could not remember ever seeing Fallon so surly and ill-tempered. His teeth were clenched, his arms folded, shoulders hunched. He'd changed back into courtly attire, but his entire form radiated the white-hot heat of suppressed anger. His mother had been steadily scolding him in a low tone and he looked ready to lash out at her in frustration. They were gathered in the great hall, awaiting the arrival of the king. King Drew, Trynne's father, and Fallon's father were discussing the mishap with Grand Duke Maxwell of Brugia in another room.

"What if he had pulled his dagger instead of the training sword?" Lady Evie said vehemently. "Neither of you were wearing hauberks . . . He could have shed your blood before Captain Staeli or anyone else intervened."

Fallon glowered at his mother, clearly still humiliated by the outcome of his altercation with Elwis. Ever since the incident, Trynne could not stop thinking about how Fallon's rash act had been motivated by Elwis's insult toward her. She felt a certain guilty pleasure from it that was confusing.

Fallon's mother held a bloodied rag to his torn ear, but he winced and lifted his arms to ward her off.

"Enough coddling, Mother!" he snapped at her.

She squinted in anger at her son and shook her head. "Don't you blame me for this, Fallon Llewellyn. You weren't thinking. You rushed into something without plotting out the consequences. It took four years to make peace with Brugia, and it was nearly wasted in a training-yard brawl."

"You think I don't realize that?" Fallon blustered. He rose and stalked away from her, casting a miserable glance at Trynne. "I already feel like a fool. There's no need to add salt to the wound."

Trynne glanced over at Captain Staeli. He had been summoned as well to account for his role in the scene. Elwis had claimed both men had attacked him, and the whole affair had exploded into flaming spurts of accusation and threats of retribution. Trynne sighed. Within hours of Myrddin's pronouncement, the kingdom was already roiling with inner conflict. Staeli had answered briefly and curtly amidst the passion and bluster. He looked calm, but she watched him pacing slowly along the far wall.

"I'm not trying to torture you, Fallon; just be sure you've learned your lesson." Lady Evie clenched the bloodstained rag in her hands. "You're nearly a man now. You can't afford to make such costly mistakes. Sometimes, we aren't given a second chance. Actions have consequences."

Fallon's mouth was twisted into a pained frown. "I know, Mother," he said softly, looking at her with hurt in his eyes. "I will do better next time. Next time, Prince *Arse-turias* will be the one bleeding on the floor."

His mother threw up her hands. "Iago Fallon Llewellyn, have you heard *nothing* I've said this past hour? He shamed you, yes. Even worse, he shamed you in front of your peers *and* in front of girls. But the blame belongs to you. You *assumed* that you were better than him. The Espion could have told you that he's been training since he was ten years old and is likely one of the best swordsmen, if not *the* best, in Brugia. He's had four or five masters."

Fallon rounded on her amidst his pacing. "And how I am to know such things if no one tells me anything? You and Father are keeping secrets from me right now." He shot Trynne an angry look as well. "What are you hiding from me?"

"Fallon," his mother said curtly, "I would tell you if I could. But we were commanded by the king to keep it silent. Even from you. I see by your angry glance that Trynne hasn't broken her word either, and I'm proud of her for it. I can expect such discretion from the daughter of Lord Kiskaddon. Apparently it's too much to expect from my own son?"

Her last blow rocked Fallon like a punch to the stomach. He stared at her, miserable, and Trynne wished she hadn't been there to witness his shame.

A wall of silence came up between them after that, making Trynne squirm inside.

The noise of approaching bootfalls announced the coming visitors, and Lady Evie walked up to Fallon and mopped the blood from his ear again. He capitulated and then went to one of the benches and sat down, burying his face in his hands.

The door opened and Trynne's father came in with King Drew, Queen Genevieve, Iago, and Lord Amrein. The wretched young man looked up at his father as he approached, waiting for another rebuke. Iago put his hand on his son's shoulder, gazing down at him. Then he patted his shoulder comfortingly and bent lower. Trynne was just close enough to hear his words.

"Buck up, buttercup. You lost a battle, not the war." He winked at his son, clapped him hard on the back, and then turned around. His wife gave him a challenging look, and Trynne saw Iago nod sagely to her, as if he agreed with her on every point.

Genevieve came over and sat next to Fallon on the bench, put a sisterly arm around him, and gently rubbed his back. He gazed sideways at her, looking sheepish. She sighed and shook her head, trying to stifle a smile. Trynne felt a flush of affection for her calming manner.

"Has Brugia decided to abandon the treaty, my lords?" Lady Evie asked with a sigh. "Out with the worst of it."

Trynne's father smiled wanly and shook his head. "Grand Duke Maxwell is interested in preserving the peace, as are we." He nodded for the king to continue.

King Drew started pacing, his hands clasped behind his back. "It's our thinking that this rupture was intended by Prince Elwis alone. It was probably even staged."

"Staged?" Evie asked with concern.

Drew nodded. "He has a deep hatred of Lord Owen for defeating his father. I think it's reasonable to deduce that his slight to Trynne was intended to be provoking. He stands to inherit his father's kingdom and doesn't want to be beholden to the throne at Kingfountain—or his nemesis. Nor does he likely want to be *bound* by the principles of Virtus. Quite simply, the young man is a troublemaker." The king looked pointedly at Lord Amrein. "It'll be best to keep an eye on him from now on."

Lord Amrein nodded. "We have two eyes on him, actually. There are some concerns, my lord, that he's attempting to woo Lady Morwenna."

The king nodded. "So she told me. That won't be a problem after tomorrow. Best if the lad cools his head across the sea in his own lands. And it seems like someone else might need to dunk his head in the icy river by Dundrennan." The king smiled at Fallon to mark it as a joke. "Your ear looks painful."

"It's nothing at all, my lord," Fallon said glumly. "I apologize for making a scene. It won't happen again."

Drew straightened and continued pacing. He glanced at Owen. "Should we tell them now, or later?"

Trynne looked from her father to the king, and then back. Were they going to share the secret after all?

"I think *now*, Your Majesty," Iago said. He rocked back on his heels, smiling broadly.

Fallon sat up, his eyes widening with interest.

"It was Lord Owen's idea, so he should be the one to tell it," the king said, gesturing for him to speak.

Trynne's father seemed abashed to take the credit. "It was just a suggestion that serves multiple purposes." He paused, and Trynne's heart raced with anticipation. Whatever he was about to say would change everything; she sensed it. "We know we are going to be invaded. We need warriors to defend our realm. There is a new generation rising—young men like Prince Fallon and Prince Elwis. In the past, they have always fought one another for fame and land. Now we need them to fight for a common purpose. Princes are ambitious by nature, so glory is a common motivator for many. My idea is to create a custom that unifies our people. We have different languages, different food, different coins even." Owen walked over to the Ring Table and placed his hand on one of the chair backs. "To earn a seat at this table, a man must pass through an ordeal of sorts. A test not just of fighting prowess and endurance, but also of wisdom and self-discipline. We want clever and judicious warriors to defend our realm, not brute soldiers. My suggestion was that each duchy should create its own ordeal—a rigorous and difficult series of challenges to set apart the champions. Young men from throughout the realm will compete against each other in each of the duchies before earning the right to try their might at the challenge at Kingfountain. The challenges can change and improve from year to year. Only the best will be allowed to progress from one duchy to the next. Accomplishing the trial will earn a badge of honor. Any contest can be attempted more than once, and they'll be held at varying points during the year." He paused before continuing. "It will provide the young men a chance to live, for a short while, in the other duchies and learn something of their customs and attributes. It reminds me of something Myrddin once told me. We only hate those whom we do not truly know."

Owen fell silent for a moment, looking across those in the room. Trynne felt a sort of hunger begin to rise inside her. For as long as she could remember, she had longed to travel, and the thought of visiting Atabyrion, Legault, Brugia, or Occitania in order to meet the challenges there was intensely appealing. Her arms were still sore from training with Captain Staeli, but she relished the idea of competing for such an honor.

Fallon came to his feet with fascination. "And a prince could participate alongside a common man?"

Owen nodded. "Precisely. The seats at this table would not be confined to those of noble blood. Some of the tests would be a trial of arms. But some would also be skills required of soldiers in battle, like climbing siege ladders or lifting heavy weights. As I said, each duchy will create their own. Within a few years' time, we'll have created a tradition that will strengthen *and* unify the people."

"It's bloody brilliant," Iago said with a grin.

"It's bloody dangerous," Lady Evie countered, looking worriedly at her son.

"It is that, Madame," the king said, walking over to her. "But so is war. And if we are going to be invaded by a stronger force, we will need to meet it with a generation of strong men. Owen will design the contest for the palace, the culmination achievement. And I think even Prince Elwis will be motivated to achieve a place at this table. Perhaps he will temper his resentment and desire for retribution in order to have the glory. I think many young men will do the same." The king smiled kindly at Fallon.

Trynne felt the hot burn of ambition inside her own heart. She found herself speaking her thoughts aloud. "What about others participating?" she asked, looking at her father. "Could *I* compete as well?"

Fallon looked at her and snorted. "Of course not, Trynne. Don't be ridiculous."

"Why is it ridiculous for me to wish to defend my own kingdom as you do?" she challenged. "Father, please! Cannot others be given a chance? The Maid of Donremy fought in battle alongside her men. She wore armor and carried that sword." She stared at him imploringly, pointing at the blade belted at King Drew's waist. The other women in the room were looking at her with concern. She knew she was being too passionate, but she could not help herself. If she started now, if she continued working with Captain Staeli . . .

"Trynne," Genevieve said, rising from the bench. She came and put her hands on Trynne's shoulders. "Your courage is commendable, but perhaps we should give this more thought. What king has ever summoned an army of women to fight in battles? It's never been done to my knowledge."

Trynne saw the looks of those around her and knew she'd lost. Genevieve was right. If she were to cross swords with Fallon, he would treat her differently because she was a girl. But if he *didn't* know it?

She closed her mouth and nodded silently. Her eyes met her father's.

He was looking at her shrewdly, probably trying to guess what she was thinking.

"It was just a silly notion, Father," Trynne said demurely.

"I'll say," Fallon muttered under his breath, his dismissiveness making her burn with fury inside.

"You've always wanted to be a soldier," Owen said with a knowing smile. "I pray to the Fountain that you will never have to be."

As he said the words, she felt a little ripple from the Fountain.

Queen Genevieve spoke up next. "What will you call this challenge? Have you given it a name?"

Lord Owen nodded. "It will be called the *Gauntlet.*"

CHAPTER SEVEN

Farewell Flowers

It was nearly time to return to Ploemeur, but Trynne was not ready to leave Kingfountain. She had been excited to attend Drew and Genevieve's wedding for months. The fallout of everything that had happened—of everything that *would* happen—had irrevocably altered her. She could feel the difference in her thoughts, and even though the palace was the same as it had always been, it felt as if her childhood were dying before her eyes. And so, in an outward act of defiance, not yet willing to let go, she visited some of her old childhood haunts to soak up the memories that she would need to sustain her in the months ahead. In a way, it was like saying farewell to the past.

She had saved one of her favorite places in the world for last—the garden on the western portion of the grounds in the lower slope of the hill. Kingfountain's palace was built atop the hill and surrounded by multiple defensive walls, each one filled with groves of trees, gardens, and the occasional fountain. She liked this one best because it was the location of the Espion porter door that her father had used to sneak to the sanctuary of Our Lady when he was a child. She had needled him to share the story with her repeatedly because it was his first memory of experiencing the power of the Fountain. He had learned that one of his gifts of the Fountain was the ability to resist the magic of others—just like Trynne could do.

That portion of the grounds was full of trimmed lawns and hedges, a spacious fountain, and beautiful magnolia trees. She had many memories of going there with Fallon. In fact, one of her earliest memories was watching him climb the crooked limbs of the trees with their glossy green leaves and pinkish-purple buds. The grove was blooming because of the spring season, and it gave the air a heady smell. Captain Staeli was back by the gate leading into the garden, leaning against the wall with one foot planted back against it, his thumbs hooked in his belt as he scanned the garden. Trynne knelt in the grass beneath one of the huge magnolias, where many of the strange seed pods were strewn about. She picked one up, touching the fuzzy skin and ridges, smiling at the remembrances of how she used to play with them after they'd fallen.

She breathed in the smells as she ran her fingers through the grass next, wishing she could take the entire garden with her to Ploemeur. She loved the city of her birth, but it had different smells because of the different trees and foliage. Eucalyptus trees were common in Brythonica and the air had the smell of the sea, even deep inland. Oh, how she longed to visit all of the different realms, to taste the food and learn about the customs and traditions, as the young men would be allowed to do. At least her little brother would inherit the duchy someday, so she would not be stuck in Ploemeur forever. She would marry, and then a new kingdom would become her home.

The wind rustled the magnolia branches and blew strands of hair across her face. She smoothed them back and closed her eyes, just enjoying the feel of the breeze. Who would she marry? The thought of Prince Elwis brought a flash of resentment and anger. No, she could never marry a man like him. That image was quickly followed by one of Fallon punching Elwis and knocking him down. She was chuckling at the thought when a fuzzy seed pod thumped on the grass next to her.

Opening her eyes, she reached out and picked it up, rubbing her thumb along the velvety edge. Seed pods were shaped like a torch, with long, striated stems that could be broken off. The bulb was soft, similar to a pinecone except velvety in texture, and each segment ended in a tiny black curl. Hidden inside were little red seeds. She'd tried eating one when she was a child, but someone had scolded her and told her they were poisonous. Nothing had ever happened to her as a result. She brushed the seed pod against the tip of her nose and then another one landed on her shoulder.

Trynne looked up curiously, but the tree was bulging with flowers and leaves. Still, she had a sinking suspicion that she was not alone. She looked away and smoothed her skirts across her knees, feigning disinterest in her surroundings as she reached out with her magic. The Fountain magic came to life within her quickly, trickling from her fingers and toes and stretching out in tendrils.

And that's when she sensed the person hiding behind another tree, off to her right. The presence did not feel threatening or dangerous, and she instantly realized that Fallon had beaten her to her favorite place. He'd seen her enter the garden and had hidden himself to watch her. Now, he was throwing seed pods at her.

Well, two could play childish games.

Trynne innocently picked up several of the pods and collected them on her skirt. She could sense where he was crouching and hiding, and now that she was listening, she could hear a stifled laugh. It made her ears burn pink. She gathered five or six pods surreptitiously and then straightened her back to him, gazing toward the distant porter door. In her mind, she could see him leaning away from the tree, arm cocked back to lob another one at her.

Her magic gave her a definite advantage. It was like having eyes all around, able to sense him and his weaknesses all at once. She sensed the pain in his ear and the dull ache in his bowels from his earlier injuries. He would not be able to move as quickly now.

Before he could follow through on his intent to hit her again, Trynne gripped a seed pod in one hand, turned, and sent it winging at him. As soon as it struck him on the shoulder, she gathered up the others and rolled on the grass to put her tree in between them.

A pod zoomed at her and missed. "That was a lucky shot!" he taunted her.

Trynne felt her stomach become giddy with excitement. She quickly scrabbled to her feet, then threw another pod at him as he changed position. That one struck the tree instead. Suddenly he was charging her from around his side of the tree, scooping up several more pods and chucking them at her in rapid succession. They clattered against the bark, but Trynne didn't stay put. She raced around the other side of the tree and hurled another one at him, catching his arm, and then raced to the safety of another magnolia. The branches were so low she had to duck, but they protected her as another pod sailed toward her. It clacked into the branches, sending down some petal wedges and more seed pods.

Although she still clutched three or four pods, she snatched another one up from the ground and flung it at him as he came charging. He dodged it, then pelted her with the ammunition he'd grabbed. She deflected one with her arm, but another hit her ribs, riling her further.

He was nearly to the tree, so she ducked beneath the branches again and ran. With his long legs, he could easily outrun her, so she dodged around the tree she'd originally crouched behind, using the forked branches as a partial shield, and sent the rest of the pods at him in a volley. Her heart was hammering with the excitement of the combat. She couldn't hold back a smile, even though she knew it made her ugly. As he reached her tree, she feinted one way, then took off another, but her hair got snagged in a branch and yanked her back. She clawed at the branch and freed herself a moment later and tried to run.

"Caught you!" Fallon yelled triumphantly and grabbed her around the waist from behind to prevent her from fleeing. She was about to start beating him with her fists when he swung her around in a huge circle. He kept spinning them both around and her stomach gurgled with the motion as he went faster and faster.

"Stop! Fallon, stop!" she shrieked breathlessly, and he set her back down on the ground before staggering back a few steps in his own dizziness and falling down on the lawn. He was laughing so hard he couldn't breathe, and Trynne took the opportunity, dizzy as she was, to grab another seed pod and throw it at him.

"Truce! Truce, Cousin!" he said amidst his fit.

Gratified by his surrender, Trynne flopped down on her knees next to him to wait for the world to stop whirling. She had to dig her fingers into the grass to steady herself.

"You . . . are . . . terrible!" she panted. "Were you trying to make us both sick?"

"I hadn't thought . . . much further than pegging you with the magnolia fruit," he admitted, rubbing his forearm across his eyes. He was still laughing. "Reminds me of when we were children." He tried to sit up and failed, which made her laugh. "I think you ate one of the seeds when I goaded you to."

She looked at him, the world still spinning. "You goaded me to do it? I don't remember that part."

"Of course not. I was far too subtle back then. And you were three, I think. It was a long time ago. I used to climb up these trees to hide from you because you were always following me like a little nuisance. Things haven't changed. You're still following me."

She punched him on the arm. "I didn't know you were here!"

"Truce! Remember the truce!"

She fumed, but it was pleasant being with him. Alone. Well, except for Captain Staeli, who could see them from his vantage point. He did not look pleased—but then again, the man rarely did.

"Why did you come to the garden?" Trynne asked him.

"I was going to sneak away from my parents and claim sanctuary at Our Lady," he said in a conspiratorial voice. "I was supposed to get on the ship for Edonburick, but part of me doesn't want to leave." He lifted himself up again, leaning back on his elbows, and gazed at her. "Wouldn't it be fun, Trynne?" He wagged his eyebrows at her. "We could claim sanctuary together and join the thieves and miscreants!"

"You are *already* a miscreant, Fallon Llewellyn," she chided.

"And you like to spoil all the fun, Tryneowy Kiskaddon. How did you know I was hiding there?"

"I heard you," she said with a superior tone.

"I forgot about that," he said with a grin. "You're like your father. You can hear any noise out of place, no matter how small." He cocked his head at her. "When do you go back to Ploemeur?"

She plucked up some strands of grass. "This evening. I'll be home before you are."

He pursed his lips. "Your mother's powers are impressive. I mean, she's a Wizr, like Myrddin. I'd love to be able to travel from place to place like she can. It's so boring to travel by ship. Are you excited to begin studying with her? You're of age now."

Trynne looked down at her hands.

"Why the pout, Cousin? You *aren't* excited to become a Wizr?"

She breathed in through her nose. "You wouldn't understand."

He pulled up the rest of the way and then sat cross-legged. "You're right, I don't. Think of what a privilege it is to learn that magic. In the stories of old, female Wizrs always had great power and influence. I mean, I could understand why you wouldn't be excited about embroidery or managing the household ledger, but what you'll be learning is rare and priceless knowledge. I'm jealous."

"Well, I'm jealous of you, Fallon," she answered. She could see he wasn't in a joking mood at the moment, which was rare. "All my life, I've been told that this is what I'll be doing. I've always been more interested in my father's powers than in my mother's. Gannon would be a better Wizr. I'd rather learn how to fight."

"Why?" Fallon exclaimed. He looked genuinely surprised. "You've always talked about it. We used to whack each other with sticks when we were children." He nodded toward the nearest tree. "I just thought you were trying to . . . to mimic me. I don't know." He raked his fingers through his unruly hair. In doing so, he put a stripe of green grass there.

Trynne was tempted to leave it there, but she reached over and plucked it out.

"Not you," she said, shaking her head. Her voice fell even lower. "My father."

He crinkled his eyebrows. "So you wish you were his son?"

She shook her head. "No, I just wish that women were given the same opportunities. You heard Myrddin's prediction. An enemy force is coming to invade us. We'll need every boy and man to help defend our realm. What if we need more than that? What if this war is so terrible that we'll need every girl and woman too?" She stared down at her lap, the secret she carried burning inside her soul like a hot coal. She wouldn't let her father be killed. She *had* to save him.

He was quiet for a long while. When she looked up, he was staring at her, and the look of respect in his eyes made her blush.

"Well, Trynne, I for one wouldn't *want* to face you in battle," he said at last. "You are the fiercest, most stubborn . . . determined little girl that I know. I may be older than you, but I'm not wiser than you." He gave her a sidelong grin. "I'm glad you're on *our* side."

She started to smile, then caught herself and stopped.

"I wish you hadn't done that," he said with a sigh.

"Done what?"

"Why did you stop smiling?" he demanded.

She stared at him, feeling a sickly cold go through her, ruining the warmth of the moment and souring his compliment. "You know why, Fallon," she whispered, shuddering. "You were there when it happened."

"I know I was *there*, Trynne. And I wish it never had. I wish you'd gone with me to fetch those pies." He pressed his knuckle against his nose. "But it did happen. You can't change the past."

"I know that," she countered, feeling defensive. "But I also can't pretend that I'll ever be pretty like Morwenna. I know that people pity me. They look at me . . . as if I'm cursed or something. I can't make my mouth smile. It's lost." There was that familiar sadness again, that bleak feeling that rose up inside her whenever she thought about the attack. Why were they talking about this now? It was ruining the moment they had just shared!

Fallon shook his head slowly. He looked as if he wanted to say something, but she wasn't sure she was ready to hear it.

"What's done is done," he said with a sigh of regret and then got to his feet. He reached down and offered his hand to help her rise. She accepted it, noticing how warm it was against hers.

"I'm going to miss this place," he said, gazing around the garden. "It may be years before I come back. But at least I know I will see you again. You see, I am determined to win the Gauntlet. So I will be coming to Ploemeur and competing for the badge from Brythonica. Try not to make the test too easy for me."

"It's a test of wits as well as stamina, Fallon," she reminded him. "You'll be at a disadvantage."

"Ouch, cruel barb!" he said, planting his hand on his chest and grimacing. "I'm reminded that being in your company is akin to dwelling amidst hornets. There's a strong likelihood of getting stung. Well, let me claim my prize from the garden. It's spring and the magnolia flowers are truly a precious thing that I will miss." He reached up and plucked one from a low-hanging branch. "This one is for you, *Cousin*. And I'll claim the better one, here, for myself." He snapped off not just the flower, but also part of the branch. "Don't eat the seeds," he said. "They're poisonous."

Trynne cupped the large flower in her hands and gazed at it. "Thank you," she said in a soft voice. There was much she wished she had the courage to say.

But she did not.

Fallon lifted the flower to his nose. "I'm eager to face the challenges of the Gauntlets, despite your jests. I intend to master them all. I hope you will cheer for me, on occasion, from the galleries?"

She gazed up at him, conflicted, all the while wondering how she could find a way to face them herself.

PART II

Knight

◆ ◆ ◆

Where there is reverence, there is fear, but there is not reverence everywhere that there is fear, because fear has a wider scope than reverence. We fear what we cannot see. We fear what we do see. We fear what we cannot know. We fear what we do know. We fear what may not happen. We fear what does happen. Death may be the greatest of all human blessings. If only because it finally puts an end to fear.

Myrddin

◆ ◆ ◆

CHAPTER EIGHT

Ley Lines

Sometimes it felt as if Trynne's heart were slowly twisting in half. She was exhausted all of the time, but pushed herself to succeed even though it felt as if her mind and body would be sundered by the double life she lived. In the two and a half years that had passed since Drew and Genevieve's wedding, she had taken to rising before the sun each day so she could train as a warrior under the tutelage of Captain Staeli. She climbed ropes fastened to rings in the walls. She lifted and hurled heavy sacks of grain. She could handle weapons ambidextrously after the constant practice, though she had been surprised to discover she was slightly better with her left hand than with her right. The training was rigorous, frustrating, and she ended each session with the determination to do better the next day.

She was equally determined to continue keeping her parents in the dark about it.

Once she had bathed and changed from the clothes of the training yard into the silks of a duke's daughter, she lived a completely different life. She accompanied her mother on her noble responsibilities as Duchess of Brythonica, and also spent hours each day poring over books that held the secrets of becoming a Wizr. They were tedious and difficult to translate, and the work did not come naturally to her at all. She often found herself daydreaming about being in the training yard and thinking of a new way to deflect and parry blows with multiple weapons. When she caught her mind wandering, she'd get frustrated at herself and redouble her efforts to learn the arcane text. But her heart was not devoted to it, and she yearned for the simplicity and innocence of her childhood.

It was a tug-of-war, in a way, between the personalities and styles of her parents. She loved them both deeply. She worried every day about her father, and that worry drove her to throw everything she had into each side of her double life. Still, she knew where her talents lay—and where they did not. Sinia's approving smile was more often earned by Gannon's efforts with his storybooks than her own with the Wizr books.

She realized she was lost in thought again, having been sitting at her desk for hours on a wooden chair. The library also boasted a comfortable couch, but she found the softness—and her early rising—made her fall asleep too easily. The daylight was streaming in through the curtained window, and she rubbed her forehead, wishing she could descend down the cliffside on the rope-and-pulley system that was used to transport supplies from the town below. It was much faster than taking a carriage down the winding switchbacks, so she'd be roaming the streets of Ploemeur all the sooner, just as she'd done as a little girl. At fifteen, she had much more responsibility, and the weight of it constantly pressed on her shoulders. The room smelled of dried lavender, a pleasant scent that mixed with the musty books on the shelves. A globe on a circular table attracted her eye, but while she was tempted to go study it and imagine visiting all the different realms, she knew how much time she would waste if she did.

Trynne sighed and stared back down at the thick leather-strapped book in front of her. The book was called *The Vulgate*. It was a collection of tales and fables relating to the original King Andrew, written in a once popular language that had died away centuries ago, a relic of the past. It had taken her months to learn to read the proud, archaic script. As a child, she had read translations of *The Vulgate* and had been entranced by the stories of King Andrew and his knights. She hadn't realized at the time that there were sixty volumes of such tales and she would be required to read them all in her studies.

At first, she had groaned through the task. Obviously someone Fountain-blessed with the gift of reading would have fared better. For Trynne, deciphering the script was a chore, and the tales and fables that had once interested her seemed tedious and full of pointless details. They were so repetitive that she began to wonder whether there was any value to reading them. But then, after several months of poring over the words and growing more comfortable with her ability to translate them, she had been startled to hear the whisper of the Fountain in connection with a particular passage.

Trynne had discovered that day that *The Vulgate* held the secret words of power.

Her discovery had earned one of her mother's approving smiles, as well as a hug and a kiss on her cheek and a hint as to where she might find another word of power.

The Vulgate began to make sense to her. It was tedious to read through so many pages about knights and damsels, tests of valor, and swords buffeting helmets. But every so often—in fact, it was painfully rare—she would discover another word of power. The word would whisper to her, and she would feel the magic of the Fountain bubble up inside of her, along with the knowledge that speaking the word aloud would unleash its power. Some words of power could break apart previous spells permanently. Others lasted only for a limited duration, the length depending on how much magic the Wizr poured into it. While many spells lost all efficacy when passing over water, others only worked in water. Sinia warned her not to trifle with the words or to play with them as toys. Some words, for example, could unravel the defenses that prevented the Deep Fathoms from drowning Brythonica. It amazed

Trynne that words alone were preventing the sea from crashing past the glittering gems on Glass Beach and flooding the city. The thought filled her with awe and respect and even fear.

And yet it did not make her wish to be a Wizr.

In the two and a half years she had been painstakingly studying *The Vulgate*, she had come to realize that it would take a lifetime to read it all. She had scarcely read four volumes in all that time, and the rest seemed like a gargantuan task that she just didn't have the heart to conquer. Why did sword fighting come more easily to her? Why was she reluctant to push her mind the same way she did her body? Every person had an aptitude for something. Trynne was different from her mother.

Realizing it was nearly the end of her study time, she marked the page with a ribbon and closed the book. She stretched her arms and then her back, feeling a little soreness in her ribs from the morning's workout. After wandering over to the hearth, she removed two pokers from the rack and began twirling them into the hourglass pattern before ducking them behind her back in the flower drill. It was a drill she had performed hundreds of times and she could do it quickly with iron bars, swords, or even staves. Captain Staeli had taught her that speed could compensate for strength and size and had hammered into her mind that she needed to be faster than her opponents in all cases.

Because of her training and exercise, the iron skewers were easy to maneuver, and she loved the grace and simplicity of the twirling movement. The metal implements felt like an extension of her body. Her shoulders rocked back and forth as she twisted to complement the motion, listening to the swish and hum of the iron as it sped past her ears. It was a glorious feeling, and while she continued it, she felt the Fountain filling her, bringing a sense of wonder and thrill. She still loved playing Wizr, and the game still fed her power as well, but the early mornings in the training yard were special to her. She never dreaded going and she always pushed Captain Staeli to teach her more.

There was a sound at the door, and Trynne hastily returned the pokers to the rack as the latch clicked. It was not her mother, thankfully, but one of the palace servants sent to tell her that her mother was awaiting her at the chapel.

Trynne thanked her and rubbed her arms, feeling alive and giddy with the thought of her plans that night. She was to travel to Kingfountain to sup with her father.

The halls of the castle sped past as she hurried to the chapel where Sinia would be waiting. Trynne hadn't discovered any words of power in her studies that day, but she was so distracted it was likely she would have missed them anyway.

Upon reaching the chapel, she heard the gentle pattering of the fountain. It was a solemn place, and it inspired Trynne's reverence. Her mother was indeed waiting there, standing by the stone plinth whereon a different book sat. The book was not kept in the library; when not in use, it was concealed inside the waters of the fountain, yet it never got wet or even soggy. Only someone who was Fountain-blessed could summon it, if they knew it was there, and draw it out of the waters.

Trynne approached on soft feet, anxious to get a peek at the page her mother was looking at. Her mother was impossibly beautiful, something Trynne knew she would never be. She loved her mother deeply and passionately, but she was a little awed by her too. Sinia was the epitome of womanhood, or so Trynne thought, and she could never compare. Her mother wouldn't sneak into the training yard or spend hours fantasizing about a dream that could never be. No, her mother was a woman of profound responsibility.

Glancing over her mother's shoulder, she spied the map with its maze of ley lines. The book was a priceless treasure, for few kingdoms had sufficient detail of their own domains let alone the domains of others. Trynne saw the jagged coastlines of the various kingdoms and spied the spiderlike scrawl of inky letters spelling the names of Brugia, Occitania, Ceredigion, Atabyrion, and Leoneyis. It was an ancient

map, created before the latter kingdom had been flooded by the Deep
Fathoms for failing to live up to the covenants of the magic.

What made this map different from ones Trynne had seen in the
library were the ley lines. The map was not marked by a grid showing
north, south, east, and west. Instead, there were ley lines drawn across
the pages. At some points, like at Ploemeur and Kingfountain, there was
a clustering of ley lines, like wagon spokes. Those clustering locations
typically marked a place where the Fountain magic was the strongest.
They were concentrated points of significance, usually on the borders
between the sea and land.

"Hello, Trynne," Sinia said, turning and greeting her with a sad
smile. In the years since the king's wedding, Sinia had often brooded
over her husband's fate. She was quick to smile and show concern for
others, but often reverted back to thoughtful silence. "Are you ready to
go to Kingfountain?"

"What were you looking at?" Trynne asked, joining her by the
plinth. The book was a closely guarded secret. Just Myrddin, Sinia,
Owen, and Trynne knew of it, and Trynne had been included only
because she was training to be a Wizr. Myrddin was the one who had
drawn the map with the ley lines during his many travels. Just looking
at all the fine details filled Trynne with wonder.

She glanced down at the page and traced the ley line from Ploemeur
to Kingfountain. A Wizr, using the magic summoned by the correct word of power, could travel to any point along the line nearly
instantaneously. From Ploemeur, she could travel to Pree, Tatton Hall,
Dundrennan, or Kingfountain. She'd been tempted more than once
to suddenly appear at Dundrennan to surprise Fallon, who had been
named the Duke of North Cumbria on his eighteenth birthday. They
hadn't met since parting that afternoon years before, and Trynne longed
to see him again. She wondered if he was even taller now.

"I was just pondering this ley line," Sinia said, gently touching
Ploemeur and then grazing her finger over the east–west line. "This is a

major ley line. See how few run parallel to it? There's one far north . . . see how it runs through Legault? And there's another east–west one to the south that runs through Brugia." She touched her chin thoughtfully. "I was just wondering why there are so few that run east–west. There are more north–south ones. It's just . . . strange."

As Trynne squinted over the map, she saw her mother was right. The only ley lines that truly ran east–west were spaced quite far apart. From Ploemeur, the ley line going south reached the southern tip of Pisan. She wondered if that was where the poisoner school was located and felt an excited tingle.

"I've not noticed that before," Trynne said, shaking her head. "There are so many ley lines, it's always confusing to look at. Is there another map showing where these eastern ones go?" She pointed to the edge of the page.

Sinia shook her head. "No, love." Her mother worked up a smile and then ran her fingers through Trynne's hair. "It keeps getting shorter and shorter, Trynne, every time I look at you."

Trynne swallowed guiltily and tried to appear unconcerned. "I don't like it long."

"Your husband might."

"I'm not even sixteen, Mother! Please don't say you and Father are planning a wedding for me already!"

Sinia cupped Trynne's shoulders in her hands and looked her in the eyes. "Would we do that without telling you? When you reach Kingfountain, please give this letter to your father for me." She pulled it from her girdle and handed it to Trynne. Her mother's handwriting was impeccable and worthy of adoration. It was a reminder of another way in which Trynne fell short—she was far too impatient to worry about the quality of her penmanship.

"I will. I'm excited to see him again. It's been a long fortnight."

"It has," Sinia said. She gave her daughter an incisive look. "Can I ask you a question, and will you be honest with me?"

Worry began to rattle inside Trynne's heart. Had her mother found out about her training in the yard? Would she get in trouble for all the times she'd snuck the book of maps out of the fountain waters and studied the pages late at night after her mother was abed?

"Of course!" Trynne said after hardly a moment's hesitation. She felt so guilty inside, yet she managed a lighthearted tone.

"Do you *enjoy* studying *The Vulgate?*"

The question caught her off guard. She wrinkled her brow. "Of course I like it. The stories are very interesting, and I love it when I discover a new word of power. I know twelve already."

Sinia clasped her hands behind her back. "But do you enjoy it? Reading it is burdensome to you, is it not?"

Trynne felt guilt wash down her body into her toes. She couldn't lie to her mother, not when addressed so honestly and openly. She knew what she *ought* to say. How many girls were given the chance to train to be a Wizr, an advisor of kings and rulers? It was a precious responsibility; without someone to utter the words of power to protect Brythonica, the duchy could be flooded. It was a duty she could not refuse until her brother came of age.

She didn't know what to say, and that seemed to be all the confirmation Sinia needed.

"I see," Sinia said with a hint of regret in her voice.

"Mother, I have *tried*," Trynne said with all the pain of her inner turmoil. "And I will not give up. I have much to learn still. I . . . I truly enjoy some of the stories. There are just so many of them."

"I'm not ashamed of you, Tryneowy," her mother said gently. And yet there was a look of sadness in her eyes again. Of disappointment. "I want to share this part of my life with you. I enjoy teaching you. But I can sense that it's not where your heart is."

Trynne was miserable. "I've failed you."

Sinia shook her head and then hugged her daughter. "No, you haven't. We are just different, you and I." She smoothed some hair away from Trynne's brow. "When I was your age, I was in love with a boy who scarcely knew I existed, one I had only seen in my visions. A ruthless and corrupt king invaded my duchy to force me to marry him, and I had to turn to a tyrant for help." Her mother looked at her with deep emotion. "I . . . I wanted to raise you in safety so that you wouldn't have to feel what I did, but that was not to be." Trynne knew her mother was talking about the attack that had stolen her smile, and also about the future they would have to face someday soon. Sinia took Trynne's hands, squeezed them, and then kissed her knuckles. "Pardon a mother's lament. You are growing up so fast."

Tears stung Trynne's eyes as she wrapped her arms around her mother and held her, suffering through her own sensations of guilt and worry and conflict.

"I love you, Tryneowy," Sinia whispered, kissing her daughter's hair. "Never forget that I always will. You are *not* a disappointment to me. I know you are trying very hard. Give my love to your father. Tell him I miss him."

Trynne smiled, wiping her tears away with her wrist. She kissed her mother's cheek and then, gripping the letter between her fingers, stepped over the rail of the fountain into the water. The water was repelled by her presence, shuddering away from her as if it were an animal afraid to be near.

Daughter and mother locked eyes until the mist rose to carry Trynne away.

CHAPTER NINE

Oath Maidens

When Trynne was a child, she had heard her mother whisper the word of power capable of transporting her across the realm to Kingfountain and back to Ploemeur. It was one of the first words she had discovered on her own. *Kennesayrim*. It drained the one who spoke it, but it also allowed him or her to use the ley lines to travel great distances. Trynne would arrive at Kingfountain in time for dinner.

Trynne loved using the ley lines to travel. It was like plunging off a waterfall—her stomach would tighten with fear, and thrill with the sense of falling. There was that moment of apprehension and concern that always happened, followed by pure giddiness when she opened her eyes and the mist parted to reveal a chamber in Kingfountain. She wasn't powerful enough to bring someone with her yet, but her father always had an Espion waiting for her arrival on the other end. Captain Staeli would have the night off, and she imagined him enjoying a tankard of ale and kicking up his boots on a table with a self-satisfied smile. He was a soldier at heart and she could never draw him into conversations about anything other than weapons, fighting techniques, or war. If she ever tried discussing politics or trade, he'd just yawn and otherwise look disinterested.

The Espion waiting for her was Pedmond, one of Lord Amrein's trusted men, and he greeted her warmly.

"Welcome, Lady Trynne," he said with a bow. "Your father is waiting in the solar."

"Any news, Pedmond?" she asked, stepping over the fountain rail and falling into step next to him. She was a little queasy from the journey, but knew from experience her stomach would probably settle within the hour.

He shrugged. "There is always news. I'm sure Duke Owen will apprise you of any he wishes you to know about."

"You are always so courteous, but rarely very helpful," Trynne complained, giving him an arch look. "I want gossip. Give me a morsel at the very least."

"There is a Gauntlet coming up in Brugia's capital," Pedmond said. "The second time this year. They like to change theirs up regularly, making it more and more difficult. The bets are all in favor that Prince Elwis will remain the champion, though my money is on an upstart from Legault."

Trynne raised her eyebrows. "What's his name?"

"No one knows. People are calling him Bowman . An archer and they say he's quite good if a bit cocksure. Maybe even Fountain-blessed. My money is on him, but the odds are in favor of the prince keeping his title."

"That is much better, Pedmond. Thank you."

"You are quite welcome, my lady. Captain Staeli wouldn't approve of me speaking so freely with you, but you did insist."

"I shall not tell him," Trynne promised.

In due course, they reached the solar, where Owen was in conference with Lord Amrein. The spymaster's hair was graying rapidly, but he still spoke with the energy and enthusiasm of a younger man. Her father's hand was on his shoulder and they were both poring over a map on the table.

As she sidled up to her father, Trynne glanced down at the map, but she didn't recognize the borders or the land shapes on it.

Her father looked up and brightened when he saw her. She gave him a hug, and he stooped to kiss her hair. "How is your mother?"

"Well enough," she said, still feeling the guilt wriggling inside as a result of their last conversation.

Owen's brow furrowed. "Is something wrong?"

"We can speak of it later," Trynne said, then looked down at the map again. "What is this?" She looked closer, squinting, but could not decipher any of the wording. The script was long and slanting, very elegant, with little curlicues and embellishments. It was a different alphabet than any she had seen.

"A map . . . well, an attempt at a map, of Chandigarl."

"One of the eastern kingdoms?" Trynne asked.

"The most prominent one at the moment," Owen answered. "There has been some blood-feuding over there in recent years, but it seems to be at an end. The region is ancient, and there have been . . . hostilities between our peoples over the centuries. In the past, Argentine kings have sent soldiers to fight in the borderlands far to the east to keep them from encroaching farther." He looked up at Lord Amrein. "Tell her the recent news."

Trynne gave the spymaster a fearful look. She loved talking politics with her father, but ever since Myrddin's prediction and her mother's vision, any news filled her with dread.

"Chandigarl has not had a single king for several generations. But there's a man who has shown some promise. He's young, according to the reports—not even thirty yet. He was driven from his capital as a boy, but after living in exile for many years, he retook his father's city and proclaimed himself king. Instead of destroying his enemies, he has been getting them to serve him . . . Many are his distant kin. There are ancient palaces and fortresses in these lands, along with vast deserts that separate us." Lord Amrein glanced at her father and he nodded. "They call him Gahalatine. And rumor is that he's Fountain-blessed. If all of Chandigarl unites under him, it may be that he'll turn his eye on us."

A queer, dark feeling blotted Trynne's soul like a shadow. "You think this is the threat, don't you?" She was looking at her father.

"In the subtle details I've been able to pry from your mother's vision," Owen said solemnly, "we were attacked by a vast host that was not dressed in our manner. These are warriors, but their culture is different from ours. We know so little about them. This map, for example, is likely very inaccurate."

"Where did you get it?"

"From a Genevese merchant," Lord Amrein answered. "It cost a fortune, and it might well be a complete fabrication. We have no way of ascertaining its accuracy, yet it and other maps like it are our only window into that part of the world."

"Are you going to attack them?" Trynne asked her father, her eyes bulging.

Owen smiled. "I have enough trouble of my own, Trynne. I'm not about to lead an army across the Marusthali Desert. Lord Amrein has Espion infiltrating the region and learning what they can. It would not be easy for an army to make the march. Hopefully, we would see them coming and fight them there instead of here." He leaned back against the table and folded his arms. "The goal is to see how quickly we can receive word from the borderlands. It takes several weeks even by ship, but we are trying to trim the delay down to days. The area is so vast, though, that this has proven to be a challenge."

"I could help," Trynne offered, staring at her father. "There is a ley line from the southern tip of Pisan that goes eastward. I could—"

Her father held up his hand. "Now just a minute, Trynne. I've seen the book, and I know the one you are talking about. I won't even let your mother travel that ley line. I'm not about to allow *you*."

"But why not, Father?" she said, shaking her head. "It may be the fastest way to get information."

The look in his eyes told her that pushing him would be pointless. "I appreciate your desire to help, Trynne. Truly." He reached out and put his hand on her shoulder. "But I'll not risk you in such a way. The ley line may go nowhere. Or it may send you straight to the middle of Chandigarl. No, I absolutely forbid you to try. If I thought you had, or were going to, I would have a guard stationed at the fountain night and day. But I know you won't do something you've given your word about. Promise me, Trynne."

He had outmaneuvered her again and it frustrated her. It was exasperating talking to someone who could think six steps ahead in a game of Wizr. But she knew he would insist on it, and if she refused, he would make good on his promise right there and then. She didn't want to do anything to compromise his trust in her.

"Of course, Father," she answered meekly. "I promise. I just wanted to do something to help."

"I know, lass," he said, smiling tenderly at her. "And I do appreciate it. When you came, you were a bit downtrodden. What is wrong?"

She glanced down at the map once more.

"I'll be in the Star Chamber," Lord Amrein said, correctly divining that father and daughter needed some time alone. He bowed and left the solar at once.

At first, Trynne couldn't meet her father's eyes, but feelings were bubbling inside her like seething soup in a kettle. Her father had given her permission to train with Captain Staeli. But he had no idea how far she had progressed, and she dared not tell him for fear he would revoke his permission. She also carried the burden of another secret: that the Fountain intended her to sit in her father's chair after he fell in battle. Although she wanted to speak freely, she couldn't, and her secrets were tormenting her.

Owen waited until she was ready to speak.

Her voice was tremulous, but she pressed on even though she hated showing weakness. "I want to do *more* than just deliver messages for you. When you were my age—"

"I was training for war at Dundrennan," Owen said, interrupting her. He had a wise look in his eyes, as if he were trying to root out her secrets.

"Yes, I know that. That's not what I'm asking. What was Lady Evie doing? Wasn't she learning battle tactics as well? Was *she* allowed in the training yard?"

His brow wrinkled. "What's this about, Trynne?"

She clenched her fists and tried to calm herself. He would not respect her ideas if she came across as too emotional. Taking a deep breath, she said softly, firmly, "I don't think that I am *meant* to be a Wizr."

He didn't seem shocked by her statement, but he waited a moment to respond, considering her words. "Is it because *The Vulgate* is so tedious to read?" he asked.

She shook her head. "Well, it *is*, but that's not the reason. What I don't understand is that if we are getting invaded by Chandigarl—"

"We don't know that for certain."

"I know, Father! Hear me out." She clasped her hands together and started pacing, trying to choose her words carefully. "What I'm trying to say is why cannot the young women my age *also* train in the arts of war?"

As the words left her mouth, the door of the solar opened, revealing King Drew, Queen Genevieve, and Myrddin. Her cheeks flushed when she saw them enter, for she realized that she had spoken loudly and passionately enough for them to have heard her.

"I'm afraid we're intruding," Drew said, looking a little taken back. "I apologize. I should have knocked first."

Owen chuckled. "This is *your* chamber, lad. No need to apologize. And we did agree to meet here for dinner. Lord Amrein and I wanted to share the map with you."

The king nodded. "We saw him leaving and he mentioned you were both here. Hello, Trynne." He flashed her a charming smile and bowed slightly. "Good to see you."

"Thank you, my lord," Trynne muttered, cheeks hot, her stomach twisting and flipping with embarrassment.

"What were you speaking to your father about?" Genevieve asked. She looked absolutely regal in her green gown studded with sparkling little beads of glass. A simple but beautiful coronet graced her dark hair. She walked up and gave Trynne a hug and pressed a kiss to her cheek. The queen had grown even more beautiful over the last few years, and had settled into her role with confidence and grace. Up close, Trynne noticed how much the dress accentuated her hazel eyes.

"I'd rather not say," Trynne stammered, her mortification growing.

"Please, I'd like to hear it. We're your friends, Trynne. We'll not laugh at you." She turned and gave the others an arch look. "It was something about wanting to train like the boys?"

Trynne looked at her father, seeking his approval even though the queen had given hers.

Owen gestured with his hand for her to proceed. He wouldn't countermand the queen.

It was an awkward and uncomfortable position to be in. What would Genevieve think of her? All those years ago, she'd been hesitant about the notion of women participating in the Gauntlet. "I was just saying, Genny, that . . ." She paused to swallow, her mouth very dry. The queen took her hands and squeezed them encouragingly. ". . . that I would rather be in the training yard than the library. I'm learning declensions and ancient court etiquette when I should be learning archery. I'm balancing weights and measures instead of a beam over my shoulders with buckets, like the boys do in the yard. If we are truly going to be attacked, should I not know how to defend myself? Do I care any less about the honor of Ceredigion than does your brother or any of the other young men?"

She had been afraid that the queen would be put off by her unwomanly sentiments. Instead, Genevieve was staring at her with startled surprise and even—if she dared assume it was such—admiration.

Her words had gotten everyone's attention, including Myrddin's. The room fell quiet.

"You are not the only one I've heard speak of this," Genevieve said, still clinging to her hands. "Since we last spoke of this, I have sought the opinions of others. Many a maiden laments that while they're allowed to pick up scythes and help harvest a field, they're barred from picking up halberds and felling their foes. Your feelings are noble, Trynne." She turned. "Myrddin? You have traveled vast distances and seen many civilizations. You have seen other worlds that are different from ours. What customs exist that grant women the right to defend their homelands?"

Trynne felt an eager fire begin to burn inside her. She gazed at Myrddin, who was giving them both a canny look as he rubbed his chin with one hand, gripping his gnarled staff with the other.

"There are many such accounts, my queen," said the Wizr solemnly. "Many indeed."

"Are there?" the queen asked. "The only one I have heard of is the Maid of Donremy. And she was a singular person for certain."

Myrddin frowned and shook his head. "Pfah, my lady. 'Tis not an exception. The queen of the Argentine dynasty also wielded a sword. I have read Master Urbino's history, and while it has some inaccuracies, that is not one of them. She was the mother of kings. She went to the borderlands with her first husband, as Queen of Occitania, and inspired the troops to fight."

"Did you hear that, Trynne?" Genevieve said eagerly, and Trynne noticed King Drew frown in concern.

"There are others as well," Myrddin said. "It usually happens after a period of war when there are but few men left to defend the land. In one world I have seen, they are called the *Oskmey*—the Oath Maidens. In another, they're the Shield Maidens. They defend the home and hearth while their husbands and brothers go to war. Sometimes they lead battles too, fighting alongside the men. One ancient queen, Vodicia, led a rebellion against a tyrant."

Trynne's heart leaped at the words. She felt a quickening inside of her, an excitement that blazed like the sun.

Queen Genevieve hooked her arm through Trynne's. "There, you see, Trynne? You must have the blood of these Oath Maidens in your veins!" Then her voice took on a more coaxing tone. "My lord husband, I would like to found an order for such maidens. They would be under my care, and I would ensure it's done properly. I think Trynne's suggestion is just what we need. There are many maidens who are anxious about the future. How could it hurt to train some of our young women? Wouldn't it be better to prepare in advance than to delay and wish otherwise later? I would take this upon myself, my lord. I have always wanted to practice with swords. I think my mother instilled that in me. What say you, my lords?"

The king was looking to Owen for his input. Trynne could see Drew was uncomfortable with the idea, especially given his wife's intention to lead the group, but he clearly didn't want to crush her idea.

Trynne glanced at her father, feeling a little guilty for her role in the discussion. But her father did not look angry or even opposed to the idea. He clasped his hands behind his back. "Let's not be too hasty," he said. He turned to Myrddin. "Are there other examples of this from military campaigns in this world? The Maid is the only one from recent memory that I've read, but I'm not as learned as you—nor have I lived for so long."

Myrddin clasped both hands atop the mushroom-shaped end of his staff. "Aye, Lord Owen. There was once a great general who was badly outnumbered by the enemies who invaded his homeland. The war lasted for several years. At one point, he threatened to arm his women *and* his children and bring the fight to the enemy's homeland." The Wizr smirked. "Aye, 'tis true. It goes against our sensibilities to force the horrors of war on our womenfolk. But there are times that it has been done. And as you said, there have been times when the greatest champion in the realm has been a woman."

When Myrddin met Trynne's eyes, she realized that he already knew her fate, just as she had speculated on that long-ago day. She knew she was right to be asking for this.

"I will not be too hasty in this," King Drew said seriously. "We will discuss it further in council around the Ring Table."

CHAPTER TEN

The Wizr's Oath

Every time Trynne went to Kingfountain, it was harder and harder to leave. Sometimes she felt more at home in that palace than she did at Ploemeur. She had rarely been to Tatton Hall and had little sentimental attachment to it. Kingfountain was the center of intrigue and decisions, the hub of power and authority. It was the seat of the kings of the past, the place of legends brought to life. Kingfountain was the place where destiny was woven. She loved everything about it, from the intangible feel of the place to its beautiful trappings. At the moment, though, the king's council was meeting behind closed doors, and she wanted desperately to know what they would decide. All she could do was pace with nervous energy, waiting and dreading the moment she'd have to return to Ploemeur.

The sun was slanting through the windows, showing the fast-ebbing daylight that made her heart wring with emotion. As she wandered the corridors alone, she passed the archway where she'd spied Morwenna and Elwis, and the memories of what had followed rushed upon her, ending with Fallon swinging her around in a dizzying circle.

That particular memory made her heart ache. She had known Fallon her entire life, and even though she loved to argue and debate with him, she secretly wished that he could someday overlook the fact that she would never be a beauty. Perhaps he needed someone like her to prick the bubble of his pride and prevent it from carrying him off.

Tapping footsteps came from around the corner ahead, and she was startled when her father's herald, Benjamin, came into view.

"Ah, Lady Trynne," he said with a smile. His father, Farnes, had served her father faithfully for years and Benjamin had inherited the role of messenger. He was in his late twenties and had a handsome and confident bearing. "Your father sent me to find you, but the queen asked to speak with you first. She's in her personal chambers. Shall I escort you?"

"Of course," Trynne answered, hastening her steps. "Has the council ended then?"

"It has," he replied with a nod.

"What did they decide?"

"I have no idea," he said with an apologetic smile. "I was not allowed in the deliberations."

Eager to find out, Trynne kept up a furious pace as they wove through the corridors toward the queen's chambers. The doorman saw them approach and knocked on the door.

"Lady Tryneowy Kiskaddon," he announced in a formal tone.

Benjamin caught her sleeve before she entered the room. "Your father wishes to see you before you return to Ploemeur. Shall I wait for you?"

Trynne shook her head. "Is he in the solar?"

"Yes."

"Then I will go there afterward. Thank you." She nodded to him and then stepped into Genevieve's rooms. The quarters had once belonged to the queen dowager and then to Princess Elyse, who was now the Queen Dowager of Occitania. Genevieve had adopted the customs and decorations of Ceredigion rather than favor her Atabyrion tastes for fancy headdresses and furs.

One look at Genny's eyes told Trynne that the decision had not been favorable. Her heart sank with disappointment.

"There you are," Genevieve said, rushing up to her and taking her hands. "Let's neither of us pout, Trynne. We must school our feelings in the face of rejection." The queen kept a hold on Trynne's hands as they began to walk in a circuit around the beautiful chamber. Trynne admired the various gowns and the huge four-post bed draped with veils and gold-threaded blankets. The backboard was nearly invisible beneath all the frilled pillows. The queen's ladies-in-waiting were arranging her gown for the evening meal and some were tidying up.

"The king said no?" Trynne asked despondently.

Genevieve's brow wrinkled. "It wasn't a *no* so much as it wasn't a *yes*." Trynne's shoulders fell.

"Don't lose heart, Trynne. I haven't. Some men need coaxing to change their minds. I reminded the council that my mother defeated an invading army at Blackpool at the age of seventeen. I also reminded them of how the Maid of Donremy was Fountain-blessed to be a battle commander. I've read many of her stories and have always found them interesting. But men are rather . . . sensitive in this area. Believe me, we went through all the arguments against it like a stage performer doffs and dons costumes. But the actor is still the same beneath them all. The menfolk are wary of us, Trynne. We are a great mystery to them. Drew didn't render a verdict. He will summon the full council within six months to discuss the matter again when my parents can also be there to offer counsel, along with the other lords of the council."

"Six months?" Trynne said, trying not to sound devastated.

Genevieve patted her arm. "Patience can be a trial, believe me, I know. But my husband is not rash. He wishes to hear all the sides before making up his mind. You can trust that I will do my part to encourage him to see reason."

Trynne let out a sigh. "It's not fair, Genny. Men get to decide so many things. They can make candles, butcher hogs, train to be knights, lawyers, scribes, or whatever they wish. Yet we, as ladies, can only hunt and hawk alongside them. We can shoot arrows at a clump of thatch, but not at a soldier trying to burn our home."

"You're right, of course," Genevieve said. "But when men feel threatened, just as a skittish horse, they must be handled with gentleness. They will come to see our view eventually."

Trynne smiled, then felt self-conscious and forced it down. "There could be a lot of training in six months. How do we know this Gahalatine fellow will not invade before then?"

"We don't," she answered. "That is why you must continue your training in secret." She gave Trynne a knowing look.

Her heart fluttered and she blinked rapidly.

Genevieve smiled and patted her arm. "You think your morning exercise has gone unnoticed? The Espion is pretty efficient, my dear. I've asked about you, and so I was told, but only because I'm the queen. I admire you more than you know, Tryneowy. So does my husband. He heard your counsel and is considering it in his own way. Give him time. I do think he'll come around."

Trynne felt a warm tingle of pleasure at the queen's words. "Thank you for telling me."

Genevieve put her arm around her and squeezed. "You have friends at court, my dear. Never forget that. Now, be an obedient daughter and go see your father."

"I will," she answered. She hesitated a moment and then asked, "How is . . . Fallon?"

The queen raised her eyebrows in a knowing way that made Trynne's cheeks begin to flush. She had tried to make the query sound casual and realized her blunder immediately. She should not have asked at all.

"He's preparing for the Gauntlet of Brugia," the queen answered with the loving care of a devoted sister. "I think he trains nearly as hard as *you*."

Trynne was flushed completely by that point, so she excused herself before the mortification made her start babbling like an idiot.

◆　◆　◆

By the time she reached the solar, Trynne had barely calmed her nerves and reasserted her composure. Why had she asked Genevieve that question? The queen was Fallon's sister—her loyalty to her brother was pre-eminent. She chided herself for being a fool and then knocked on the door of the solar. She waited outside to be admitted.

The door handle jiggled and she saw her father in the gap, his expression haggard and fretful. He seemed relieved to see her.

"What's wrong, Father?" Trynne asked. As soon as she stepped into the room, she realized they were not alone. The king was sitting at the table, looking dumbstruck. Myrddin stood at the far end, his hands pressing on the wood. The Wizr looked grim. "What has happened?" Trynne asked, her insides twisting into knotted ropes as she firmly shut the door behind her.

King Drew stared up at her, obviously rattled. "Myrddin has just informed us that he must go."

Trynne felt a moment of pure panic. She gazed at her father and then at the Wizr.

"It's true, little sister," Myrddin said in a kindly way. "The Fountain bids me go and I must obey. There is trouble brewing in another world. I must tend to it."

"Do we not have troubles enough in *this* one?" the king said with a hint of anger. He rose from his seat and began to pace. "I am your king, Myrddin. Will you not obey my will? Why can you not stay?"

Trynne's world was rocking. It felt as if a huge stone were being dragged across the floor. It felt like the magic of the Wizr board was at work.

"Was it not the Fountain that put the crown on your head, lad?" Myrddin said. "Was it not the Fountain that gave you the sword?"

"Actually, I arranged it," Owen said with a half chuckle.

The Wizr gave him a piercing look. "Aye, 'tis true, my lord. But did you find that blade in the ice caves of the North by *chance*? Was it not *put* there for you to find? We may as well argue with water not to tumble off cliffs. Yet still it will fly as water is wont to do."

The king let out a pent-up breath and shook his head in frustration. "Myrddin, we *need* you!"

The Wizr, who was still leaning on the table, straightened. "I know, lad. Sometimes, there are greater needs. I go where your ancestor once went after the sword of his bastard son skewered him. He went to a realm where such a wound can be healed. A realm where stones sing with water from the Fountain. A land of orchards and lavender. Of pretty gardens, which have been neglected of late. Alas, it is no longer a land of Virtus kings," the Wizr said somberly, his countenance falling. "Their *need* is greater."

His words were so softly spoken and mournful that it made Trynne feel like weeping. She stared at the Wizr, unable to imagine the knowledge he had acquired after living for so many centuries, on so many worlds. He was a man of quirks and wise sayings. But he was full of wisdom that exceeded anything she knew. Still, her heart rebelled against him leaving, knowing it would make her father more vulnerable.

"I cannot say I relish this parting, Myrddin," Owen said, shaking his head. He approached the portly Wizr and put his hand on his shoulder. "I have learned much from you these many years and had hoped to learn more still. *You* are one of the Fountain's blessings. And I admire you." Owen's voice thickened with emotion. "Is there anything that can be done to aid you? Would you take my scabbard with you for defense?"

Trynne nearly gasped her disapproval, but her eyes grew hot at her father's offer.

Myrddin reached out and patted Owen's shoulder. "No, lad. But it was generous of you to offer. You are not a *pethet*. And I mean that." His own mouth quirked into a smile and he arched his eyebrows. "Unlike some *others* in this room who dissent against the Fountain's will with their brooding thoughts." He gave the king a pointed look. Then he softened a bit. "Were the need not so desperate, I would stay. I made oaths that I would obey the Fountain when it called on me. These oaths I must fulfill. And so I leave you."

"Forgive me, old friend," the king said, shaking his head. "And take my hand and with it my blessing. I have relied on your wisdom and counsel these many years. A seat at the Ring Table will sit empty for you until you return." The two men clasped hands, their grips sturdy and strong. The king's voice was haggard when he continued. "I've been preparing all this while to lose my right hand. To lose my left of a sudden was . . . more than I was prepared for. Forgive me, Myrddin."

The Wizr gave him an approving smile. "Thank you, lad. I have not felt so appreciated in all my travels. There are rapids in the river ahead. Perilous times are coming. Be courageous. Paddle hard." He grinned dangerously. "Avoid the rocks if you can."

The Wizr and the king hugged one another. Trynne's father's emotions were obviously churning, so she went to his side and held him. For once, she was the comforter rather than the comforted, and she hardly noticed when his arm slipped around her shoulder.

Myrddin smiled at them, and then she experienced the rushing sensation of the Fountain magic as he vanished before their eyes.

◆　◆　◆

There was a long, stunned silence in the solar after the Wizr disappeared.

The brazier coals were fresh and sizzling and the windows were still open from the day, letting in the night air. It was nearly time for Trynne to go home, but her reluctance to go had only grown.

"I can't believe he's gone," Drew said. He stood by the chair at the end of the table, gripping it so hard his knuckles were white.

"I think I just supposed he would be with us the whole time," Trynne's father said. "It never occurred to me that he might be called away elsewhere." He sighed. "I should have foreseen it."

Drew gave him a sidelong look. "You can't always predict *everything*, Lord Owen."

He nodded. "I wonder that Sinia didn't tell me. Perhaps the Fountain warned her not to." He seemed to suddenly realize that Trynne was still there. "You'd best return and tell your mother this news." He bent down and kissed her hair, and she hugged him fiercely, stifling a sob.

"Shhh, lass," he soothed, stroking her back. "In some games of Wizr, it is impossible to predict the outcome. We are not defenseless. No enemy has conquered this city since before the first Argentine ruled it. There is a massive river protecting us, not to mention multiple rings of walls and hills. If Gahalatine or another ruler seeks to conquer us, he will have to earn it."

She looked up at his face, the fear of losing him unbearable at the moment. But she would be brave. She would be a soldier, like him. Unable to speak, Trynne nodded and then mastered herself. Standing straight, she gave him another hug.

"Give your mother my best regards," the king said, smiling kindly at her. "She's my only Wizr piece now. I will need her counsel more often, I think. Your father leaves notes for her in the waters. I may have him start including mine now." He grinned.

"Yes, my lord," she said.

He waved aside the pleasantry. "You've been in Kingfountain so often over the years, Lord Owen. I know you miss your wife and your other lands. You are as steadfast as Duke Horwath was in service of his king. I miss that old man still. I was just a little boy when I first came here," he said, looking up at the stone buttresses holding up the ceiling.

Then he smiled to himself. "And so were you, Lord Owen. Sometimes I feel as if the true owner of the castle is the Fountain, and we are just here as its guests."

Her father let go of Trynne and started pacing. "We are more than just pieces in a game," he said. "At least, that is my hope."

Trynne bade her father and the king good night and then hurriedly walked to the chapel where the small fountain awaited her. An Espion trailed her the entire way, keeping a discreet distance. She wondered how she was ever going to accomplish anything with so many people minding her. There was news to share with her mother. There were tears to shed on her pillow where no one could see them. Her emotions were wrung out and she was weary.

Trynne stepped over the lip of the fountain and stood amidst the dry stones. In her mind, she thought of Ploemeur and prepared to utter the word of magic that would bring her there.

But before she could, she heard another voice mutter it. A man's voice.

And suddenly her muscles were locked and she felt as if she were drowning.

CHAPTER ELEVEN

The Broken Ones

The sensation of drowning sent ripples of panic through Trynne's body. She was falling through the magic, being pulled down as if into the very depths of the sea, and the crushing weight of it was squeezing her chest, her legs, her throat. Unable to move, unable to see through the dizzying vortex, she cried out in her mind for something to cling to, something to stop the fall.

The magic ended in a jarring crash that left her collapsed on a cobblestone floor. Even though the ground was solid, the world seemed to pitch up and down, and she knew she wouldn't be able to stand for several moments. A strange blue light masked her surroundings, and the sound of sandals scuffing on stone hung in the air. Her stomach gave her only a moment's warning before heaving her dinner onto the floor. She knelt, pressing her hands against the stone, and allowed the convulsions to ripple through her as her bowels constricted. Her lungs expelled water to join the sickening mess.

"*Ach*, I forget that happens sometimes to those who are new at it," Myrddin muttered. He was busily shuffling around, his voice moving this way and that.

The fear in Trynne's heart began to ebb. Her blurry vision was sharpening, but her strength was too spent for her to lift her head, so she stared down at the tiles beneath her. She rubbed her lips on the back of her wrist, feeling better after vomiting so hard. The seasick feeling was settling and the whirling of the room was slowing down, like a wagon wheel coming to rest on its axle after being upended.

She saw a pair of sandaled feet by her, and then Myrddin thrust a flask toward her. "Drink this, little sister. Fresh water."

She gratefully accepted it, then uncorked the stopper and quickly drank. The taste was leathery, but it was satisfying and helped remove the flavor of bile from her mouth. She handed it back to him, still unable to fully lift her head. There was a pattern on the tile floor, she noticed, a mosaic of sorts. The shape was an octagon with a large cross through it. It was made of light and dark tiles and pieces, not the traditional black and white of a Wizr board. She had never seen the symbol before.

"Where did you bring me, Myrddin?" Trynne asked hoarsely. She coughed against her fist and found her voice again. The room was shadowed and dark, lit only by blue stones glowing in the wall. The place had a run-down feeling, and beneath the stench of her sick, there was the stale smell of an ancient crypt. The stones beneath and around her were mottled with broken pieces. The room was a small cupola, but there was an arch on one wall leading to a dark corridor beyond.

"This is an in-between place," Myrddin said. As she looked up, she saw he was wearing a traveling cloak and had a large sack with a strap across his chest. He gripped his gnarled walking staff in one hand and the pommel of a sword in the other. He looked prepared for a long journey.

"In between what?" she pressed. "Why am I here?"

Myrddin crouched on one knee to bring himself down to her level. "I don't have time to explain all this, little sister. The Fountain bids me go, and so I must, but it has also bidden me to speak to you ere I go too far. Your king is in danger, and I will not be there when he faces it. You must do so. He has enemies who seek the hollow crown. The Fountain wills you to be his champion, his protector." Myrddin sighed and shook his head. "So much I *want* to say, but so much I *cannot*. Heed me, little sister. The fate of Ceredigion rests upon your shoulders. If you fail, the Deep Fathoms will reclaim not only Kingfountain, but all the territories the king has gathered into his peace. You cannot fail. I could not see how you could fulfill your destiny, not when there is so little *time* before it will come to pass. But your words triggered a memory. The Oath Maidens!" He smiled confidently and with energy. "You must bring the order back, to restore it anew. There will be many men who will seek to undermine you. They are *pethets*. If you do not stand by the king in his hour of need, then all will be lost and ruined." He wagged his finger at her. "But *if* you are an Oath Maiden, you will be able to stand."

She gazed at him in bewilderment. "I can hardly stand now. What are you saying, Myrddin?"

"*Anthisstemi*," Myrddin whispered, gripping her elbow and helping her rise. As he uttered the word of power, Trynne felt strength fill her legs and wash away all of her queasiness and discomfort. She was refreshed and suddenly alert, her mind cleared of the fog of the journey.

"I do not have time to explain this all to you, little sister," he continued, keeping his hand on her elbow. His voice was hard and determined. "*Brachio*, I would that I did! I must obey the Fountain's summons. You were meant to be an Oath Maiden. One of the Broken Ones. If you accept the oaths, you will be empowered by the Fountain to do the work it has for you. You will be tempted to violate the oaths. You *must* not!" His eyes were fervent, almost wild. "There are grave consequences, sister. If you accept the oaths, the Fountain will personally guide you and direct you. You will be an emissary of its will, like the Maid of Donremy. She was an Oath Maiden too. But the people in her day were not ready to follow her. They were unworthy of it, so she was taken and executed. Her heart was broken. To be an Oath Maiden, to be a Broken One, you must endure hardship and suffering and not flinch from it." He screwed up his brow and said the next words in almost a whisper. "No pain that we suffer, lass, no trial that we experience is ever for naught. Hardships teach us qualities we can get in no other way. Like patience, faith, fortitude . . . and humility. These are the true principles of Virtus. All that we endure, especially if we endure it patiently," he added, wagging his finger at her again, "builds up our character, it purifies our hearts, and it expands our souls." He paused, sighing deeply. "It makes us more worthy to be called the children of the Fountain. Now I have told you the Fountain's will for you. I have delivered my warning that once you go down this path, you cannot go back upriver. If you forsake your oaths, there will be terrifying consequences. You are only fifteen. This is a heavy burden to put on you, but those even younger than you have had to bear it. The Fountain will not force you to accept it. But this it commands me to offer you. Will you accept it?"

Trynne stared at the Wizr, her heart near to bursting at his words. She felt the magic of the Fountain surrounding them, felt its power behind the words he had used. He was speaking on behalf of the Fountain, inviting her to become what she had always dreamed.

She wanted to say yes. But she felt completely overwhelmed. "Will I be able to tell my parents?" she asked.

Myrddin stared at her, pausing a moment, as if listening.

"No," he answered curtly.

The answer hurt as if he had stabbed her, and she winced. It would be a painful decision. "Is there no one I can tell?" she said in anguish.

Myrddin stared at her, his lips pursed in a frown. He released her elbow and settled his meaty hand on her shoulder. "The queen. She must know that you are to be her husband's protector. The Fountain also bids me to let you tell Captain Staeli. He is loyal to you, little sister. You will learn how much before your journey is over."

Trynne felt a surge of relief and a prick of apprehension at the same time. What did that mean? From the look in Myrddin's eyes, she dared not ask.

"Will you accept this?" he asked her forcefully.

"I will," she answered, and as she did, she felt the grating feeling of stone again, a feeling of destiny that was accompanied by the determination to succeed. In her heart, she experienced the swelling of the Fountain's approval. It was such a powerful feeling that it made her eyes well with tears.

"Kneel once more, little sister," the Wizr said. "And prepare to receive your oaths. There will be five. If you honor them, then someday you will receive four more. After you have proven yourself a true Oath Maid."

She dropped down to one knee. "What is it like, Myrddin? How will I feel?"

He smiled again with that knowing smile. "You will never be the same again."

◆　◆　◆

When Trynne awoke in her own bed well before sunrise, she wondered if it had all been a dream. The sheets had their familiar smell, and the pillows were just the right softness. She blinked into the shadows and gloom, full of memories of what had transpired with Myrddin. Had it only been a flight of fancy?

"My lady, are you awake?"

It was Captain Staeli's voice coming from the shadows. It was time to head out to the training yard.

"I am. I'll be down shortly."

"Very well, my lady."

Trynne pushed herself up in bed, her stomach tingling with apprehension. How could she know whether it had truly happened? And then she felt it rising up inside her, an awareness not just of the distant calls of songbirds or the muted rumble of the surf. No, it was an awareness of the lives of countless others who had shared her calling. As she closed her eyes and bowed her head, she could almost hear the screams and ringing steel of ancient battlefields. Myrddin had called it the "wellspring," the source of the Fountain that had collected all the lives and experiences of others, which she could tap into and drink from. She no longer felt like a girl of fifteen. She carried with her the wisdom of ages past. Oath Maidens had once protected Leoneyis. And they had all been destroyed by a king who'd forsaken his oaths. After he had murdered the last one, the Deep Fathoms had drowned his entire kingdom.

Then she remembered the oaths—the promises she had sworn over a handful of small stones. Five oaths in all, though she would ultimately be asked to take four more. They were the origins of the code of Virtus, the symbol of true knights. Oath Maidens were the defenders of the kingdom. Their strength came from protecting others, not from seeking to harm. Each of the five oaths whispered into her mind. If she failed in any of them, there would be dire consequences.

Never slay a man with a spear or arrow. In return, she could not be slain by such herself. Never take a life unawares or out of revenge. Never hearken to greed or take a bribe. Never swear an oath falsely. Never refuse to serve when the Fountain calls—even at the peril of life and loved ones.

The memory of the oaths made her breath come quickly. She hastily stole away from the inviting sheets and put on her training garb, her mind whirling with the snatches of memory from lives of women she didn't know, but who were suddenly a part of her. Her fingers tightened the lacings of her leather tunic, and she wrapped the girdle around her waist and cinched the buckles. Her leather bracers were on the floor and she stooped down and strapped them on next, then tied her hair back with a band. She breathed in and out slowly, trying to master the churning tide of images that came and went with each breath. Myrddin had said that it would take time to grow accustomed to the insights and flashes sent to her by the Fountain. Patting her stomach to quell her nerves, she marched away from the changing screen and joined Captain Staeli in the hall.

He never spoke much, just followed her down to the yard, performing his duty with efficiency and honor.

When they reached the training yard, she was nervous and a little breathless.

"It's been a few days since we trained with daggers," Captain Staeli said as he walked in front of her to the weapons chests. "You've done well with underhand attacks, but today we will do overhand."

She felt a smile tug at her mouth. In her mind, flowing like water, she instantly knew all the variations of knife fighting that had ever been taught or tried. She supposed this would be as good an opportunity as any to demonstrate to him that she was different.

Brugia, the Fountain whispered to her. *You will compete in the Gauntlet. Bring him with you.*

Yes, Trynne answered in her thoughts, accepting the charge.

Captain Staeli rummaged through one of the chests and withdrew a long-bladed dagger. "This was made in Atabyrion," he said, examining it. "Fair blade. See the diamond shape near the hilt?" He handed it to her. "Now, hold it with the blade downward, along your forearm—yes, exactly like that."

Trynne stepped away from him into the yard, summoning her Fountain magic into a trickle of power.

"Let's see how you do for starters," he said, hunching his shoulders as he came at her with an underhand thrust. He began to feint toward her, as if he were a street brawler with only a dagger. "How would you use the blade to defend yourself? Just see what comes naturally to you."

Trynne nodded to him, keeping herself perfectly still and not mimicking his aggressive posture. She could sense which attack was a feint and which was real, so she didn't waste energy pacing or stepping from foot to foot. Trynne kept the blade up near her face, watching his entire body at once.

She saw the look in Staeli's eyes as he noticed her unusual posture. Then he lunged at her.

Since she was the one defending, the magic rushed in to aid her. Trynne deflected the attack with the dagger, then stepped around and trapped his arm against her side. Dropping to her knees, she pulled him off balance. He was already moving to free himself when she pivoted on her heel and dropped lower, using her position to throw him off balance. Staeli landed on his back, his arm still trapped in her armpit, his wrist torqued around. She pulled his pinky, and when the dagger fell out of his grip, she caught it before it hit the ground.

She released his arm and rose, holding both daggers.

The look of startled surprise on his face was worth all the strawberries in Plowman's Field.

"Swords next," she said. "Swords against daggers. I'm ready for you, Captain. Get on your feet."

He blinked and then quickly rose, chafing his elbow and giving her an appraising look. "I get the swords?"

She nodded and then held both daggers underhanded.

Staeli fetched two short swords from the chest and began slicing the air with them as he shook loose his arms and shoulders. His face was one of determination.

"Are you going to attack me, Captain?" she asked. "Or do you just want to swing your arms about?"

He gave her a bemused look. She normally didn't taunt him like that. Then he rushed at her, swinging both weapons at once in a hasty lunge that brought him close in just a moment. Trynne had him unarmed in less than a minute, one of her daggers at his throat. His response was to grapple her arm and try to fling her down, and that's when the fight became more interesting.

Captain Staeli pulled out all the various tricks from his arsenal. She countered each one, seeing how it would happen just a moment before it did and knowing exactly how to counter it to her best advantage. Her movements were short and swift and devastatingly effective. After several minutes, she had him on the ground again, controlled by a locking bar hold on his arm. His breathing was huffing with the effort and with a little hint of pain. She did not feel winded at all.

He looked about to surrender, but her new senses told her that he was going to try to kick her foot and trip her. She waited until he did, then bent her knee so that his blow missed, following up by dropping her knee down on his calf muscle, making him grunt with pain.

"Do you yield?" she asked him, tightening her grip on his arm.

He nodded, his nose crinkled with suffering, but he bit back the pain.

Trynne released him and then helped him rise. He kneaded his calf, grimacing. The dawn still had not broken yet, and he was clearly winded.

"What happened while you were away?" he said, shaking his head at her. "You're not the little girl I trained yesterday." He straightened, rubbing his arm next.

She let out a sigh. "I am not, Captain Staeli. I have been chosen by the Fountain to protect the king. I am different now. I *feel* different. I guess you could say the Wizr cast a spell on me. The Fountain bids me go to Brugia and compete in the Gauntlet. Captain Staeli, I no longer need your protection."

His eyes widened as if she'd suddenly slapped him in the face. In that brief unguarded moment, she saw real hurt. She was not an assignment to him, she realized, but almost like a daughter. He had watched over and protected her for much of her life. He had enjoyed training with her in the mornings, and the thought of being dismissed from her service was unbearably painful to him. But he was a soldier and a man, and would brook his disappointment with grim resignation. In that moment of decision, she saw his lip curl into a sad frown.

"If that is my lady's wish," he said solemnly.

She shook her head no. "Captain, I no longer require your protection. But I would appreciate your *companionship*. The Fountain bids me keep this secret from my parents and even from the king. I have been permitted to tell Queen Genevieve. And you." She gave him one of her rare smiles.

His look softened considerably and a proud grin lifted his normally stoic mouth. "Truly? The Fountain . . . the Fountain knows *me*?"

"Yes, Captain. It does indeed. And I am grateful that I do not need to bear this secret alone. Have you heard the legends of the Oath Maidens?"

CHAPTER TWELVE

Brugia

Trynne's relationship with Captain Staeli changed significantly in the days following her humbling of him in the training yard. In fact, their roles reversed, and she became the teacher. Their early morning jaunts in the training yard started with him picking various weapons and asking her to teach him the techniques revealed to her by the Fountain. A rigorous master, he proved to be an equally adept learner. He hadn't expected his charge to turn the tables on him, but there was no denying the power of her Fountain magic, and he was eager for the opportunity to test and improve his abilities.

As the time approached for the Gauntlet of Brugia, Trynne grew more and more anxious about how she was going to attend. She didn't want to break her parents' trust by using the ley lines without their permission. But taking a ship would likely be more dangerous, and it would certainly be more time consuming. Brugia's capital, the city of Marq, was at a major intersection of ley lines. It was due south of Kingfountain, along a major north–south axis. It was also on the same east-west axis as the ley line that ran through Pisan, the one Trynne speculated ran eastward all the way to Chandigarl. There was a ley line from Ploemeur to Marq, so she could travel to that city instantaneously, which she felt in her heart was the best option. But she worried her mother or father would find out and banish her from the fountain rooms.

While she worried about her upcoming travel, she and Captain Staeli visited some Brugian merchant shops in Ploemeur. She was grateful that Brythonica was a trading nation, giving her access to the fashions from both continents. She bought a lovely dress from the merchant shop on her visit with Captain Staeli. The fashion for girls was a skirt with dark colors, deep maroon or violet or gray, with a front-lacing kirtle worn over a voluminous white chemise with garters at the wrist, elbow, and upper arm. It was also a Brugian tradition for both maids and men to wear stiff velvet hats in black with silver ribbons stitched into the base. These were not the puffy caps worn in Kingfountain; they fit closer to the head and fluted out slightly. Staeli also bought a costume in the Brugian fashion, one that was big enough to cover his hauberk. He grudgingly bought the black hat as well, though he was the sort of man who preferred leather hoods to such ceremonious attire. And he bought an extra costume for his "nephew"—one that Trynne would wear after arriving in Marq.

Trynne waited anxiously for the fortnight to pass, growing increasingly nervous. Her mother's mood had gone somber after she'd learned of Myrddin's departure. The king needed Sinia's counsel more and more, and her responsibilities at Kingfountain had disrupted her duties as Brythonica's duchess. But while Trynne's mother was distracted, it remained to be seen whether the voyage to Brugia could be made in secret. With Sinia's frequent departures, Owen's parents were staying at the castle to help keep the order and ensure Gannon was diligently practicing his studies.

Trynne's mother had a busy day of duties scheduled for the day of the Gauntlet, and Trynne hoped to depart Ploemeur after breakfast and return by the evening meal. She wondered if she would get to see Fallon while she was there—and if he would be able to recognize her in her disguise. The idea made her feel smug and excited at once.

The last day of waiting arrived, and that morning she found herself checking her pack once again to make sure it was ready. There was a knock at her door and Trynne was startled to find her mother's lady-in-waiting behind it. Her name was Blanche.

"Tryneowy, your mother would like to see you ere she departs for the House of Pillars. Can you come?"

"Of course," Trynne answered, her stomach suddenly aflutter with nerves. She knew it was the Fountain's will that she go to the Gauntlet in Marq. But it had left the arrangements to her. Walking nervously to her mother's sitting room, she took a deep breath and then entered, trying to appear calm and free of worries.

"Yes, Mother?" she asked. Her mother was sitting at the table, brushing her golden hair, but she looked ill at ease. When Trynne entered, Sinia set down the brush and quickly rose.

"What's wrong?" Trynne asked her, giving her a concerned look.

Sinia approached and took her hands, her expression brooding. "I had a strange vision last night," she said in a low voice, and Trynne's stomach began to flop like a fish tossed on a plank.

"You did?" she replied, trying to hide the tremble in her voice. "Of what?"

Sinia's brow furrowed even more and she clutched her daughter's hands. "You will be sixteen soon and I know I should trust you more."

A spasm of fear shot through Trynne. Her mother knew something was amiss. Her skin went cold and she felt a tremor starting in her knees.

"I had a vision of you in Brugia," Sinia said, all but confirming Trynne's worst fear. Would her mother forbid her from going? Why was her assignment turning out to be so difficult?

Trynne's mouth was so dry she needed to swallow. "Brugia?"

"Yes. I've not been there myself, but it was very clear to me in the vision that *you* were there. I saw you with Captain Staeli."

Before Trynne could form any response, her mother continued. "Trynne, there is an old sanctuary in the capital city of Marq. There are a lot of waterways, so there is an abundance of bridges and boats. It's very lovely. I saw you and Captain Staeli at a bookmaker's shop across the bridge from the sanctuary. You were holding a book in your hand. A rare copy of *The Vulgate*. It was in the window of the shop. I saw you buy it." She sighed. "Trynne, I believe the Fountain wishes you to go to Brugia to retrieve that book. It may help with your Wizr training. I have to admit that I'm very nervous about letting you go. Brugia is not friendly to our family, and you are not used to bringing people with you on the ley lines."

A gush of excitement and gratitude flooded Trynne's heart. The Fountain was aiding her! She willed herself not to smile, but she couldn't help beaming.

"I *know* that you have always wanted to travel," her mother said, shaking her head. "Perhaps it is the Fountain's attempt to meet your wishes. It does respond to our thoughts in its gentle way. Trynne, do be careful! I will worry about you until you return. Marq is full of waterways, and you remember how sometimes water affects the magic, don't you? Water can protect you, of course, but it sometimes breaks apart other spells.

"Do you think you are strong enough to take someone with you? If you'd like, I could bring Captain Staeli there myself to make sure all is clear. I don't know why the Fountain isn't sending me; I could be there and back in half a moment. But I think it wants to test you. To give you an opportunity to develop your power." Sinia gave her an encouraging smile.

"I would relish this opportunity!" Trynne said, squeezing her mother's hands hard. "Thank you, Mother!"

Sinia gently touched her hair. "In my vision, I saw you wearing a dress in the Brugian fashion. It would help conceal your identity, at any rate. There are those from Brythonica in Brugia, though not many. I'd feel better about this journey if you did go in some sort of disguise. And I trust Captain Staeli. He is an able protector."

"I would like to try bringing him through myself. If I'm too sick or weak, then you can do it, but I'd like to try, Mother. If that's all right."

Sinia sighed again as she hugged her daughter. "You are growing up too fast, Tryneowy. I wish you could be a little girl for a while longer."

Trynne felt so grateful for her mother in that moment, for her wisdom and for her devotion to the Fountain, how she heeded its directions even though her mother's heart worried.

"Mother?" Trynne asked. "Tomorrow is the Gauntlet of Brugia. I believe it is being held in Marq."

Sinia nodded. "Actually, it is," she said warily. "The city will be very crowded."

"But can I go? Would you let me?" Trynne gave her mother the most pleading look she could muster. Her heart shuddered with eagerness.

Sinia watched her thoughtfully, her brow wrinkling in concern. "Well, since Captain Staeli is going with you . . ." She let the thought dangle, and Trynne grinned and kissed her mother's cheek.

"Thank you! I will return after the Gauntlet tomorrow."

Sinia patted her hands and then turned to go back to her dressing table. "You can tell me who won," she said, and Trynne felt a throb of mischief in her heart.

♦　♦　♦

The city of Marq was the most fascinating place that Trynne had ever experienced. It smelled different, looked different, and sounded different—and she was thrilled to the quick of her soul to be there. The sanctuary of Our Lady of Marq had been built centuries ago, commissioned by a past ruler who had shared affinity for the religion of Occitania and Ceredigion. The people of Brugia were not devout, and no one but visitors threw coins into the fountains. The sanctuary was made of brown-gray stone and it was much shorter than the edifices she had seen in Brythonica and Ceredigion, and certainly not as impressive as the island sanctuary of Our Lady of Toussan. But it had beautiful arched windows, decorated stone apexes, and flying buttresses that held up the central spire. The grounds were vibrant and green, full of meticulously trimmed, blooming trees that were uniform in height, each surrounded by knee-high hedges that were carved to form paths around the grounds. Larger, more ancient trees intermingled with the wizened buildings.

When they left the grounds of the sanctuary, they passed over a narrow stone bridge crossing a lane of brackish water. There were little plants growing in the cracks and seams along the bridge's face, probably wisteria. As Trynne crossed, trying not to look as excited as she felt, she watched the small gondolas pass beneath, full of passengers wearing the fashions of Brugia. She decided she'd have to ride in one before she left. It looked enchanting.

The air smelled of dampness and mold and smoked cheese and she leaned on the bridge rail, inhaling the pungent fumes with enjoyment. The magic thrummed inside her and she realized she was not at all depleted by the trip. If anything, she was stronger because of it. The ley line paths had been so easy to follow.

Captain Staeli, however, looked a little greensick. Trynne waved at him to follow her across the rest of the bridge, and he heaved a sigh and did her bidding.

Another strange thing she noticed about the Brugians was their penchant for dogs. On the sanctuary grounds, in the crowded streets—everywhere she looked there were lithe whippets. At least one in five people had one on a leash. She absorbed the information greedily, again feeling her magic swell and increase. If she had her choice, she would cross to distant lands every day to watch and learn.

As she walked with Staeli through the busy streets, seeking the bookmaker's shop her mother had described to her, Trynne remembered one of her father's lessons. He had once traveled in disguise as a knight of Duke Horwath, and it had taught him how much appearances matter. Wearing the badge of another duke, looking the part of a household knight, had changed the way people treated him. Whereas he was usually the focus of attention when he traveled as the Duke of Westmarch, he had been ignored as a household knight, and it had allowed him to operate undercover. The principle was on display before her. No one paid her any special attention because her style of dress matched that of the other young women her age.

How strange her magic had become after taking the oaths. Its power had grown so vast, and it roiled inside her. She felt unstoppable, full of potential.

"I think that must be the shop," Staeli said, gesturing to a bookmaker's shop. Trynne paused at the grimy window and peered inside. The shop was crowded, and the wonderful smell of old books exuded from it. There it was in the window—an old text with a battered leather cover. Her mother had told her to look for the red ribbon sewn into the spine. It peeked out at her.

Trynne went into the shop. She wasn't concerned about speaking to the owner. She knew the word of power to master languages and whispered it before entering. *Xenoglossia.*

The owner was an excessively chatty man in his midthirties with dark hair and a self-confident demeanor. He insisted each book in his shop was a particular masterpiece, citing to Trynne how many days each one had cost him in labor and materials, and seemed almost reluctant to part with any of them. When she pointed to the one in the window, he confessed he hadn't made that one, that it was expensive because it was so old, and few people could read the ancient script anymore. Only a collector would want it.

"It would be valueless to a young thing like you," he said breezily. "It's full of old tales of lords and ladies and the like written by some gout-ridden deconeus, I imagine. Are you sure you want it? I have a newer version over here that was translated by Tibbet. I printed it myself, so it's of the finest craftsmanship. It will cost far less."

"No, I like the antique look of it," Trynne said, turning the book over in her hands.

"It is an antique," the owner said, taking it from her and rubbing his palm across the cover as if it were a beloved friend. "I don't even know why I put it in the window yesterday. I hadn't planned on selling it. Are you sure you want it? It is nearly unreadable. I think you'd like Tibbet's translation of *The Vulgate* better. Really, lass, I'm not sure I want to part with it."

Trynne felt annoyed that he was playing such games.

"Well, I think I saw an older-looking book down the street," she said, glancing at Staeli. "Maybe I'll spend my coins there instead."

"Don't be hasty, don't be hasty," the proprietor said, flashing her a cunning grin. He bobbed his head a few times as he continued to stroke the book. "Since you really just want it for a *decoration*, as I fancy you do, then perhaps I could be persuaded to . . . I'm not sure . . . perhaps around thirt— twenty florins?"

A sudden feeling prickled in the air, nearly drowning out the man's words. There were other patrons in the shop as well, poring over books and waiting for a turn to haggle with the owner. But Trynne sensed that Fountain magic was approaching the store from the outside. Even though the streets were crowded with people and their dogs, she sensed the disruption in the current. That feeling was getting closer.

Trynne frowned, feeling suddenly vulnerable. Had her arrival attracted unwanted attention? Had her use of the magic in changing languages alerted another Fountain-blessed that she was there?

Her stomach thrummed with worry. She gave Captain Staeli a warning look and watched his hand drop to the hilt of his short sword.

"Was it thirty or twenty?" Trynne demanded, feeling harried to be done.

"Which can you afford?" he pressed.

"How about twenty-five, or I'll leave without purchasing anything," Trynne shot back.

"I'm sure your father can afford five more florins?" he said, nodding to Staeli.

Trynne felt the presence of the magic press up against the window of the bookstore. She felt her insides writhe with worry.

"Thirty, then," Trynne huffed. She dug into her purse and produced the proper coinage. The shop owner took the money and then handed her the book.

"A pleasure, lass," he said, wrinkling his brow as he looked over her shoulder at the window.

Trynne felt someone watching her. She could sense someone who was Fountain-blessed standing outside, beyond the glass, looking in. She knew that they could sense her just as she could sense them. Angry at being discovered, she turned to the window to see who was staring at her.

There was no one there.

◆ ◆ ◆

Revenge is drinking poison. One who is injured ought not return the injury, for on no account can it be right to do an injustice; and it is not right to do evil to any man, however much we have suffered from him.

Myrddin

◆ ◆ ◆

CHAPTER THIRTEEN

Dragan

Fear struck Trynne's chest like a javelin. She could sense the presence of another Fountain-blessed, as clearly as if he were standing before her, but there was no one visible. Almost a decade after her attack, she still remembered the sensation of being a little girl alone in her room, sensing that someone was there. Her father only knew one man who had such a cursed gift from the Fountain. The thief known as Dragan, her father's mortal enemy.

For a moment, she was transfixed with terror, reliving the experience of the pain and trauma that had not only stolen her smile but had made her afraid of the dark and of being alone. She had worked hard to conquer those fears and disappointments. And she was an Oath Maiden, not the helpless youngling she had once been. He would not get the best of her again.

"What is it?" Captain Staeli said in a growl, noticing her altered state. He followed her gaze to the window.

"*Apokaluptis*," Trynne breathed in a low, quavering voice, invoking another word of power. It was the word used to unmask a disguise, to reveal the true nature of something hidden. She felt the pulse of Fountain magic in her mind, as if a large boulder had been catapulted into a lake. The ripples shot out from her in all directions, totally unnoticed and unfelt by those around her.

But there was suddenly a man standing at the window.

Her father had described Dragan as a handsome man, though riddled with pox scars, with long sideburns and a hawkish nose. The sideburns had grown to a short beard flecked with gray. He wore clothes that would have marked him a nobleman except for the abused, patchwork quality of them. His eyes, though—his eyes were like staring into death. They were haunted, menacing, and utterly ruthless. They were staring at her with such hatred it made her insides turn oily and weak.

"Dragan," Trynne whispered hoarsely, still in shock from having encountered him in the city of Marq.

Her weakness lasted for just another moment before a vengeful fury blazed up inside her like an iron poker yanked from the depths of the furnace, glowing with power and heat. It startled her with how hotly it burned. This was the man the Espion had been hunting since before her birth. She had unmasked his illusion, noticed him as he had noticed her, and she was going to drag his sorry carcass back to the palace of Kingfountain so he could stand trial for treason. But no matter what he'd done to her, to her father, she would not kill him. No, she had sworn an oath never to do that.

She shoved the book she had just purchased into Captain Staeli's surprised hands and rushed to the door.

Dragan fled.

"I can wrap that in paper if you want to protect it?" the bookmaker called after her, but Trynne was heedless of his words. Another patron opened the door. Trynne collided with him, but she didn't even pause to apologize before slipping past him. Dragan's fancy ratty jacket stood out, and she fixed her sights on him and hurried through the crowd, not quite running but trying to gain ground.

He walked with a brisk vigor, tapping his hat politely at those he passed and stealing from several with deft hands that infuriated her, knowing that it was deliberately done because she was watching him.

Staeli caught up to her, his voice a growl. "Is that the one?" he seethed. "The false noble? He's of the age. Are you sure?"

"I have never been more certain," Trynne answered, her heart thundering in her ears. Dragan was keeping just ahead of them, slipping through the crowd. She felt him trying to cloak himself in his magic, but the force of her spell was still at work and he couldn't hide yet.

"Then it's no accident we were here today," Staeli grumbled. He stuffed her new book into his pack as he walked. He sounded more emotional than usual, and Trynne realized it was because he harbored his own deep resentment against Dragan. He had been called as Trynne's protector because of him. Their fates were all entwined.

"Faster," Trynne said, breaking into a jog. She wished she had a moment to change from her Brugian-style dress into the men's clothes she had brought to compete in the Gauntlet. People were looking at her with annoyance for barging through the crowd, but she couldn't care less as she dodged past the whippet dogs. Her eyes were fixed on the back of Dragan's head, popping in and out of sight amidst the rabble.

"If we lose sight of him . . ." she whispered under her breath.

Suddenly Dragan broke into a run, cutting through the crowd, deftly weaving through several people.

"He's going for the bridge!" Staeli warned, and began to run as well.

Trynne wondered if she should cry out to enlist others to help, but they were close to him. Surely they would make it. Dragan jogged up a narrow stone bridge, plowing his way through the crowd as people grunted and hollered at his rudeness. Some of the dogs began barking with the commotion, and soon it sounded as if the entire city was joining the chase as the yaps and barks spread like wildfire.

Captain Staeli reached the bridge first and elbowed his way through. Trynne was hot on his heels, trying to keep sight of Dragan and failing amidst the sea of bobbing heads. She felt another prickle of Fountain magic and sensed that he had turned invisible on the bridge. Her spell had ended over the water. She remembered her mother had once said that some spells didn't work over water at all; it was a natural barrier that provided protection from some of them.

Staeli stopped halfway across the bridge, searching the crowds, his face growing agitated with anger. "I lost him!" he snarled.

"I feel him still. Follow me," Trynne said. She could sense his power, although she could not see him, and knew he was just ahead of them. In fact, she sensed him along the rail. "He's almost to the other end!" she shouted, hurrying forward.

Staeli responded immediately and continued to press against the crowd. The hostile glares and occasional counter-shoves ended when they finally reached the other side. With all the distractions swirling around her, Trynne focused her thoughts and sensed the direction he was going. She was the only one who could lead them and she knew invoking the word again would be useless. All he would need to do was dart over another bridge, or run far enough out of range.

Dragan led them through a crowded main street before darting into an alley. She followed, drawing out a small dagger hidden in her girdle.

As she and the captain slowed to a brisk walk, Trynne sensed Fountain magic coming from behind them. There was another Fountain-blessed person in the area.

Had Dragan assembled other criminals who were Fountain-blessed? Was he luring them to a place where they'd be outnumbered and then murdered? But how could that be? How had Dragan known that Trynne would be there in the first place?

"I sense another one behind us," Trynne said, touching Staeli's shoulder. He jerked his head at her in surprise. He could not see their foe at the moment, but it was obvious he trusted Trynne's powers. His faith in her was heartening.

"How far away?" he asked, glancing backward.

"Not far. They can feel me just as I can feel them. We're being followed as well."

"I don't like this," Staeli said, shaking his head. "We'd better catch him before the other catches us."

"I agree," Trynne said. "Then we run."

She started down the alley, still sensing the invisible thief ahead of them. Staeli stayed close, but he continually looked backward, keeping watch for their tail. The alley was full of twists and turns and overcrowded hovels built atop each other. There was very little room to maneuver and side streets opened up quickly around them. A noxious sewer smell hung in the air.

Dragan kept pressing forward, going down and sideways, forcing Trynne to follow him. It did feel like he was leading her through a maze, one that he knew and she didn't.

Soon, they came across a street gang dicing in the midst of one of the alleys. Dragan slipped through the band unnoticed, pausing only to shove one of them hard into his fellows, which startled them and then made them aware of Trynne and Staeli.

"That was clever," the captain muttered darkly under his breath as the gang rose up, their clothes in tatters. Trynne felt the presence of the other Fountain-blessed closing in from behind. They were going to be trapped between the gang and their pursuer.

"Oi, looks like these two have lost their way," said the leader of the band. He had a jaunty, foul look and much bravado.

"A pa and his little waif," snickered another.

Trynne sensed Dragan slip around the corner ahead, and that blazing poker of anger inside her flared white-hot. He was getting away! As soon as he joined the main street again, he could slough off his magic, making it impossible for her to track him from afar.

Captain Staeli drew his swords. He might not have understood their language, but there was no misunderstanding the tone.

"He's got weapons, man," one of the gang said worriedly to the cocky leader. "Could be the prince's spies . . ."

"Nah, dressed too well," said another.

"The girl is ugly enough," snorted another man.

Trynne and Staeli had slowed down and stopped. The other Fountain-blessed person would be arriving soon.

She looked at the captain and then nodded. "Be quick."

Captain Staeli grunted with a smirk. "It won't take long."

Then her protector rushed into the gang like a dog itching for a fight. He struck with the flat of his blade and his elbows, stomped with his feet, and used his shoulders to crush them into the brick walls. Several tried to grab him and gang up on him, but Staeli was efficient, brutal, and adept at cracking skulls.

One of the gang slipped past him with a dagger. "Oi, lass! I'll take that purse if you please," he said, jutting his chin toward her purse and wagging his dagger at hers. "The blade too. It's nicer than mine."

"Take it, then," Trynne said, turning the hilt to face him. He looked a little surprised by her quick acquiescence, but he reached for it all the same. She deliberately dropped it, and as soon as his eyes tracked toward it, she kicked him in the face, breaking his nose and dropping him.

Her magic twinged in warning as another man rushed up to grab her. Spinning to the side, she dodged the outstretched arm and felt the weakness of his momentum through her magic. With a quick snatch, she grabbed his wrist and used his charge to spin him around and into the wall. He collided with the stone, grunting in pain and shock. Trynne grabbed the back of his shirt, then kicked the side of his knee sharply.

Trynne glanced up just as their pursuer entered the alley. It was a woman, wearing a hooded cloak and a beautiful dress in the Brugian style. Their two magics clashed for a moment before recognition settled in.

It was Morwenna Argentine, the poisoner of Kingfountain.

Captain Staeli kneed one of the gang members in the stomach and then shoved him down. Between the two of them, they had mastered eight or nine men, and most were collapsed in a heap.

"Morwenna!" Trynne gasped in surprise. She did not release her grip on her magic, which she quickly used to search for the poisoner's weaknesses. Their meeting like this was highly suspicious, especially after the close call with Dragan. As Trynne's magic worked, she sensed the poisoner was armed with three daggers, a needle comb, and an assortment of poisons, including vials and powders and a spring-loaded ring on her finger. Trynne sensed that Morwenna's body was disciplined and fit from her training at the poisoner school. But through the defenses, she sensed one glaring weakness. Morwenna's neck was vulnerable. She could be choked, strangled, drowned—anything that could stop her breath. It was a little surprising to see such a thing. Morwenna was trying to gauge her in the same way, but the poisoner's magic could not penetrate hers—it parted around her like a river around a stubborn boulder.

The two stared at each other with suspicion and then, almost as if by mutual agreement, let their magics subside.

The poisoner approached warily, casting her gaze first to Trynne and then to Staeli. She noted the bodies sprawled in the alley.

"Well, you're certainly the last person I expected to find at the end of this chase," Morwenna said, her eyes still showing a bit of mistrust. "I was following two Fountain-blessed. Where is the other?"

"What are you doing here?" Trynne asked, still feeling wary and confused. "I thought you were in Pisan?"

Morwenna's eyebrows lifted. "I was. I finished the school a year ago. I've been on assignments for my brother ever since. Did you come here through the ley lines? Of course you did, why am I even asking. That's how I came as well."

Trynne's eyes bulged with surprise at that. The ley lines were a closely guarded secret, normally used only by trained Wizrs.

"I learned about them in Pisan," Morwenna said. "Who were you following? I heard one of the competitors for the Gauntlet was Fountain-blessed. An archer from Legault. Was that him?"

Trynne shook her head. "No. I was after a man named Dragan." She looked at Morwenna carefully to see if she recognized the name.

Morwenna did startle, her eyes widening with surprise. "The man who attacked you?" she whispered. "That was him? Where is he now? I don't sense him anymore." She was staring down the alley warily.

"He led us into this rabble before slipping away. He's not using his magic right now."

"If he's here," Morwenna said firmly, "I need to find him and arrest him. The Espion has been hunting him for years."

"But why are you here? Are you on a mission to hunt Dragan?" Trynne asked, still not certain how to handle all the information she had just received.

Morwenna blinked with surprise. "No, I'm here because of the Gauntlet. Fallon asked me to come. Does he know you're here?" Her eyes lit up with interest. "He didn't mention you were coming too."

That uncomfortable nauseating sensation blossomed in Trynne's stomach again.

CHAPTER FOURTEEN

The King's Poisoner

Trynne was so shocked by Morwenna's statement that she stumbled over her next words and felt her cheeks flush. "No—that's not—I wasn't—"

"I've embarrassed you," Morwenna said, touching her arm. "Forgive me. I'm still so surprised to find you here. This isn't the proper place to become reacquainted." She glanced down at the writhing bodies of the gang and smirked. "I'm glad Captain Staeli was with you, so you didn't have to use much of your magic," she added conspiratorially. "The last word you uttered was what drew my attention. I felt it from far away. Come, let's go the way you felt Dragan going. What did he look like? How would I recognize him? I've heard very few have actually seen him. Some have taken to calling him 'the Ghost.'"

Trynne quickly described what they had seen him wearing as they all walked briskly to the end of the alley. Shortly thereafter, they arrived at the main street on the river's edge. Everywhere Trynne looked, there were dogs on leashes, men and women in identical black velvet hats, and street vendors. The air hung heavy with the scents of food and the blooms in a nearby flower wagon.

The foot traffic went both ways, and there were gondoliers in the river scooping their way along in both directions as well. Morwenna clung to Trynne's arm as they stood in the alcove, watching the crowd.

"I love watching people," Morwenna confided. "But now we're trying to spot a man in shabby nobleman's clothes. One *without* a whippet." She clucked her tongue. "If only I'd come sooner. I'm going to *hate* having to report this to my brother and your father." Morwenna frowned at the thought, still searching the crowd. Then she turned and raised her eyebrow in an almost accusing way. "I do *need* to report this, Trynne, despite our friendship. Does your father know you're here? Will he be upset if he finds out?"

Trynne was still battling her inner demons and almost didn't hear the question. Morwenna had been *invited* by Fallon to meet her in Brugia? What did that mean? How did she know about ley lines? Trynne's curiosity was screaming to know the answers.

"Father doesn't know I'm here," Trynne said, shaking her head. "But my mother does. She sent me to get a book—"

"From the bookmaker's shop!" Morwenna said, suddenly interested. "It was that old copy of *The Vulgate*, wasn't it? I saw it in the window yesterday when I arrived."

"You know about *The Vulgate*?" Trynne asked.

"Everyone *knows* about *The Vulgate*, Trynne," Morwenna said, dropping her voice lower. "What they don't know about is the secret that's hidden in plain sight. You know of it, of course, or I wouldn't be talking about it. Your mother is a Wizr, after all. I'm so jealous of you, Trynne. You get to be tutored by a truly exceptional woman. I tried to get Myrddin to tutor me, but he insisted that I must discover the words on my own. You're special, though. What you have access to at Ploemeur is infinitely better than the scraps I found in Pisan." She squeezed Trynne's arm. "I can see that I've concerned you, so let me catch you up quickly. Then I want to take you to Oberon's—that's where Fallon is hiding until the Gauntlet starts," she added in an undertone.

"It starts today, doesn't it?" Trynne asked hopefully.

"Actually, it starts *tonight*," Morwenna said. "The trials begin at dusk, so there's still the whole day ahead. The darkness makes the challenges harder. How unlike the house of Asturias to make things complicated!" She gave Trynne a pretty smirk.

Morwenna had truly become a beauty since they had last met at the royal wedding. Her confidence had expanded and she seemed very aware of her alluring looks.

"So you didn't come to see Fallon face the Gauntlet?" Morwenna asked.

"No, I didn't," Trynne said. "So he's in hiding, then?"

"Of course! Prince Elwis hates him and has his men out searching the streets for him. He's offered bribes to innkeepers to rat him out." Morwenna grinned mischievously. "He's staying at an Espion stronghold, so of course they won't find him. He's going to the Gauntlet in disguise so that nothing interferes with him winning the badge fairly. You're clever to dress up as a Brugian as well." She only glanced at Trynne occasionally, her eyes still searching the crowd for Dragan.

"Any luck spotting him, Captain?" she asked Staeli.

The captain, who was keenly observing the crowds, just shook his head no in response. His bearded mouth twisted into a discontented frown. "Too many people."

"How do you know of the ley lines?" Trynne asked.

"A fair question. I have a very curious nature," Morwenna answered. "There are lots of books at the poisoner school in Pisan. Some are translations. Some have been handed down for centuries—very musty. Those I like best! I came across one in the map room. The poisoner school has the best maps because it has kept track of the boundary changes between kingdoms for generations. Older maps are rather useless, so nobody looks at them very often, preferring the newer maps that have more current information. But I like studying the past. I grew up reading stories from translations of *The Vulgate*. I used to spend hours reading them by the fire while Father dozed." She had a faraway look in her eyes. "Then one day I came across a map that was very different from the rest."

"How so?" Trynne asked, but she felt she already knew.

"Well, most maps—the good ones—contain lines vertical showing north and south and horizontal ones showing east and west. Other maps mark sea routes that connect ports to ports. The map that I found looked like both, but the routes were neither sea routes nor were they simply cardinal points. What intrigued me about it was that the lines seem to gather and connect around certain cities. Like Kingfountain and Ploemeur and Marq. The lines spread out from those cities like wagon spokes. All across the map, I kept seeing those same spokes. That's what I called them then. I didn't know the true name. None of the people I asked about the book could explain what it meant. They offered explanations like wagon routes or some other nonsense to try and discourage me. But I would not be deterred. I'm really quite stubborn, Trynne. Especially when I want to know something."

"But what about your poisoner studies?" Trynne asked. "I thought you wanted that?"

"I do, of course! It's just that I've always been blessed with a very strong memory. I can hear a detail once and recall it later. So much of poisoner school is repetition. They teach you these little sayings and chants to help memorize plants and flowers and such." She shrugged. "I only needed to hear things once to remember them. It normally takes three years to finish training, but I finished the studies in a year. The physical training takes longer, of course—I wasn't going to skip that! But I had a lot of free time to read and that's when I discovered the truth about *The Vulgate*. You already know this, right? That the ancient text holds words of power? If you're Fountain-blessed, you only need to say the word—or even *think* it—to trigger the magic. I was so intrigued! As I read one of the older copies of *The Vulgate*—I think it was volume twelve—I came across the story of Myrddin using his magic to travel great distances. I discovered the word in that book. So then I went to the map room to try it out. Well, I didn't want to startle anyone at Kingfountain by just showing up, so I tried to get to Glosstyr to see my father. But somehow I overshot it and ended up at Dundrennan instead."

Trynne was so fascinated by the tale that she had stopped looking for Dragan. She knew Fallon had been spending much of his time at Dundrennan since becoming the duke of the North.

"The magic completely exhausted me," Morwenna continued, shaking her head and chuckling softly to herself. "I was so spent . . . so sick . . . after leaving the fountain's edge, I threw up and fell unconscious. The servants were startled to find me, and when I was finally strong enough to open my eyes, Fallon was there as my kindhearted nurse. He was very curious to find out how I had gotten there without anyone knowing." Morwenna sighed and smiled with the memory. "He's a good friend." Then she paused, her brow wrinkling. "I've said something wrong. You look pale."

Trynne felt as if a dagger had been plunged into her heart and was slowly twisting. She could hardly breathe. Her mouth was hot and dry and she was suddenly light-headed.

"Did I offend you?" Morwenna said in a worried tone.

"No . . . not at all." It was difficult getting the words out.

Then Morwenna's eyes widened. "Oh," she whispered. "Oh, I see." She began to nod her head slowly. "I'm sorry, Trynne. I was so caught up telling you my story that I hadn't noticed it until now." She licked her lips and glanced at the throng passing the alley entrance. "I should have picked up on it sooner, but you are very discreet. He doesn't know; you can be certain of that."

"Doesn't know . . . what?" Trynne asked in confusion.

"How you feel about him," Morwenna said as if Trynne were a simpleton. "I've an unfair advantage. Most women can spot such things quickly enough, but I've been trained at the poisoner school to notice such little signs of . . . tenderness. You mask yours well, Trynne, I'll give you that. It's the injury. Most people give themselves away with their mouth. But it was your eyes that told me." She put her hand on Trynne's shoulder. "Let me be perfectly frank with you. Fallon is my friend and I know that he is also yours. He speaks of you as if you were his own sister . . . with as much respect as he has toward the queen. He's handsome and quite gallant," she added with a droll smile. "A girl could get a bit breathless around him. But I assure you that I harbor no romantic feelings toward him." She then sighed and looked directly into Trynne's eyes. "He may be a bit . . . interested in me. I haven't encouraged it, and I won't, especially because I can tell that would hurt you. I do consider you a friend, Trynne. It was Fallon who persuaded me to tell the king and your father about my discovery. And your father explained the ley lines to me and told me what they are properly called. As I said, I've been a little jealous of you all these years. You know these things already, and I've had to struggle to learn each of the words. I'm sure you know so many more than I do. I won't ask you to teach me, for that wouldn't be proper. I'm a poisoner, not a Wizr. But I do serve my brother. As for why I'm here, I think it would be best if Fallon explained it to you himself."

Trynne blinked with surprise. "I'm not sure . . ." She could not think of a reason why she shouldn't stay. Nor could she summon the will to say no because she had only seen Fallon rarely during the last few years, and each time she had, her heart had been in commotion for weeks afterward.

Morwenna gave her a pointed look. "I won't hear any objection. Everyone in this city is trying to find him right now so that Elvis can stop him from participating in the Gauntlet or humiliate him during it." She rubbed Trynne's arm. "I know he'll be happy to see you. Come, let's go together. If Dragan's smart, he's already on a gondola where the water will protect him from our magic. I just wish there were a waterfall nearby so that we could throw him over the edge!"

♦　♦　♦

The Oberon was a small home built along a waterway so that it couldn't be approached on foot. The walls were made of red brick, and there were stained wooden planks fastened to the bricks in the front. It was two stories high with a long row of windows, each one small and paned with glass embedded with diamond-shaped wires. The roof from the upper level sloped toward the river, exposing four different dormer rooms of varying size. Two stubby chimneys appeared in the middle of the roof, and a section of the lower floor jutted slightly out over the river into a wide bay window with an additional piece of roof covering it. It was distinctive and interesting and crowded between other brick houses on one side and a brick wall on the other, which had a small landing pad and a locked iron door. The wall implied there was a small yard on the other side, but it was impossible to tell. Vines crept up the wall and the side of the bricks near the door.

Trynne's heart was thumping painfully in her chest as the boatman guided their gondola toward the landing with a staff. The boat swayed a little. There were lily pads clustered around the base of the house, and Trynne spied a dragonfly buzzing over one.

She was nervous about meeting Fallon again, especially in light of Morwenna's tale. After hiring the gondola, they had gone on a brief tour of the city of Marq with its waterways and crowded streets. Trynne would have enjoyed the adventure more had she not felt so heartsick. After learning about the ley lines, Morwenna had used them to come and go at Kingfountain's palace, much like Trynne did, except the poisoner's visits were much less predictable and scheduled. Morwenna had been to most of the kingdoms already, it turned out, and she'd learned a lot about the different customs in those other lands.

She was living the kind of life that Trynne had always coveted.

The boat reached the platform and the iron door opened, revealing two men who made and received Espion hand signals. They quickly ushered the two ladies and Captain Staeli off the boat and in through the door.

As Trynne shuffled down the corridor of the Oberon, gazing at the beams supporting the roof and taking in the sights and sounds, she heard voices and laughter from the common room ahead. She recognized Fallon's voice amidst the din. Her mouth went dry again and she wiped her hands on her dark skirts. The corridor was stifling hot and the smell of wood rot and smoke hung in the air.

Morwenna unfastened her cloak and took it off, preparing to hang it as they entered. Trynne noticed that the chemise she was wearing beneath the cloak was pulled open at the shoulders, leaving only the kirtle straps to cover her skin. She felt another flush of jealousy, especially as they entered the common area and all the men's eyes instantly shot to Morwenna. The girl seemed to glow with the sudden attention she was receiving.

A few of the Espion glanced at Trynne, but their attention was quickly drawn to the more alluring woman.

Trynne saw Fallon sitting jauntily in a seat, leaning back on his chair so that the front legs were lifted up. He looked older than she remembered, his face fuzzy and unshaven. His dark hair was a mess and he looked so casual. His eyes lit up when he saw Morwenna enter, burning with frank hunger. There was no sign of the indifference with which he'd viewed her years before, when the three of them were last together, and a sick feeling seized Trynne's chest. Greed. Jealousy. Her oaths had warned her of this too.

Then his gaze shot to Trynne.

His expression transformed, looking almost guilty when the recognition settled in.

"Cousin?" he belted out in surprise and wonder.

CHAPTER FIFTEEN

Spurned

It wasn't long before Trynne's embarrassment and discomfort melted away in the face of Fallon's personality. He could chase away a thunderstorm with one of his witty sayings and a smile. It was clear he was quite at home amongst the Espion and that he and Morwenna had become closer. But it was equally clear that he was grateful for whatever tides of fate had brought Trynne to his table.

"So your mother sent you to Marq to fetch a dusty book," Fallon said, stroking his chin. "And you brought Captain Staeli—the stouthearted Westmarcher—as your guardian. Can't argue with the choice—the man is all ice and iron. Welcome, Captain!"

Staeli shrugged off the younger man's exuberance with narrow eyes, ignoring him utterly, and headed to the periphery of the room to speak in low tones with some of the Espion gathered there.

Fallon smirked at the snub and leaned forward, thumping the table with his elbow. "Cousin, Cousin, Cousin, so you *didn't* come to Marq to watch me face the Gauntlet. I'm crushed. Truly. But how did you find Morwenna? You look like a local girl," he added, tugging at the garter around her elbow, then letting it snap back against her arm. She pulled her arm away from him.

"I found *her*," Morwenna added with a sly grin, "chasing after the thief Dragan."

Fallon startled, sitting up, his expressive eyes widening. "Truly? The blackguard is here?"

Trynne nodded. "I felt his magic and he felt mine. I don't think he realized whom he had stumbled upon until he saw me from the window of the bookshop. He fled when Captain Staeli and I went after him."

"Of course he did!" Fallon said, his brow wrinkling. "Now there's a man I'd like to drown in the Deep Fathoms. So he took one look at you and tucked tail and ran." He shook his head. "Well, if I run into him, then I'll be sure to punch him in the mouth for you. Ere I turn him in to the Espion for greater tortures." He reached out and playfully pushed her shoulder. "I can't believe you are here. I hadn't expected it."

"I knew *you* were here," Trynne said, giving him an arch look.

"A lucky guess, perhaps?"

She screwed up her nose. "No, your sister told me."

"So you've been to the palace recently? How fares Genny? I've not seen either of you in months!"

"She is in excellent health," Trynne replied. Her stomach was still a little giddy, but each moment with him made her feel more at ease. "There are many cares at the moment."

"Aren't there always? People worry too much about things they cannot control. Never greet a devil till you meet one or cross a bridge before you've reached it. Ten times out of nine things aren't as bad as we fear them to be."

"Don't you mean nine times out of ten?" Morwenna quipped.

"That's how I heard it originally," Fallon said, giving her a wicked smile. "But every saying can bear a little improvement. So, *Cousin*," he said, addressing Trynne again. "You no doubt wonder why I am here with the king's poisoner."

"It had crossed my mind," she answered in a neutral tone.

"Well, Morwenna stumbled into Dundrennan . . . did she already tell you? Ah, she did. Yes, she literally stumbled there, sprawled out on the floor. What a mess. I was able to coax a few secrets from her, namely, how she arrived using magic. You know how much I *loathe* secrets." He gave her a slightly challenging look. "In order to get a seat at the 'Table of Splinters' and become a permanent member of the king's council, one must pass all the Gauntlets. There are only so many seats, you know. I intend to be the first who passes all of them. I've passed the one in Edonburick, naturally. I've also been to Legault. Theirs was easy. Legaultans have no imagination. It's no secret how much Prince Elwis and I hate each other. Our fathers have sworn that they will do everything they can to keep us apart. But I know dogs like Elwis never sleep without dreaming about mischief. Elwis is eager to see me fail. So I hatched this idea of getting into the city before anyone learned I was here. The Gauntlet is this evening at dusk, and I intend to win it and then vanish before Elwis's nose." He wagged his eyebrows. "Poisoners know the arts of disguise, and Morwenna especially so." He glanced at the king's half sister again and gave her a knowing look. "I can't wait to see Elwis's face when he realizes he's lost to me."

Trynne felt a little wary by the tone of the banter. "Will Elwis be competing? I thought he was already a champion of Brugia?"

Fallon shook his head. "You are right. He already bested it. He's also won the badges of Occitania and Legault, but that's it."

"So you're tied?"

Fallon shrugged. "Not for long. When I get this one, it will put me ahead. That I do it under his nose will add salt to the steak."

Trynne felt a guilty throb in her heart. Fallon didn't realize that *she* intended to pass the Gauntlet as well. Right under *his* nose.

"So this is your first time to Brugia, is it not?" Fallon asked, scratching his bottom lip and arching an eyebrow.

"It is," Trynne answered. "It's a beautiful city."

"It smells like dead fish," he bantered.

"So does Edonburick, I hear."

"Only down on the docks, not up in the cliffs. I miss our chatter, Trynne. So you are training to be a Wizr yourself? Do you know how to whisk yourself away now like your mother does, or did she bring you?"

Trynne felt a little offended. "I came on my own."

He held up his hand repentantly. "Good, that's good. So why haven't you come to Dundrennan to see me? Now that I know you can, I'll be expecting it."

"I can't really just . . . *go* wherever I want," Trynne said, glancing over at Captain Staeli.

"Why not?"

"Because my parents trust me, Fallon. My father may not be the head of the Espion anymore, but he may as well be for all they tell him."

He waved his hand. "That's an excuse. You don't because you are afraid." He pitched his voice lower. "You've had that bodyguard with you ever since you were attacked."

Trynne's heart was starting to burn with discomfort. She wished Morwenna were not witnessing the conversation.

Leaning forward, his elbow planted on the table, Fallon tapped his lips on his clenched fist. "I'm sure your mother is worried sick about you right now. That's what parents do. She probably gave you a very short leash for this visit, but you're nearly a grown woman now, Trynne. Time to leave the nest." He reached out and snatched her hand. "We are going to sneak away and steal a boat. Right now. Morwenna, would you distract the captain for a few moments?"

Trynne jerked her hand away, her cheeks flushing. "I will not do that, Fallon Llewellyn."

"Why not?" he challenged. "Because you're afraid. No one is going to recognize us. No one is going to hurt you. I'd love to show you some of the sights. We'll be back, get a scolding, and then you can watch me win the Gauntlet before you leave. Morwenna? Help me persuade her."

Trynne was tempted. The thought of riding in a gondola with Fallon, just the two of them, was enticing. The truth of the matter was that she wasn't afraid of being away from Captain Staeli. She was afraid of breaking her parents' trust in her, the oath she'd made never to go anywhere without a guard. What was more, she could almost hear Myrddin's voice in her head—*never swear an oath falsely*. Yes, this was about more than a simple afternoon.

"I don't think she wants to be persuaded," Morwenna said, reaching out and touching Trynne's arm. "You're very impulsive, Fallon. She is not."

"So you are both against me?" he said defensively, leaning back in his chair. He looked at Trynne with obvious disappointment. "Someday you will need to make your own decisions. You'll need to stop trying to please everyone."

Trynne's cheeks flushed. Fallon didn't know the conflict that raged in her heart. He was judging her unfairly.

"I think it's time for me to go," Trynne said, pushing away from the table.

Fallon shrugged. "If you must." His eyes burned with repressed anger.

Trynne stood, wanting to shove him backward in his chair and knock him on the floor. He had no idea what she was capable of. He believed that in teaching her to rebel against her parents, he would be helping her gain some freedom. She would have thrilled to spend time with him alone. But it felt wrong.

"I wish you luck in the Gauntlet, Fallon," she told him, trying to hide the quaver in her voice.

"If you think I need it," he countered. His brow furrowed with displeasure.

Trynne swallowed and stepped away from the table, her insides writhing with disappointment. It was not how she had hoped things would go between them.

Jeff Wheeler

As she walked away, she heard him sigh with anger. Morwenna murmured something back to him. A jolt of jealousy went through Trynne's heart, but she stifled it. She should not be jealous of the beautiful poisoner. Yes, she was graced with beauty and certain freedoms and gifts. But Trynne would not have wished for her familial disadvantages for all the world. The poisoner had grown up in the shadow of her father at Glosstyr. Her mother spent half of the year at Kingfountain, sometimes more. There was sadness that was a part of Morwenna's life that Trynne didn't understand.

"Shall we go, lass?" Captain Staeli asked in a low voice. He glanced over her shoulder at Fallon, his eyes narrowing.

"Yes," she answered solemnly.

"I'm proud of you," Staeli said, giving her a small, approving smile.

She raised an eyebrow. "You heard?"

Staeli said nothing, only gave her a wise look and escorted her back to the door.

♦ ♦ ♦

The sun had begun to lower in the sky, but the city of Marq was far from being ready to sleep. For the rest of the day, Trynne wandered the streets and bridges with Captain Staeli, developing a feeling for the beautiful land of Brugia. Without a gondola, the only way to cross from one section of the town to another was over the bridges. Each bridge was distinct and shaped to meet the need and size of the crossing. Most of the homes were two-story dwellings, packed close together, but there were also many parks and sculpted tree lanes adding shade and variety to the landscape. It was like being in a living maze.

She would have preferred to spend the afternoon with Fallon, but after the way he'd reacted to her refusal, she was glad she hadn't gone with him. He was used to getting his way, used to his parents' indulgence, and clearly didn't handle disappointment well. He was also too impulsive and didn't think through the possibilities of his actions. The whole city was looking for him, so going out on a gondola ride with her would have been fraught with risk. Why couldn't he see that?

There was much she had admired about him when they were children, but he was changing in ways she wasn't sure she liked. Staeli was not a very talkative companion, and she had a lot of time to ruminate on the encounter and play it over and over again in her mind. She wished that she could have parted with Fallon on better terms, but she was angry at him for being so spoiled and haughty, for making such uncharitable assumptions about her motivations. She deserved better than that.

As dusk neared, Trynne and Captain Staeli approached the central island, where the Gauntlet event was being held at the duke's palatial manor. When they got to the bridge protected by the duke's men, she found a bathhouse to change in. She emerged shortly thereafter, her dress bundled up in her pack, which she handed to Captain Staeli. She was more comfortable in training clothes, the kind she wore in her practice sessions in Ploemeur. As her mother had noticed, she had deliberately had her hair trimmed shorter and shorter over the past months, and it was tied back in a queue.

The final bit of her disguise she had planned for months. She knew it was a tradition in Atabyrion for warriors to paint parts of their faces with paste made from blue woad. She had applied it over the non-paralyzed part of her face. The vibrant color would help guarantee her anonymity. She had always been short and lean, and her training had given her muscle where it counted.

Captain Staeli smirked at her disguise after taking her bag. "Well, lad," he said with a wink. "Do us proud, eh? Show these Brugians what you are made of."

"I will," Trynne answered, giving him one of her rare smiles.

"The guards yonder have been blocking out all but those who will compete. The Gauntlet must be kept a secret, so no witnesses are allowed over the last bridge. I'll meet you back here when you are done."

Trynne shook her head. "No, meet me back at the sanctuary. I can feel a ley line from here to there. It'll be faster. I don't plan on staying long afterward."

"Good luck," he said, clapping her on the back as he would a son.

Trynne straightened a bit and then marched confidently toward the bridge.

As she approached the guards, she sensed Fountain magic ahead. She was not using any herself, but she felt its subtle ripple. The guard wearing Grand Duke Maxwell's badge frowned at her.

"Are you fourteen, lad?" he asked her sternly.

"Sixteen," she responded, adding some husk to her voice.

He wrinkled his brow. "It's your skull. Go on."

Trynne passed the guards and walked across the narrow bridge. There were archers posted on the other side, armed with arrows with black shafts and silver heads. The men wore colorful garb, purple and yellow, along with frilled Brugian neck pieces and pointed helmets. Trynne followed the sense of the Fountain magic. On the other side of the bridge was the entrance to the manor, guarded by more men.

"Any knives? Weapons?" one of them said as he examined her.

Trynne shook her head. Combatants could bring in nothing but a sturdy pair of boots and the clothes on their back. The guard quickly searched her, examining her boots mostly, and then waved her through the doors. Her stomach thrilled with excitement.

The feeling of the Fountain magic swelled as she entered the manor, accompanied by the noise of jumbled voices. Trynne gazed at the decorations of the hallway, impressed by the huge gold-framed paintings of regal figures, presumably previous rulers of the Brugia. She recognized one of the subjects as an Argentine, the dowager queen who was Severn's sister. Looking into her eyes, Trynne felt as if the matronly woman were watching her.

She was ushered into a room filled with other participants. It was a cavernous space, made more so by the vaulted ceiling. Guards wearing the duke's colors were stationed everywhere, probably thirty in all, and each held a polished black staff. The combatants were of all sizes and shapes, but most were big and young and they were talking and jostling each other as young men tended to do.

She cast her gaze around the room, feeling out of place and strange. Slowly, she walked around, seeking the source of the Fountain magic. The feeling came from a tall, gawky lad who was probably sixteen. He had straw-blond hair, ears that stuck out, and a narrow face that was quite ugly. The gangly look was almost comical.

And she realized, almost at once, that it was a disguise. It was as if the waters of the Fountain parted around her. Upon a closer look, she noticed the ring on the young man's hand. She could literally feel the magic burning from it; it was the source of both the power and the feeling.

The lad was Fallon.

Almost as if in answer to the thought, the young gawky man looked at her, his eyebrow lifting. Had he recognized her? Her stomach shrank and she kept moving, not giving him a second look. She cursed herself as he started to approach her. It was Fallon. She was sure of it.

"From Edonburick?" said a voice behind her in a thick brogue. It was Fallon's voice.

Before she could answer, a loud gong sounded, sending ripples of noise through the hall. The chattering and nervous voices stilled at once.

"His Excellence, Prince Elwis Asturias!" shouted a voice, followed by a ribbon of trumpets.

Trynne couldn't see well amidst the throng, but she recognized the prince's voice. "Welcome to Marq. Welcome to the Gauntlet." He sneered the words as he walked forward, casting his eyes over those assembled. "Only some of you will actually be able to compete this evening. The rest are going to end up at the healers with broken bones. But you are here now, and it is too late for you to back out. To compete in the Gauntlet, you will need a black staff. Try to wrest one from one of my guards. Now!"

At his command, the guards with the black staves came rushing toward the middle of the room, striking the young men with the very weapons they had been charged to take.

In a moment, all was mayhem.

CHAPTER SIXTEEN

The Gauntlet

Each of the realms under the sovereignty of Kingfountain had their own Gauntlet, and each was given the right to conduct it as they saw fit. Trynne was shocked to see this one begin in such a brutal manner. The guards went after the foreigners first, but they were soon wrestling with all the contenders for their weapons. She heard the crack of wood against bone and watched people slump to the ground only to be trampled on in the melee.

Trynne's magic rushed in without being summoned. The murmur of waterfalls in her ears guided her through the haphazard violence. She identified a guard, the strongest, who was bringing down a man with almost every stroke, and chose him to disarm. Keeping her eyes fixed on him, she ducked a blow aimed at her forehead and prepared herself to strike. The guard saw her approach, grinned viciously, and swung the staff down in an overhand arc. She twisted sideways, feeling the wood hiss in front of her. When it clacked on the stone ground, she grabbed the quivering pole with both hands and used it to absorb her weight. She kicked the guard in the knee and then the groin, and wrenched the pole from his hands as he bowled over in pain. Whirling the staff over her head, she brought it down on his neck to stun him before kicking him in the chest to knock him down. Through her efforts, she felt her store of magic draining rapidly.

The gawky blond who could only be Fallon had already seized a weapon and was charging through the only open door. She hesitated a moment, wondering if she should go after him or help some of the others struggling in the room. Was this a contest of brute strength or a test of the principles of Virtus?

Another competitor had managed to grab a staff, but he was bleeding profusely from his scalp. So many had crumpled onto the floor, where they were writhing in pain, befuddled by the blows they had received. Very few would be competing in the rest of the Gauntlet, it appeared. Trynne struck a guard behind the knee and then whacked him upside the head. Not enough to knock him out, but enough to jar him. Another guard saw her do this and rushed at her. She kept the staff at the ready and then parried his blows effortlessly before countering with a sweep that knocked his legs out from under him. Curiously, using the magic for defense only sapped a little from it. A cheer rose up from the mob—people had seen her stop to help. The man with the bleeding face rushed past her to follow Fallon. Trynne tried to subdue her anger. She wanted to stay and humble all of the guards, but the delay would cost her later, especially if her power vanished before she made it through the other obstacles.

Trynne watched a smaller fellow grab the fallen staff of the guard she'd just injured. He gave her a grateful nod; after nodding back, she fled down the path.

The corridor was lit with fluttering torches and lined with tapestries, which made shadows wriggle and dance on the walls. She heard the sound of bootsteps rushing up a set of stairs and hurried to follow, feeling her heart thrum with excitement in her chest. The corridor took a sharp turn ahead, and she reached out with her magic to search for any obstacles. She sensed a bar had been fixed to the wall, about chest level, meant to surprise and harm someone running recklessly. Prepared to meet the challenge, Trynne ducked as she went around the bend, keeping her staff parallel to the floor. She dodged the bar easily, not losing her stride, and rounded another corner, where she found a cramped stairwell leading up to one of the manor towers. The sound of a slamming door came from above.

Trynne could hear the sound of boots from behind her as well, so she hastened up the stairs, taking them two at a time. She was grateful for her training with Captain Staeli. Her endurance was more than a match for the challenges she'd faced so far. When she reached the top of the stairs, there was a heavy iron door blocking the way. She remembered hearing it slam, which seemed odd until she noticed the pulley mechanism next to it, tied to heavy sandbags positioned above. Blinking quickly, she deduced that opening the door triggered the trap that would apply sudden pressure to the door. That meant there was something dangerous on the other side. Reaching out with her magic, she sensed that the tower led outside in a precipitous drop. She realized the drop below led to the moat.

Every use of her power diminished it, and she felt the edges of it shrinking, which made her stomach quiver with worry. What if it ran out when she needed it most? But there was no time to fret. The person coming up behind her would reach the landing soon, so Trynne heaved on the door. As she wrenched it open, she felt the wind and saw two torches hanging from sconces on the wall, the flames hissing in her face as they were drawn in by the wind. The moat was indeed below. Did that mean she needed to swim? Her eyes caught two iron bars extending down from just above the door, almost like rails that went down at an angle. She couldn't see the moat in the darkness of night, but she could smell it, and she heard someone splashing in the water below.

Then she understood. She could place the staff over the bars and then hang on to it as she went down. She couldn't see where she was going or how steep it was, but it was better than—

Click.

The trap released the sandbag and the door closed behind her, shoving her out of the tower. She managed to reach out and grab one of the bars with her left hand and dangled from it over the dark pool below. Gritting her teeth, she swung the staff up and over the bars, then quickly snatched it with her other hand. Suddenly, she was gliding downward along the poles. Her stomach thrilled with the feeling of flying, but she couldn't see where she would land. There was a lawn on the other side of the moat, lit with braziers and sputtering torches that began to loom ahead. The ironwork rods she glided down eventually came to an end on the lawn.

As she hurtled downward at an accelerating pace, she saw the iron poles curled into circles at the ends and were attached to two wrought-iron columns at the end of the lawn. The circles were designed to absorb her momentum, she realized, and when she hit them, her body swung up and around once in a full circle. She dropped to the grass gracefully, just as someone spluttered in the water behind her. Turning, she saw the man with the wounded forehead trying to climb up onto the stone, looking tired and worn out from the swim with the staff. He glared at her as he swung up his legs.

Trynne pulled her staff out of the rings and raced ahead. There was a series of stone obstacles she needed to evade to cross the remainder of the lawn. Some were benches of varying heights. Some were pedestals. A tall wall loomed at the end, about twice the height of a man. She blinked quickly, trying to discern a pattern in the debris. Fallon was scrambling to get up the wall, but as high as he jumped, he could not reach the top edge. It would be impossible for her, for she was much shorter than him. He stepped back, tossed his staff up and over the wall like a javelin, and started shimmying up two of the pillars, which were close enough to provide him with leverage. Trynne started through the maze, jumping over one obstacle, darting past another. By the time she reached the pillars, Fallon had managed to fall forward and catch the lip of the wall. He pulled himself grunting up to the top.

She started up next, mimicking his movement by throwing the staff over it first. She then jammed her hands and feet against one of the pillars, pushing herself up the other. The other man arrived as she reached the top of the pillars. Trynne fell forward and barely managed to catch the edge of the wall. She felt a hand grope at her boot and realized the man below was trying to grab her and pull her down. She brought up her knees and heard his hand slap on the stone. It infuriated her that he was cheating!

The young man glared at her and then uttered an unflattering epithet in Legaultan at her as he started up the pillars himself. Was this the one they called Bowman?

Everyone who passed the Gauntlet earned a badge, but the one who came in first always won the champion's badge and a hefty bag of gold. Others received lesser prizes. The money was intended to help a champion pay the costs of becoming a knight of the realm. This competitor was clearly willing to cheat to get the money and the fame. Trynne's fingers burned and her arm muscles strained to hold herself up, but she had practiced for so long in the training yard that she knew what her body could do. She began rocking her hips and then pulled, swinging herself onto the top of the wall.

From that vantage point, she saw another competitor coming down the poles as she had while two more were trying to swim across the moat. Then from her position, she saw that the pillars were of varying heights. She could have jumped from one to the other across the maze, and a final leap would have brought her to the top of the wall.

So each challenge had a difficult way and an easier way to pass it. The bloodied man below swore under his breath and began shimmying up the pillars too. Trynne swung over the edge, lowered herself until she hung from the other side, and then dropped and fetched her staff. Lamps had been hung on iron poles lighting the path to an enormous hedge maze. As she ran toward it, she felt it waiting to swallow her up in darkness.

As Trynne entered the hedge maze, formed by a wooden trellis covered in thick jasmine vines, she heard rustling from the foliage. It was, she realized, the perfect hiding place for guardsmen. Suddenly a pole jabbed at her head from one of the clusters of leaves and Trynne ducked to avoid it, then raced ahead toward a crook in the maze. She had no idea which way to go, but somewhere ahead of her, she heard grunts, followed by a bark of pain.

Was it Fallon? After the way he'd treated her earlier that day, she wanted to win just to spite him.

A whisper of leaves was the only warning before someone thrust a pole at her chest. Trynne parried it with her staff, but she realized that the longer she kept still, the more guards would strike at her. She breathed hard, feeling the fatigue Myrddin had warned her about. Her magic was dwindling, and if she used it all up, she'd be comatose. She wouldn't pass the Gauntlet.

Then another idea struck her. The trellises for the star jasmine vines were made of wood. She ran the length of maze on her right, and when she got to the end, she swung up the staff across the trellises on either side of the maze and pulled herself up. From this position, she could see a burning pit fire along the far wall of the maze, marking the exit.

A staff lunged from the foliage and struck her ribs. She'd been too slow to dodge it. Grunting with pain, she dropped down, fetched her staff, and hurried off in the direction she had seen the fire. The maze turned her around a few times, but she kept moving, listening to the sound of rustling and whispers from beyond the wall. In the daylight, the hedge maze would have been much easier to navigate. The darkness and shadows made it difficult to find offshoot corridors. But Trynne was persistent and pulled herself up several times to spy her way. She was getting closer to the end when she heard the noise of people entering the maze behind her. It sounded like the five others were coming in at the same time.

As she drew nearer to the glow of the pit fire, she saw more details amidst the green leaves of the vines of the maze.

Then she heard a series of thumps, followed by grunts of pain. With a twinge, she recognized Fallon's voice.

"You craven *gunnnghh*!" It sounded as if his words had been broken off by a blow.

"I thought it was you," Prince Elwis muttered darkly. "What magic is it that disguises your face, Llewellyn? Hold him fast!"

The voices were coming from Trynne's right, but when she hurried to reach them, she found herself at a dead end. She'd gone the wrong way. She was about to turn around and walk away when she heard the voices coming from behind her.

"A ring, is it? Where did you get this?"

Trynne felt the stream of Fountain magic, which she'd sensed throughout the competition, suddenly vanish.

"Pizzle in the Deep Fathoms," Fallon cursed at him. There was the noise of fist punching stomach and another groan.

"I'll take it as a keepsake. You thought you could trick us, Llewellyn? Well, you won't be getting past the hedge maze. At least not tonight."

"When I get out of this," Fallon wheezed in warning.

"You'll do what? Weep to your mum?" His voice took on a childish taunt. "Life is so unfair. 'I have a scrape, Mum. Will you kiss it?' You pampered nobles disgust me."

Trynne wondered if she should climb up the trellis and jump down to the other side, but then she realized that perhaps it was the right way to go. The jasmine vines were thick enough that they could overhang a gap and only *look* like a wall. She pushed her way through the vines and was suddenly at the end of the maze.

There was Prince Elwis with four of his guards. Three of them were in the process of chaining Fallon to the trellis to stop him from competing.

"Ah, the painted knight. The Atabyrion," Elwis said dispassionately. "The *short* one." His expression turned sour. "I don't like the thought of one of your countrymen winning my kingdom's Gauntlet either, Llewellyn." He gave Trynne a cold look. "You'll stay here too, Woady. Take him," he barked.

Trynne was ready for the attack from behind. She'd seen Elvis's eyes dart behind her, and her magic had warned her there were men sneaking up. Trynne did not have time for a sustained fight, so she twisted into a low stance and swung her staff up and over her head backward, cracking it against the skull of one of her attackers. As she untwisted her legs, she brought it around again and dropped the second man.

Elvis's eyes widened with surprise.

Trynne went after him, but two of the guards closed ranks in front of him, blocking her. She dispatched both of them in seconds. The magic of the wellspring filled her with knowledge, but her magic and strength were both gushing out of her. She heard a sword clear its scabbard and saw Elvis was armed, his eyes dark with menace.

"You think that you can best *me*, boy?" Elvis sneered.

Trynne adjusted her grip on the staff. Pole against sword. Little though he might know it, Elvis was already at a disadvantage. She had the longer reach. She maintained a defensive posture and waited for him to attack her, slowing the ebb of her magic.

"I warn you," Elvis taunted. "I've never been defeated. If you face me, you won't be walking out of this maze. You won't be walking anywhere."

But in a few quick moves, Fallon bested one of the guards trying to subdue him, wrapping an arm around the man's neck and struggling to choke him.

Trynne did not answer. She didn't want her voice to shake. She wasn't afraid of Prince Elvis and she hesitantly reached out with her magic, looking for a weakness to exploit. The truth of the matter was that he was just as capable as he claimed to be. He had trained and practiced for years, had pushed himself to succeed in every imaginable way. He was a disciplined warrior, not opposed to using tricks and deceit to win. He'd even been trained at the poisoner school. She could sense his skill brooding beneath the surface.

She bowed to him, saluting with the staff, and then waited for him to make his move.

Elwis charged at her, using his sword to jab and thrust at her. He was trying to injure her. She defended herself, her only goal to stay conscious and knock him senseless. She could see no recognition in his eyes. Her soldier's garb and woad stains had completely fooled him. Magic leached from her faster and faster.

The sword came down and Trynne caught it, then jammed the end of her spear into the prince's stomach so hard he bowed over, clutching his chest. He couldn't breathe, but he fought on. When she whipped the staff around to crush his cheek, he ducked and rolled forward, a dangerous move, and tried to stab her. Trynne pivoted and the blade rushed past her harmlessly. She trapped his wrist against her side, then jammed her knuckles holding the staff against his throat and flipped him over and onto his back. He struck the stones so hard that he blacked out.

Trynne stared at the body, gasping hard and feeling her knees tremble. Captain Staeli could not have done any better.

The other guard slumped to the ground, also unconscious. Fallon, free of his disguise, was staring at her keenly. Did he recognize her? She wasn't sure. She couldn't get enough air and felt the black edges closing in around her eyes.

Trynne knelt down by Elwis, keeping her painted profile facing Fallon. She felt his neck to make sure he was breathing. His pulse was ragged, but he would survive and awaken with great pain. At his collar, she saw the champion necklace and the little gold badges affixed to the chain. He had four of them. It was one of the rules of Virtus that a knight who was challenged had to fight a duel, and if they lost, they lost their tokens. Trynne hadn't challenged Elwis in words, but he had challenged her by attacking first. By rights, the necklace he wore so proudly was hers. She snapped it off his neck and cupped it in her hand.

Fallon chuckled. "You've made a mortal enemy," he said with a grunt. "Believe me, I know. What's your name?"

She kept her voice low. "Fidelis, my lord. They call me Ellis." She had chosen the name earlier as a nod to the Atabyrion word *fidelis. Faithful.*

Fallon wrinkled his brow. "You've done me good service today, Ellis. Do I know your family? You look familiar."

Trynne dug her hand into Elwis's pocket and found the ring that he had taken from Fallon. She could sense the Fountain magic inside it, radiating like smoking coals.

Before she could pass it to Fallon, he smiled and shook his head. "Let him keep it," he whispered conspiratorially. "It's cursed, actually. I meant for him to have it all along."

At those words, Trynne realized that Fallon was more clever than she had realized. How had he come into possession of a cursed ring? A certain dark-haired poisoner came to mind. Trynne started to smile and then caught herself in the act. Fallon's gaze began to narrow, his eyes crinkling at the edges. She stuffed the ring back into the prince's pocket.

She straightened and then jangled Elwis's chain. "I'll take this, then. I've won enough today, my lord. This Gauntlet is yours." She gestured for him to precede her, hoping she wouldn't faint.

He pursed his lips, then shook his head. "No, you're the one who earned the champion rank. I'll not claim it unfairly. Take the honor, Ellis."

Trynne shook her head, feeling her body start to wobble. "No, I'm spent, my lord. You claim it. If I don't flee now before he rouses, I'll not live through the night. I need to get far away." She jiggled the necklace in her palm. A Brugian badge already hung from it, so she didn't need to earn it twice. "This is enough."

"It means we'll both have four badges. I'll see you next in Occitania. And I'll win *that* one without your help." He gave her a nod of respect.

She waited for him to go ahead through the archway leading out. Then she sucked in her breath and prayed she had enough Fountain magic to make it to the sanctuary where Captain Staeli was awaiting her.

CHAPTER SEVENTEEN

The Wizr of Chandigarl

Trynne's magic was so depleted that she had collapsed after stepping outside the well of the fountain. She slumped onto the cool tiles, listening to the patter of the waters behind her as she sunk into the darkness, her body unable to rouse itself.

She awoke sometime after midnight in an unfamiliar cell. There was a little oil lamp giving off a small glow of light. She lay on a reed-sewn pallet with a small blanket covering her. Captain Staeli sat with his back to the wall, his head drooping, but he was not asleep. There was a small bowl and a crumpled, blue-stained rag nearby. Her mother would be worried about her, but she still had no strength and there was not even a prickle of awareness from the magic. She was defenseless.

"Rest, lass," Staeli whispered. "I'm keeping watch."

She gazed at him, grateful for his loyalty. The Gauntlet had tested her and it was harder than she had thought. Not because of the challenges themselves but because of the dishonorable conduct of the Brugians. Weariness overwhelmed her and she drifted off to sleep again.

In the morning, she changed from the men's clothes back into the Brugian dress. Staeli assured her that the blue smudges on her face were gone. She looked and felt like a different person. She stuffed the necklace she'd taken from Elwis into the bottom of her pack and gingerly reached out to try to sense the magic. There was still nothing left. Part of her wanted to panic, but she knew what she needed to do.

Together, Trynne and Captain Staeli walked the grounds of the sanctuary and came to the spot where men often gathered to play Wizr. Several old men were already playing matches, but there was an unused set at an empty table. She and Staeli sat across from each other and started a game. As soon as her fingers started moving the pieces, she felt the whisper of the Fountain flowing into her. With it came tingles of gratitude.

The sound of boots came into the area, and she spied two men wearing the badge of Brugia. One of them had a bruise on his cheek. She recalled him from the previous night at the Gauntlet, so she kept her gaze fixed on the table.

"The sexton said there was a man and a lad who spent the night in a cell," the bruised man muttered to his companion. "The prince will have our heads if we don't find him."

"I've never seen him so angry," said the companion.

"Nor I," agreed the other. "The lad took his chain."

"I know, I know. Did you see the fight?"

"No, I got struck down in the main hall and was being tended by a pretty healer."

"I would have loved to see Elwis knocked down. He's too proud by half."

"Hush, man. Too many ears." The guards walked past, but one stopped and stared at them playing the game. Trynne felt a twinge of dread.

"Excuse me, kind sir," said the bruised man.

Staeli frowned and looked up at him, folding his arms.

"But have you or your daughter seen a young man in the sanctuary this morning?"

Staeli frowned deeper and jogged his shoulders.

Trynne was afraid his accent would give him away. "What did he look like?" she offered in a sweet voice.

"Hard to say. It's an Atabyrion, though. Half his face was painted blue."

Trynne gave him an innocent look. "If we *do* see someone like that, should we tell the deconeus or the sexton?"

"Aye, lass. Please do. Sorry to intrude on your game."

"It's no problem. Can you tell me who won the Gauntlet last night? I was not feeling well and was abed early."

The man frowned. "Prince Fallon Llewellyn took the prize. Followed by a Fountain-blessed lad from Legault. But the Atabyrion prince insists that he didn't *win* the Gauntlet. He credited the blue-faced lad for being the victor and said he would hold the bag of gold for him in Edonburick. The whole city is trying to find the lad. They're calling him the painted knight."

"Thank you," Trynne said, feeling a flush of approval for Fallon. She looked back at the game, trying to suppress her enjoyment of the situation.

"It's your move, Father," she said to Staeli, giving him a knowing look.

"Threat," he said, blocking her early move with one of his own.

By the end of the game, she had summoned enough power to bring them home.

◆　◆　◆

Trynne withdrew the book she had purchased in Marq from her bag and handed it to her mother, whom she found in the library. "I'm so sorry we were late," she apologized yet again. "I was so drained that I needed to rest before coming back."

Sinia did not look concerned at all, which was a relief. "I was waiting up for you, but then saw a vision of you returning this morning." She patted Trynne's cheek. "I think you will need to practice traveling the ley lines more, Trynne. It's the only way you'll get stronger at it."

She didn't reveal that the trip had taxed her very little. It was fighting the street gang and competing in the Gauntlet that had done that.

Her mother examined the book, opening the pages with a sense of reverence. Trynne could see how much her mother loved to read old books. She wished she could share that obsession, but she would rather have been in the training yard or visiting the Gauntlet that had been constructed at Ploemeur. She'd not been allowed to visit it, as only the participants and those helping were given permission to see it. Her plan was to save her own duchy's test for last, prior to entering the Gauntlet in Kingfountain.

"How was the Gauntlet?" Sinia asked her, making Trynne blink with surprise. "Who won?"

"Fallon," she answered truthfully, clasping her hands behind her back.

"Did you see him while you were there?"

Trynne bit her lip. "Actually, yes. He was staying at the Espion safe house. Prince Elwis doesn't care for him."

Sinia nodded knowingly. "It was both courageous and foolish of him to compete in Brugia. But I'm glad he did well."

"He's been spending time with Morwenna," Trynne said, trying to keep any hint of jealousy from her voice.

Sinia nodded. The news didn't seem to surprise her. Her mother smoothed her hand over the book cover and walked to the table.

"Morwenna told me that she has learned some of the words of power," Trynne said, trying to draw her mother out more.

Sinia glanced back at her, her brow wrinkling.

"I think she'd make a better Wizr than I would," Trynne said seriously. "Have you considered training her? Could she be trusted that much?"

Sinia looked at her, and she could feel her mother's compassion as well as her disappointment. Trynne knew her own lack of interest must be difficult for her mother, who cared so much about the magic and the tales of old.

"Your father and I have discussed Morwenna's . . . aptitude before. And the risks."

Trynne experienced that wriggling self-doubt again. "And?"

"She serves her brother best as his poisoner," was her simple reply.

"But you do see the talent she has," Trynne pressed. "More than mine. I'm not jealous of her, Mother. If you want to train her, shouldn't you?"

Sinia's lips tightened. "You have such potential with the magic," she said. "You're depleted right now, but I can sense the vastness of your reservoir. You remind me of your father at this age. Your powers will grow."

Trynne felt frustrated by the promise she'd made not to tell her secrets. How she longed to tell her mother that she was an Oath Maiden, following the Fountain's directives. She was not supposed to be a Wizr. And perhaps Morwenna was not supposed to be a poisoner either.

She licked her lips, trying to find her courage to speak up for herself. But she didn't know what to say.

"What is it?" Sinia asked. She set the book down and approached Trynne, taking her hands and squeezing them. "You look conflicted. Is it because of what you heard about Fallon and Morwenna?"

A stab of anguish went through her. "What do you mean?"

Her mother squeezed her hands again and then stroked her shoulder. "As a parent, it's difficult to know what to say or when to say it. Our family is already coping with so much. We didn't want to concern you with court gossip."

"Fallon likes her," Trynne said, feeling her heart was going to break. "But she doesn't like him. She told me so herself."

Sinia gave her a pained smile. "But it still hurts, doesn't it?"

Trynne squeezed her eyes shut, trying not to cry. "Is this how you felt?" she whispered, gazing at her mother, seeing the shared pain in her eyes. "You fell in love with Father from your visions of the future. But he didn't know who you were. Or that you were meant to be together. At least you knew, though." A sickening feeling came into her stomach. She wondered that she hadn't thought of it before. "Do you know . . . do you *know* who I'm going to marry?"

Sinia stared at her, her eyes filling with tears. She nodded, but it was not a pleased look. It was not a delighted look. It was full of sadness, which made Trynne feel even worse. What did it mean?

"Mother?" she gasped in a questioning tone.

Sinia shook her head and turned around. "I cannot tell you what I've seen." When she looked back at her, her expression was full of resolve.

There was that scraping feeling again, that sensation of something ineffable happening. It rumbled through Trynne like an earthquake. Sinia's eyes widened with surprise. She blinked a few times, the faraway look of a vision.

"We must go to Kingfountain," Sinia said, taking Trynne's hand firmly. "A Wizr will arrive from Chandigarl. I saw both of us in the throne room with your father and the king. We must leave at once; the city is in peril!"

♦ ♦ ♦

For her mother to leave Brythonica unprotected was a sign the peril was real. When Sinia did leave to consult with the king, which happened more and more often lately, Trynne was always put in charge of the duchy. This time, mother and daughter traveled together, and it was Sinia's power that brought them through the fountain waters. Trynne's brother, Gannon, was still in Ploemeur, of course, so there was an heir.

Being back at Kingfountain filled Trynne with excitement, but she was also worried about what they would face. A Wizr from Chandigarl? Such a thing had never happened before.

They walked hurriedly to the throne room, where the guards admitted them without comment. The king and queen were at the Ring Table, conferring with Owen and some of the other lords of the realm.

"Lady Sinia?" King Drew asked with confusion, seeing her there.

Owen jerked his head up and started to walk around the huge table toward them.

"What is it?"

"He's coming," Sinia said breathlessly, an edge of panic in her voice.

The torchlight in the great hall flickered. A darkness seemed to descend, like a shadow blocking out the sun. Shivers shot down Trynne's arms. The mood in the chamber shifted palpably.

A man suddenly appeared out of the aether.

What struck Trynne first was the power of his presence. She could feel the Fountain magic emanating off him in waves, both from his person and the magic artifacts he carried. He was nearly seven feet tall, but very slender and tapered. His long, white-blond hair fell past his chest, and his intricately designed tunic was held closed by a spider-shaped brooch embedded with a jewel that sizzled with energy. He gripped a staff that was as tall as his chin and ended in a sphere wreathed in roots. The man's hand gripped just beneath the ball, drawing attention to a huge turquoise ring on his middle finger. The scarab-shaped bauble dominated his hand, almost like an insect attached to him. His eyes were blue and possessed a strange glow. His skin was quite pale, but he was muscled and fit and wore a curved sword at his hip, suspended by a leather belt with the raven symbol on it. The tunic fell well past his knees and was covered by a burgundy velvet jacket that collected on the floor around him like a cloak.

"My name is Rucrius," the man said, his accent as impeccable as any native of Ceredigion.

King Drew rose from his chair at the Ring Table, planting his hands on the surface of the polished wood. "We are honored by your visit, Lord Rucrius," he said, his voice firm despite the shock of the man's unexpected appearance.

"We have no such titles in my realm," Rucrius said dismissively. "All pay homage to the Overking. I come at the behest of Gahalatine, my master. Long have our people watched the squabble and bloodshed of these lands. You claw and fight over titles and land like children over sweets. You murder and poison and defame. But you, boy king, have managed to unite the realms, a feat that has not been done in centuries. Still, it will not last. You are ill-tempered children in need of a master." His voice lowered into a threatening tone. "My master bade me to tell you that he is coming. He challenges you for the right to wear the hollow crown. We will prove our cause with our blades and with our wills. Willingly have the rulers of Chandigarl knelt to their new sovereign. And so will you kneel as well. Gahalatine will conquer these lands and place true men and women as his vassals to rule in his name. You have little time to prepare for him. Behold, he comes swiftly."

The room was quiet save for the mutter from the torches.

Rucrius straightened even more, bringing up his chin slightly. "In these petulant lands, honor is broken on a whim. My master speaks only the truth. To prove my words, I give you two signs. The game you have played for centuries to teach your rulers humility and discipline has ended." Rucrius lifted his staff and then thumped it on the tiles. There was a cracking noise, louder than thunder, and Trynne felt as if someone had stabbed her. The tile beneath the staff was broken, but something told her that wasn't all . . . She had the notion that the ancient Wizr set hidden in the fountain waters had been broken in two.

"Second," Rucrius said forcefully, "your predecessor defied the rites of sanctuary. They will no longer protect you from the Deep Fathoms. *Anemoi!*"

It was a word of power. Trynne felt it jar her soul, and suddenly a keening wind began to howl outside the palace.

♦ ♦ ♦

Ordinary people have an unlimited capacity for doing harm. What they do not see is they also have an unlimited power for doing good. In my long, weary travels, I have often seen the Powers choose the most undeserving of wretches for works that profit the most people. A peasant girl to fight a war. A child too timid to speak. A foundling abandoned at a sanctuary. In this way, the noble and powerful are forced to eat the sour crust of humility. The only true wisdom is in knowing that you know nothing.

Myrddin

♦ ♦ ♦

CHAPTER EIGHTEEN

The Flooding of Kingfountain

The keening wind outside the castle turned into a hurricane. Screams began to echo through the palace. The Wizr of Chandigarl stood there smugly, absorbing the chaos his spell had caused. There was the clatter and smash of crockery breaking. The king's herald, a man named Silas Meeks, burst into the throne room.

"My lord!" he shouted with raw terror in his eyes. "The river is turning!"

"The river?" Genevieve gasped.

"Aye, my lady! The wind is blowing the river backward. The falls have stopped!"

It was unimaginable. All of her life, Trynne had seen the mighty waterfall thundering next to the palace. With a word of power, the Wizr had turned its course.

"Lord Owen, arrest him!" King Drew said with a firm, angry voice. The king's eyes were like daggers. He stood, planting his fists on the Ring Table, and glared at the intruder.

Trynne's heart leaped within her bosom, driven to a frantic pace by utter fear. Was this the moment that her mother had seen in her vision? Wasn't there supposed to be a battle? The fury of the wind shrieked through the castle like a host of untamed spirits. Owen drew his sword and advanced on the Wizr.

Rucrius cast a disdainful look at him. The scarab-like ring on his finger pulsed and glowed blue.

"I will stay until my message is fulfilled," Rucrius said archly.

"Then you will stay in the dungeon," Owen pronounced. He gestured for Kevan, and the two men advanced. Suddenly Kevan went rigid and froze in place, his eyes wide with panic. He couldn't move.

The Wizr's lip curled into a sneer. But Owen continued to approach him.

The ring on the Wizr's hand flashed a second time. Trynne felt the rush of Fountain magic as it tried to engulf her father, but it passed harmlessly away from him. Owen increased his pace and lifted his sword.

"Kneel!" the Wizr commanded, stretching out his staff. The orb nested in the top sparked to life, projecting a blinding shaft of light. There were cries of terror, and the people in the room cringed. Trynne watched through the sun-bright radiance as her father rushed the Wizr and swung the sword around in an arc, aiming for the Wizr's neck.

At the last moment, Rucrius raised the staff and caught the blow. The sword bit into the wood with the jarring sound of steel on stone. The blow rocked the Wizr back on his heels and gouged a chunk out of his staff. His eyes widened with sudden panic as he realized his magic did not and would not work on Owen Kiskaddon.

Then he vanished before Owen could strike at him a second time.

Trynne felt her mother grasp her hand.

"Protect the king!" Sinia called out to her husband. Then she invoked her magic and yanked Trynne with her down a ley line.

They emerged in an instant on the island of the sanctuary of Our Lady. The hurricane was hitting the structure full force. Debris from the city gusted past them—wooden shingles, laundry linens, pennants, and shards of broken crockery. They stood at the rear of the sanctuary, near the docks, and Trynne gaped when she saw that the herald's words were true.

The river had turned on its back and lifted like a raging beast.

It was shocking to behold: the mighty river was being blasted back by the fierce winds. It was like staring into the maw of some other-worldly giant, its teeth of foam gnashing and biting to devour the city below. The water was expanding and filling like a giant lake above the city. Her knees knocked together as she took in the impossible scene. With a word, Rucrius had turned her world upside down.

"I need to release the spell before more water builds up," Sinia shouted over the wind. "Or the city will be flooded!"

"We need to evacuate the bridges and the island!" Trynne retorted, still clinging to her mother's hand.

"There is no time. I won't be able to hold the water for long. Stand by me in case the Wizr tries to stop me. His magic won't work with you near me. I need you to raise a shield."

"A shield?" Trynne gasped.

"Yes! Now! *Siopa! Pephimoso!*" Sinia cried out, her hands held forward, fingers splayed, her head bowed.

At her mother's words, the gale blowing at the river was silenced.

When the wall of water came rushing down the dry riverbed to flood Kingfountain, mother and daughter stood to face it. Sinia's eyes were fierce and determined, her fingers tensed and hooked like talons.

"The shield!" she reminded her daughter.

"*Aspis!*" Trynne stammered. Her well of power was still so depleted from the trials she'd faced in Brugia that she knew it would not last very long. Magic gushed out of her, as if she were a broken jar spilling water. Then she felt her mother's magic weave inside hers, filling up her stores so that the supply wouldn't be emptied. It would drain her mother twice as fast, but she felt the lake of her mother's power compared to the pond of her own.

The avalanche of the river rushed toward them, and Sinia began a complex weaving with her arms. Some of the waters diverted and struck the docks at the shores of the palace, crushing them into splinters. Another wedge of water was sent smashing into the trees on the far bank. But the brunt of the flood Sinia summoned toward where they were both standing, and Trynne started to scream with terror as it rushed them.

At first she thought that she was going to drown as the river flooded the island sanctuary. But it smashed into Trynne's shield instead. She had always wondered what it would feel like to be inside a waterfall—and now she knew. It was all surging foam and chaos and raw, menacing power. The noise was louder than the thunder of a thousand horses. Her store of magic would have been depleted in less than ten seconds if her mother hadn't latched her power to Trynne's.

In the maelstrom of the flood, Trynne sensed her mother's spells at work. Somehow the sanctuary itself was swallowing the river. The force of it made Trynne's knees buckle, and she felt blackness tear away at the edges of her vision. Her shield started to crack.

Hold it longer! Sinia pleaded with her thoughts.

I can't!

Trynne was sinking, starting to black out. The strain against her mind and her power was agonizing. She would have collapsed earlier if her mother hadn't been sustaining her. The stress and fear of failure kept her struggling.

It's almost over, it's almost over! Hold on!

Trynne could see nothing through the waves. She could hear nothing but the roar of the waters. She couldn't hold the shield. It wasn't that she didn't want to. Her strength was failing.

Another thought joined theirs.

Aspis!

Suddenly there was a third well of magic. It was strong and determined and supplanted Trynne's as hers guttered out. She sank to her knees, trying not to vomit, trying not to weep at her failure.

The river melted back into its proper channels. As Trynne lifted her head, she saw the shattered docks on the palace side and the shattered trees on the other. Her shoulders slumped and she started sobbing with relief and shame.

There was a hand at her shoulder, an arm around her back. She thought it was her mother at first, but when she glanced up, she saw it was Morwenna. The shame twisted into despair.

Sinia gasped and also knelt down on the ground.

"Lady Montfort," Morwenna said with deference and even a touch of reverence. "I've never seen . . . never known . . . such power. You saved Kingfountain."

Trynne squeezed her eyes shut, stifling her sobs and trying to master herself. If she hadn't expended so much of her power in Brugia, she would have been able to hold the shield easily. Yet the Fountain had bidden her to compete in the Gauntlet. Why? She couldn't make sense of it—she didn't want to try. Inside, she felt ruined and stricken with remorse. So many people could have died . . . She didn't know how she would have borne the grief. And yet she'd followed another oath, hadn't she? *Never refuse to serve when the Fountain calls . . .*

So why did she still feel so empty inside?

"Thank you for joining with your power, Morwenna," Sinia said, clasping her hands.

"What I did was such a little thing," Morwenna said meekly, "next to what *you* did. Truly you are Fountain-blessed."

When Trynne looked up at her mother, she saw the disappointment in her eyes. She would never admit to her displeasure aloud, but she could no longer hide that from her daughter.

◆　◆　◆

King Drew had summoned the members of his council to meet at the Ring Table following the aftermath of Rucrius's display of magic. Trynne didn't feel she deserved to be in the room, but she had been asked to stay. Her parents were both there, which was unusual enough. It turned out that Morwenna had brought Fallon to Kingfountain following the Gauntlet of Brugia. They had arrived amidst the commotion. Fallon had attended the meeting to represent his parents, and Morwenna had also been invited to stay. Lord Amrein and the queen rounded out the group.

Trynne wished Myrddin were there as well. She couldn't help but believe that his presence would have prevented the disaster.

The king sat at the table, strumming his fingers on the polished wood. "My friends, what do you make of this calamity?" he asked in a bewildered tone. "Lady Sinia, if you hadn't come when you did, all would be in ruin. There would be no city left to save."

Sinia had been weakened by the ordeal, but she was still strong. "I came because of a vision," she said. "I saw Trynne and myself holding off the flood. I knew I had to come, my lord."

"A thousand times thank you," Drew said. "You are the savior of Kingfountain today. Truly, the Lady incarnate. What was the purpose of this attack?"

"A declaration of war, surely," Lord Amrein said gruffly.

"Indeed," replied the queen. "In the olden days, kings would send challengers to issue their threats and warnings. It followed the principles of Virtus."

"Did it?" Drew challenged. "They nearly drowned the city!"

Trynne's mother shook her head. "That may not have been Rucrius's intention."

"What do you mean, Sinia? Say on?" The king gestured, keenly interested.

"He came here to issue the challenge. His display of magic was intended to show us that he knows more than we do. By stopping the river, he was proving that the protections of our sanctuaries wouldn't protect us from him. Perhaps he wanted us to *ask* him to release the river tamely. To beg for it."

The king's eyes narrowed angrily.

"To force our humility," Owen said thoughtfully. He took his wife's hand. Trynne's heart lifted slightly at the show of affection.

Fallon stopped pacing. "So what I understand is that this Rucrius fellow came and said that this pretend-king Gahalatine would launch an attack, fight all nobly and honorably, and then claim our kingdom fairly? Is that the gist of it? Well, I think it's a gambit. They want to draw all of our forces away from Kingfountain and then attack it while it's undefended. Isn't that what *you* would do, Lord Owen?"

Trynne wished she had the courage to speak up at that moment. But her self-confidence had been shattered. She felt her magic slowly returning, trickle by trickle, but she didn't even have the power to get back to Brythonica.

"Fallon could be right," Owen said, looking concerned. "It could be a diversion. Or perhaps Chandigarl does not operate under the same bans that we do. Sinia's vision from earlier showed that there was going to be a great battle."

Fallon's eyebrows arched with surprise. "What vision?"

"Never mind that," the king interrupted, waving at him to be still. "Say on, Owen. What did you make of this Wizr?"

Owen rubbed his lip. "He was overconfident, to be sure. When he arrived, he tested each one of us to see which were Fountain-blessed. He was here to issue a challenge, but also to determine our weaknesses. He was clearly surprised that his magic didn't work on me. I sensed his vulnerability and would have been able to slay him. He knows that now. I don't think he did before."

"So we've startled him, eh?" Drew said. "He left in a hurry. And we didn't need to beg him to stop the flood either. This puts our situation in a better light in my eyes. But I'm alarmed that our enemy was able to arrive in the middle of our stronghold without invitation or prevention. Is there no way to lock down these ley lines, Lady Sinia? To prevent others from using them?"

Sinia smiled sadly. "There is only one way, my lord. And that would be to destroy the sanctuary."

"That's not exactly an option, is it?" the king said, bemused. Then he glanced at his blood-sister. "We have been preparing for this conflict for some time. You once told me, Lord Owen, and I believe you gained this wisdom from Ankarette Tryneowy, that the Fountain's most valuable gift is that of discernment. We have clues about our enemy, this Gahalatine. What we need is more intelligence. Master Amrein, so far the Espion has only been able to speak to those who have *been* to Chandigarl. We've had no luck sending someone there?"

"Not yet," came the solemn answer.

The king nodded and sniffed with frustration. "I think it's time we sent our own emissary to Chandigarl." His eyes shot to Morwenna. "We need to understand the character of our enemy. If the ley lines work both ways, then perhaps we should use them to our advantage as well."

Trynne saw the look of fear in Fallon's eyes. His teeth clenched and he took a step forward. "I will go with her. My lord king, grant my request."

Trynne's heart shriveled with blackness at the sight of the desperation and disquiet in Fallon's eyes.

King Drew studied the young man but did not answer right away. He leaned back in his chair and then glanced at his wife.

Genevieve's look was one of steel. "Impossible."

"Sister!" Fallon seethed.

"I am speaking as your queen," she said, rebuffing him. "To risk one life is not an easy decision. But to risk more unnecessarily?"

Fallon gripped the top of one of the chairs, clenching the wood so hard his knuckles burned white. "Remember when Severn sent Mother and Lord Owen to Atabyrion? He was dressed as one of her father's men. Why not use such a ruse now? Morwenna has power. But we all know that if a Fountain-blessed is pushed too hard, they grow weak." His eyes glanced quickly at Trynne and she was absolutely mortified and stung by the insinuation.

"Your argument has merit," the king said. "But that does not imply we should send *you*. Take your emotion out of this, lad. There is no doubting your bravery. But you have ever been reckless."

It was a gently given rebuke, but it clearly stung. Fallon's eyes widened with offense, although he could not argue the point. No one who knew him well could.

"My lord," he said pleadingly, looking miserable.

"I would hear other thoughts," the king said, glancing around the table. "Weigh the merits of this decision. I will not risk my own sister's life needlessly. Owen?"

The room filled with anguished silence.

Owen stared at Morwenna. So did Trynne. The poisoner looked a little fearful, but it was clear she intended to rise to the challenge of the mission. She looked confident and poised. Trynne felt vulnerable and weak.

"I think we should send her," Owen said, his brow wrinkling. "Alone."

CHAPTER NINETEEN

Broken Friendship

"Trynne!"

It was Fallon. His voice and the sound of his stride announced him as he hurried down the corridor to catch up with her. The halls of Kingfountain were bustling with servants in a state of consternation from the otherworldly display of power that had wreaked havoc on the city. The citizenry had been flocking to the sanctuary of Our Lady, some to drop coins in the water to offer thanks, others driven by the fear that the sanctuary could no longer protect them.

The king's council had adjourned and Trynne had been instructed by her parents to return immediately to Ploemeur to ensure all was well at home. She didn't want to return, but she was walking down the hall to the chapel fountain, her heart raging with conflict. In her hand, she squeezed the champion's chain she had taken from Prince Elwis the day before in Brugia. She could hear the murmurings of the wellspring magic again, though faintly. Yet her failure to maintain the shield still tortured her.

She stuffed the chain necklace into her bodice to hide it from Fallon. She did not want to see him so soon. Her heart was too raw. It was clear as day that he was obsessed with Morwenna.

"I have to get back to Brythonica," she said, turning around and giving him a dark look.

"I know, but I wanted to speak with you ere you left," he said, pausing to catch his breath. A butler shouldered past him down the hall, earning an angry frown from Fallon.

Trynne folded her hands behind her back, squeezing her thumb sharply to distract herself from the pain in her heart. She moved aside, realizing they were causing obstacles for the palace staff, and leaned back against the cool stone wall. She looked up at him, disliking the fact that he was so tall.

He pressed his forearm against the wall and gazed down at her. "I hate how they treat us like little children," he said in an aggrieved tone.

Trynne blinked in surprise. "We are young, Fallon."

"I know that, but they deprive us of experience we need. Our parents were doing so much more when they were our age. I'm not afraid to go to Chandigarl. Don't you feel we are being wronged?"

"Not really," Trynne said truthfully.

He looked at her in annoyance, his cheek muscles twitching with suppressed anger. "They were having grand adventures. Your father went to Edonburick in disguise."

"Only because he was Fountain-blessed," Trynne explained. "King Severn could only trust someone who wouldn't be deceived by the magic."

"I know that!" he snapped. He flushed, no doubt aggrieved with himself for losing his temper, and when he spoke again, it was in a steadier tone. "I didn't come to fight with you, Trynne. We've both heard the stories all our lives. But *you* are Fountain-blessed too. You have gifts that I cannot have, no matter how hard I work. I've trained and I've pushed myself and done everything I can do to prove myself worthy of a single, meager gift." He shook his head. "Yet I hear nothing. Nothing." He gazed down the hall, his expression brooding. "Sometimes I wonder if it's even real."

She stared up at him, surprised that he was being so vulnerable with her. But considering how he had treated her the previous day, she was determined to be frosty.

"It's real, Fallon," she said. "And this isn't a game for children. If you want to be trusted, stop acting like one."

He shot her a surprised look. "What?"

There were so many people in the corridor, many of them glancing their way, and she felt uncomfortable with all the spectators. She didn't wish to argue with him in front of strangers.

"Admit it, Fallon. You're only angry because they won't let you go with Morwenna."

"Of course I'm angry! She's the king's sister . . . his blood-sister, and she's being used like a political pawn."

"She *is* a political pawn," Trynne said with annoyance. "That's exactly what she has wanted to be."

He looked at her in confusion. "You're jealous of her. I cannot imagine why."

Trynne shot him a hot look. "Because she's beautiful and accomplished and deadly and capable. She's like Ankarette—"

"Tryneowy," Fallon said softly, reaching out and brushing a strand of hair from her forehead. The way he said the name made her bones want to melt, but was he referring to her or the famous poisoner?

"What?" she said sulkily, trying to hide the tremor in her voice. Why did he have to make things so difficult?

"She's like Ankarette Tryneowy," he said, dropping his voice lower. "That's why you are jealous of her. But don't you realize that she is jealous of *you*? Her father used to be the king, but now is a pariah who lurks in Glosstyr like it's his prison. Her mother dotes on her older brother. Both of your parents dote on you."

"They do not," she stammered.

He reached down and tipped up her chin. He was looming over her, his smell washing over her, and her insides were fluttering like a mass of whirring butterflies. Was he going to kiss her? She pressed the flat of her hands against the wall to steady herself.

"They *do*," he said with a wry smile. "And so do I. We've been friends since we were little children, Trynne. You are so disciplined and methodical, like a Wizr set. So stern, sometimes. You have an old soul. I'll admit I'm too hasty and impetuous. I was an utter jack in Brugia, and I hate that I hurt you." He stared up at the wall, shaking his head. "That feels so long ago. I'm still sporting bruises where Elvis's lackeys punched me. They couldn't abide me winning the Gauntlet under their noses. I'll get my revenge. But I digress. I was trying to apologize." He gazed down at her again. "I couldn't stand to lose you as a friend, Trynne. Say you forgive me."

Pressing her lips together, she gazed down at the floor and nodded, her throat too thick from the storms raging inside her to speak.

"Can I ask a favor?" he asked in a sly way.

She glanced up at him, wrinkling her brow.

"I'm going to be facing the Gauntlet of Occitania next. I want to be the first who beats them all. Would you come . . . watch me? Ploemeur is not so far from Pree. Would your mother let you? Captain Taciturn can come too, of course."

Trynne bit her bottom lip, trying not to smile.

"Stop that," he said.

"Stop what?"

He brushed his thumb along her lip and teased the corner of her mouth. "Stop *hiding* your smile. You are so self-conscious about it. You have been for years. You have a pretty, lopsided smile, Trynne."

"I am *not* pretty," she said forcefully.

"Yes you *are*," he said back with a chuckle. "Why do you think I've always teased you so much? You are too sensitive. It has shattered your confidence for too long. So . . . will you come with me to Pree? Occitania is very different from Brugia. Or so I've heard; I've never been there. We could take the ley lines if you want?"

Someone was approaching them, and Trynne glanced over and saw that it was one of the queen's ladies-in-waiting.

"Lady Trynne, the queen wishes to see you before you depart."

Fallon sighed and gave the girl a dark smile. Trynne watched as the girl flushed nervously, reacting to his attention the way most women did. Fallon was undeniably handsome. *Fionan*—as the Atabyrions said.

"Tell my *sister* that Lady Tryneowy will be right there. Off with you, lass." He waved her away rudely like a household pet.

"That was unkind, *Farren* Llewellyn," Trynne said, letting herself smile.

"Cousins can be *so* annoying," he quipped. Then he pinched her chin. "What's your answer?"

"I will try," she whispered. She had already *planned* on going to Pree for the Gauntlet.

"I will hold you to it," he said. "And I will come to you so we may go there together. Tell my sister I'm leaving for Edonburick with the tide to deliver the king's messages to our parents. Then I'll be back in Dundrennan. You could always . . . visit me . . . you know. In fact, I wish you would. There's nothing wrong with being a *little* impetuous, Trynne."

He winked at her and then strode down the hall while her insides slowly started to calm.

♦ ♦ ♦

When the servant announced Trynne's arrival, Genevieve met her with a kiss. She took Trynne's hands, brought her to the balcony doors, and the two went outside together. The rush of the falls greeted them, but the signs of the river's destruction still scarred the land. It made Trynne's stomach tighten.

"I do need to get back to Ploemeur," she said. "What do you want from me, Genny?"

Genevieve gazed out over the river, her face a little pale and very serious. The queen linked arms with her.

"Do you remember when we last spoke about Oath Maidens? How I said it would be six months before we discussed it again?"

Trynne swallowed. "Yes."

Genny turned to her. "Trynne, I don't think we have time to waste. The threat of Gahalatine is real. He is coming. What we saw from Rucrius is just a taste of what's to come. They have magic that's stronger than ours. I've spoken to the court historian, Polidoro Urbino, and learned what I could about Chandigarl, but we still know next to nothing. I fear we cannot wait for Morwenna to complete her mission." She sighed and looked down. Then she squeezed Trynne's arm. "I'm going to found the order despite my husband's hesitation. I don't like to do things in secret, but I keep hearing Myrddin's words over and over in my head. The Oath Maidens once protected the Argentines. The first Argentine queen was one. I believe I can trust you with this secret. I believe I can entrust you with this task."

Tell her. It's time. The Fountain had given her permission already.

"My lady," Trynne said, glancing back to be sure no one else was nearby. The noise of the river and the falls would have smothered their conversation anyway. "The Fountain bids me tell you."

"Tell me what?"

"Before Myrddin disappeared, he took me to another place. It may have been another world." She screwed up her courage. "Genny, I am already an Oath Maiden. I made the five oaths and received a blessing from the Fountain. I was tasked to protect the king."

The queen's eyes widened with surprise. "Tell me everything."

The words came gushing out of Trynne all at once. She described the ceremony of the oath magic, shared the oaths she had made and how she had already been tempted to break most of them. Trynne described how the wellspring worked, including her realization that she had greater power when she acted in defense. She confessed that she had been at the Gauntlet of Brugia and had rescued Fallon, who had not recognized her.

Genny's eyes gleamed with delight when she learned that part, and they shared a secret laugh. "So you're the painted knight they're all speaking of!"

Trynne went on to tell her how diminished her power had been after the Gauntlet—and how that had handicapped her when it came time to defend Kingfountain from Rucrius.

There were some confidences she did not share. She wasn't sure if she should confide what the Fountain had whispered to her about taking a seat at the Ring Table, so she didn't divulge that part. Nor did she say a word about her feelings for the queen's brother. But it relieved a huge emotional burden to be able to share so many secrets.

The queen listened to her story with eagerness and asked many questions. As they spoke, their hearts knit together, strengthening the friendship they had long enjoyed.

"Trynne, you cannot understand how relieved I am to hear this news," the queen said. "I was very disappointed when my husband wouldn't allow me to found the order. I felt it was the right thing to do. Obviously Myrddin did as well, or he wouldn't have chosen you before he left. Sometimes I cannot understand why the Fountain acts as it does. We need Myrddin so desperately, yet he is gone."

Trynne stared at her and nodded thoughtfully. "He said the need was even greater elsewhere."

The queen patted her arm. "Thank you for sharing this with me. You spoke of the conflict you've had within yourself. The disquiet of trying to please your mother while desiring to be like your father. You cannot reach your full potential with your soul riven apart like this. You must talk to your mother, Trynne. Lady Sinia is wise and powerful. She will understand. I know you've been forbidden to tell your parents certain things. But this, I think, you can say. Your heart is not in your studies. And I need you to train other girls to defend Kingfountain.

Your passion is to study war. I cannot help but believe the Fountain is grooming you for this purpose, just as it called the Maid of Donremy long ago."

Trynne's shoulders slumped. "She will be so disappointed in me."

Genevieve nodded. "Yes, but she's a mother with a mother's heart." Her voice thickened midway through the words, and she dropped a hand to her abdomen and slowly rubbed it in a circle.

"Now it's time that I told you *my* secret. One that I've shared with no one else. Not even the king."

PART III

Lady

◆　◆　◆

The young are hasty in falling in love. Youths always wish to hurry romance and commit their hearts. King Drew was such and told me he wished to have a bride. By all means, marry, I told him. If you get a good wife, you'll become happy; if you get a bad one, you'll become a philosopher.

Myrddin

◆　◆　◆

CHAPTER TWENTY

Toy Soldiers

Trynne found her mother in the castle library with her younger brother. She paused at the doorway, gazing at the pair, and was nearly brought to tears. It was past the lad's bedtime, but there was no sign of his grandmother. No, instead her mother was nestled on the couch, her legs tucked underneath her as if she were a child again. There was a book spread open on her lap, but Gannon showed no interest in it. He was playing with lead figures on the floor instead, doing a mock battle of some sort typical of a young boy. Sinia's fingers caressed his fair hair in a tender gesture, and Trynne could see a look of sadness on her face. Then she lifted her eyes and found Trynne in the doorway.

"Your sister is home."

Gannon's head shot up, and he smiled broadly at Trynne before returning to the lead toys, hunched over them with his twiggy legs and jutting elbows. He was such a spindly thing.

Trynne pushed open the door and entered, though she felt her resolve start to fracture in face of her mother's vulnerability. Sinia looked so very spent from her miraculous conjuring at the sanctuary of Our Lady. Truly she was the unsung hero of the moment. But such a display of Fountain magic would have exhausted anyone with the gift.

Trynne came up behind the boy and then knelt to look over his shoulder. "Who is fighting?" she asked in his ear.

"Papa and King Severn," he said innocently, clashing the pieces together. His childish words struck her with pangs, especially because of the innocence with which they were spoken. It was a story for the ages. A magical winter threatening to sheathe Ceredigion in ice. A duke who betrayed his king in order to save the people and usher in the Dreadful Deadman, the king who was prophesied to bring all the kingdoms together. Would the coming days of peril threaten to overshadow their father's legend? Did the fallen king still fester with resentment at being overthrown? Trynne's heart felt black at the thought.

"You should be abed," Trynne said, glancing up at her mother, wanting to be alone with her.

Gannon's brow wrinkled. "I know, but Mama wanted me to stay." He smashed the pieces together again as he made hissing and clashing noises.

Sinia closed the book on her lap and set it aside. "Your sister and I have much to discuss. Off to bed."

Gannon pouted a bit, but he was an obedient lad by nature. He stuffed the lead figures into his pockets and then gave Trynne a willing hug and a sloppy kiss. Sinia held him for a moment, a contented smile on her face, and patted his cheek before he bounded out of the library.

"Sometimes, when I look at your brother," Sinia said wistfully, "I remember that your father was about his age when your grandmother sent him away to Kingfountain to be a hostage. It makes me weep sometimes, the thought of what it must have done to her. Seeing her in the palace so often reminds me of it. He's such a little boy. With no guile." She took one of the couch pillows and hugged it to her breast. "Sit with me," she said, brushing a tear from her eye and then caressing the cushion next to her.

Trynne's throat was thick. She sat down at the edge of the couch, miserable. "You probably already know what I'm about to tell you. It's not fair."

Her mother played with some strands of Trynne's hair. "Some things I know through visions, Trynne. But I can guess at enough through my own observations."

"It still isn't fair," Trynne said, shaking her head.

"Very little in life *is*," Sinia replied. "A philosopher said, 'Only by joy and sorrow does a person ever know anything about themselves or their destiny.' They learn what to do and what to avoid."

Trynne entwined her fingers together, twisting them as her emotions battled inside. She let out a deep sigh. "I'm not meant to be a Wizr, Mother," she whispered.

The stroking hand on her shoulder stopped its ministrations. Trynne felt tears burning in her eyes. She hung her head.

"I suppose not," her mother said, her voice throbbing with sadness.

"I have *tried*. But in my heart, I would rather be . . ." Trynne's words failed her.

"Preparing a castle for a siege?" her mother supplied. "Well, it seems you may get your wish after all."

Trynne turned her head abruptly, staring at her with surprise. "What do you mean?"

Sinia had a pensive look. She was mastering her disappointment, but Trynne could still see it in her eyes, in her dejected countenance.

"One of the things we discussed in the council was the defense of the kingdom. You already know that the Wizr board has been broken. Rucrius's magic cracked the stone. That special set has been a key to our kingdom's defenses for centuries. No one could ever surprise King Drew because the board showed him plainly who was friend and who was foe. It also showed us which direction the enemy pieces were coming from. Who was moving against our king. We've been struck blind."

Trynne reached for her mother's hands worriedly. "And the pieces?"

"They are just stone now. They do not change color when someone switches sides."

"Can you fix it?" Trynne asked hopefully.

Sinia shook her head. "That set was created long ago. It's a relic of the Deep Fathoms. Myrddin said that it was a gift to the original King Andrew, and he used to play the game with his knights. It was stolen, along with the king's sword and the scabbard, before the battle leading to his grave wound."

Trynne's heart shuddered. "Then I should not do this!" she said with anguish. "My duty is here. You are needed at court, Mother. The king needs you."

Sinia clasped Trynne's hands and stroked them gently. "Your duty is *not* here, Trynne," she said. "As much as I might wish it were otherwise, I can see that your heart isn't fulfilled by the study of magic. It is a burden to you." She shook her head, gazing away a moment, as if preparing herself to speak difficult words. She let out her breath and then straightened her shoulders. "Daughter, the king's men will be arriving shortly with an embassy from the palace. Your father and I have discussed it. The king and queen are investing you with the title of countess. Along with the title, you will be given lands, certain freedoms, and a royal pension. You are to be the Lady of Averanche shortly."

Trynne's heart whipped into a frenzy. "Can this be true?"

"I would never lie to you, Trynne," her mother said with an arch smile.

The thought was almost too much to consider. Her? A part of the royal court in her own right, and not just because she was the daughter of powerful parents?

Her mother wasn't done speaking. "You will hold that title independently. It was going to be invested on you when you turned sixteen, but in light of recent events, it will happen straightaway. You did great service to the people of Kingfountain. You have earned the king's trust and demonstrated responsibility belying your youth. We chose Averanche because it is between both of our duchies and closest to Pree. Without the board, we cannot see threats coming. You will be responsible for defending our borders and preparing soldiers to fight with the king when the invasion comes."

"I will be part of the battle?" Trynne gasped with wonderment.

"Of course not!" Sinia said, wrinkling her brow. "No, Trynne. You will help defend the homeland. The queen has been given command over the home army. She will choose one of the dukes of the realm to be her battle commander. Westmarch will go with your father to fight Gahalatine. Brythonica was chosen to help defend Ceredigion. When it's time for battle, your army will march under your father's banner whilst you remain here in Ploemeur. I will away to Kingfountain to advise the queen."

Trynne felt the wrongness of the plan. It was not her destiny to remain behind. She *had* to go with the king to protect him when the time came.

"I thought you'd be pleased with this news?" Sinia said, looking concerned at her reaction.

"I am pleased," Trynne said anxiously. "The Lady of Averanche. I had no idea. I'm just so surprised."

Sinia seemed to accept her change in tone. "I knew you would be. For too long you have lived under the shadow of the past. And your father and I have perhaps coddled you more than we ought. You are a capable young woman. Captain Staeli will go with you—not as your protector, but as your captain. He served under your father for many years before joining the Espion. You will have your own household, your own herald—your father said that you cannot have Benjamin, but Farnes is willing to come out of retirement to help advise you." She reached out and brushed some locks of Trynne's hair away. "My heart is bursting right now, Daughter. Have I taught you enough? I led all of Brythonica when I was younger than you. That was *forced* on me when my parents died. You need to grow up so fast. It won't be much longer before . . ." Her voice thickened and tears spilled from her lashes.

Trynne hugged her mother fiercely, burying her mouth against her neck. The vision of her father's death hung like storm clouds over them. Mother and daughter tried to comfort each other. The grief of the moment was too powerful for words.

CHAPTER
TWENTY-ONE

Lady of Averanche

The castle of Averanche commanded a stunning view of the sea. It was built atop a hill along the coast, the town nestled inside a sturdy wall that had withstood sieges for generations. The battlements were usually windy, but Trynne loved to scale the stairs leading to them and walk alone, staring out over her domain, wondering at all that had befallen her in recent weeks.

The Lady of Averanche.

Her days were no longer solely devoted to books and the study of swordplay. She had been given a household staff to help her manage her responsibilities and rarely had a moment of peace. But she loved every moment. Trynne was decisive by nature and had good instincts. She often saw smiles and nods of approval from the mayor, who brought many of the city's disputes before her. She dispensed justice but tempered it with mercy. Her banner bore a castle with a fish over it between two moons. In the game of Wizr, her piece would have been a tower. It was a defensive piece, which felt right. Averanche had always been a border town and had changed sides between Occitania and Ceredigion many times over the centuries. It had been one of her father's castles since he was about her age.

She leaned forward against the battlement wall, the wind whipping her hair in front of her face. In the distance she could see the island sanctuary of Our Lady of Toussan. Ploemeur was tucked into a cove beyond it. The air carried the tangy smell of the sea and she let herself smile because no one was watching her.

Part of her still wished that she hadn't let her mother down. Sinia took her responsibility to protect the people of Brythonica very seriously. She needed an heir to maintain the defenses, and Trynne had always been the logical choice because she had shown signs of being Fountain-blessed at a young age. Gannon, on the other hand, had not. But he was still young; there was still a chance.

No, Trynne knew she would feel guilty for years to come, but it felt right deep down to her bones. She was answerable to the queen and took her commands from her instead of her own mother. The queen who was with child at such a calamitous time. Queen Genevieve had sent Trynne several missives—sealed, of course—telling her to prepare for some new arrivals. The queen was handpicking young women from throughout the realm to become Oath Maidens. They would be summoned to the court, sworn to silence, and then sent to Averanche to be trained by Captain Staeli and Trynne herself. Trynne bubbled with excitement, anxious to see who would be chosen.

Standing there on the battlements, squinting at the distance, she tried to make out the sanctuary of St. Penryn's. She loved her freedom. She had used the ley lines to travel a little bit more, visiting places—mostly sanctuaries—that she hadn't seen in a long time. The deconeuses and sextons all knew her on sight, and none asked who had given her permission to visit. She was a lady of the realm; it was her right.

The sound of shuffling steps came from the stairs alongside the battlement walls. Farnes reached the top wheezing; his hair, mostly gray now, ruffled in the breeze.

"My lady . . ." he gasped, stiff jointed and walking gingerly, "you have a visitor."

That was no longer uncommon. She leaned back against the stone wall. "Who is it?"

She saw him before Farnes could respond. Fallon had followed the aging herald up the stairs, obviously sneaking.

Farnes, who plainly hadn't seen him, began to speak, "It's—"

"Cousin!" Fallon boomed, scaring the old man nearly out of his boots.

Trynne gave him a half smile.

"Thank you, kind father, for showing me the way up here," Fallon said, clapping Farnes on the back. "If you'd just pointed, I would have saved you the arduous journey up the stairs. Hello, Cousin," he said, bowing gracefully in front of Trynne. "I've come as promised."

Farnes was clutching his heart, his eyes still wide from the surprise. He looked at Trynne for her orders. Now that she was the Lady of Averanche, she was no longer expected to have a constant chaperone. She could be alone with Fallon if she chose.

"Thank you, Farnes. I'll be down shortly."

"As you will, my lady," he said, giving Fallon a wary look. He started shuffling back toward the stairs.

"You nearly killed my herald," Trynne scolded.

"I couldn't help it," Fallon replied with a grin. He walked to the edge of the battlements and leaned down, resting his elbows on the wall. He faced the sea. She faced away from it.

"I thought we were going to meet in Ploemeur?" she said, raising her eyebrows.

"That was *before* you became so important," he said with a dark look. Was it jealousy?

"I'm glad you found me nonetheless. You came from Dundrennan?"

He shook his head. "No, Edonburick. I had reason to go there first." He glanced at her surreptitiously and then looked away.

"What is it, Fallon?" she pressed.

"You wouldn't understand," he said, gazing down the cliff at the water dashing the rocks below. The harbor was small and easily blockaded. His normal jovial nature was wilting before her eyes. He looked fidgety. Uncomfortable.

"I might if you tried to explain," she suggested.

He turned slightly, leaning his weight on his elbow, and gazed at her. With his crouched position, he was nearly eye level with her.

"I don't think you would, Trynne." He sighed. "You always follow the *rules*."

She narrowed her gaze. "What's wrong?"

He had a sullen look. "Just a hunch, really. A suspicion." He gave her an intense look. "I think Duke Severn is plotting a rebellion."

CHAPTER
TWENTY-TWO

Impossible

At Fallon's words, Trynne's heart clenched with dread. Severn was no longer the power he had once been. The duchy of Glosstyr was autonomous, which gave the former king his independence, but it was a seat with little power. It had never hosted the Assizes or the king's court. It was a bruise on the skin.

"If you know something, you must tell the king," she told him with concern.

Fallon's smile was patronizing. "I have nothing to *accuse* him of, Trynne. Not yet."

She turned to face him more directly. "What evidence do you have?"

He scratched along the side of his neck and then pursed his lips, considering her words. "If I'm wrong . . ."

"Just tell me!" she insisted.

"Very well, Trynne," he said, holding up his hands. "You keep your own secrets, you know."

She sighed with exasperation.

"That wasn't fair. Forgive me. Lord Amrein once said, and I believe he heard the saying from your father, that a wise ruler keeps his friends near and his enemies nearer. I don't think they've followed their own advice in regards to Severn. He's been isolated for far too long, and I know he wishes revenge against your father."

"How do you know this?" she pressed. "From Morwenna?"

He nodded curtly. "She is worried her father's loyalty was broken by his defeat. She's his own daughter, and you can imagine she feels the conflict most keenly. But that is not my only evidence." He rubbed his hand along the stone rampart. His hair was tousled by the wind, and she had the urge to smooth it out. "For the last few years, I have been . . . how do I say this? . . . getting to know the Espion better." He gave her a rakish look. "There is so much that happens in this realm. So much intrigue that never is discussed in wider circles. Lord Amrein isn't getting any younger. I flatter myself that perhaps the king will choose me as his replacement. In the future," he hedged, holding up his hands. "Your father was younger than me when he was entrusted with the duty," he added under his breath, and Trynne once again heard the throb of jealousy in his voice. Fallon had long bristled at feeling underused, forced to live in the shadow of the older generation. "Be that as it may—I don't know why I am rambling so much—I've gotten to know many of the Espion on very familiar terms. They love to boast and brag. When we were in Brugia, for example, you found me at their hideout. That's not the first time I've been to one."

"You *are* rambling," Trynne said, shaking her head. "Just say it, Fallon. What do you know?"

"The Espion has said that the old king has some *new* acquaintances. Men, or so it's *believed*, who wear black robes and silver masks. The masks hide their identities. Several of them have arrived at Glosstyr within the last year. No one knows where they come from or who they are."

Trynne's brow wrinkled. "What does Morwenna say about them?"

He held up his hand abruptly. "I haven't asked her that. And I'm not sure she would know. They started coming after she left for poisoner school, and she's not been back very often. These men in silver masks do not stay long. The Espion struggle to stay informed in Glosstyr, as you well know, so by the time we hear about them, they are long gone. Men in masks, Trynne? Does that not sound like a conspiracy to you?"

"It does," she answered, her insides roiling even more. "My father knows, doesn't he?"

Fallon shook his head. "I've not said anything yet, as I have no solid proof. Only suspicions. Why do you think I've been acting so interested in Morwenna? To rankle Elwis, naturally, but also to create the idea that I would be interested in becoming part of the conspiracy."

Trynne stared at him in shock.

"You should see the look on your face!" he said, laughing. "I suppose I have enough guile for both of us." Her hand was also resting on the stone, and suddenly he put his hand on top of it. "I wanted you to hear this from my own mouth, Tryneowy Kiskaddon. I am loyal to the king. I am loyal to my sister. And I am loyal to both of your parents. If I *seem* a bit angry and petulant, especially in public, please understand that I'm trying to be useful to the crown in another way. A spy is only as good as his deception. I'll not ask to go to poisoner school or anywhere like that. But I have been training secretly with the Espion in Dundrennan. Clark has been a mentor of mine for many years." He squeezed her fingers. "And you have been my dearest friend since childhood. You deserve to know the truth, especially if you hear rumors or nonsense about Morwenna and me. Rest assured; I do not love her. My affections have been elsewhere for some time." He lifted her hand to his lips and pressed a gentle kiss on her knuckles. "Just so we understand each other."

Her mouth had gone totally dry at his words and she felt a flush creeping into her cheeks. Her mother had once warned her that she would not marry Fallon Llewellyn. That thought had disappointed her, since they were such dear friends and companions. Should she tell him this at such a tender moment? How would he react if she did?

"You're speechless," he said. "That's a first. I blurt out my feelings for you and you gape at me like a codfish." There was a gleam in his eye as he heaved a theatrical sigh. "Well, I've probably startled you. Think on what I've said." He squeezed her fingers again, then released her hand and brushed his thumb against the corner of her mouth, the part that could smile. "Why do you think I've teased you with the name *Cousin* for so many years? I often say the opposite of what I feel. I'm an inconsiderate jack."

"Stronger words than *that* come to mind," Trynne said at last, finally able to unloose her tongue. She'd been wrestling with her feelings, at the surprise—nay, glee—that his words had unleashed inside of her.

"Let's have them, then!" he said with a delighted smirk.

"First off, you are cruel," she said with a smile of her own. "You've taunted me for years. You're saying that all this time you were declaring yourself?"

"Some men woo with honeyed words. I woo with vinegar." He shrugged.

"You are impossible."

"Impossible, incorrigible, incomprehensible, infallible, impassible, and incontrovertible as well."

"You forgot *unintelligible*," Trynne muttered darkly, enjoying the banter and the shared memory.

"Only because I ran out of breath!" he added with laughter. Then he looked over her shoulder. "What a sunset," he breathed. "Look at it." He grabbed her shoulders and turned her around to face it. The sun was making the ocean molten silver. A few wispy clouds hung on the horizon, flaming orange and purple. The surf crashed against the cliff walls. She felt him behind her, standing close, his fingers still resting on her shoulders.

"And here I am, flirting with the Lady of Averanche. Well, tomorrow I will flirt with you in Pree." He rested his chin on the top of her head. "My, but you are *short*. Sometimes I think you're still only twelve."

She butted him in the ribs with her elbow, hard enough to make him gasp.

"*Guff!* I deserved that."

"You did." The breeze smelled of sea and salt and wildness. She leaned back against him, knowing she should break the spell he was casting around her heart, as his arms wrapped around her shoulders. Her mother had seen a vision of her marrying someone else. She wondered, obliquely, if that future lover would be a stranger who didn't know her past, her deformity. She blinked rapidly, feeling pain strike her heart in a way that nearly made her flinch. No, she wanted to savor this moment with Fallon. She wanted to watch the sunset with him before going down to the solar and entertaining him as an honored guest.

Love was such a fragile thing.

♦　♦　♦

The next morning, before dawn, Trynne was in her room, fastening on a leather arm bracer, when a knock sounded on the door. Her maid, Adalie, was a sprightly girl of fourteen. She rushed to the door and stopped there.

"Who is it?" she asked in a whisper.

Trynne didn't hear the muffled response, but Adalie quickly unlocked the door and opened it. Captain Staeli strode in, already wearing his training gear. She gave him a concerned look. "What's wrong, Captain?"

He scratched his beard. "I thought it best if you knew before coming down. The lord of Dundrennan is in the training yard. Should I send him away?"

Trynne blinked in surprise. "I didn't think he rose this early."

Staeli shrugged, unruffled as always. "It's *your* castle, my lady. Do you think he suspects you?"

"Suspects me of what?" she asked.

"That you were the one he saw at the Gauntlet."

Trynne frowned. "He hasn't said a word about it. But I don't think it would be wise if he caught us in the training yard this morning. I support canceling our regular training for the day. I should go entertain our guest."

"Wearing that?" the captain asked archly.

Trynne shook her head. "No, I'll change first. Thanks for the warning, Captain."

He bowed and then turned away.

Adalie gave her a mischievous grin after Staeli was gone. "He's rather handsome, my lady," she said slyly.

"You think so? Captain Staeli has never struck me that way."

Adalie's smile grew even wider. "You know that's not who I meant. Which gown would you like me to fetch?"

"Preferably one I can still swing a sword in," Trynne answered with a raised eyebrow. "The blue one with the silver sleeves."

After the quick change, she walked down to the training yard of the castle. It was much smaller than the one she was used to in Ploemeur, but it served the need. She had presumed that Fallon would linger abed all morning. She was a little surprised at his self-discipline, but then, he had been training for the Gauntlets.

When she reached the yard, he was sweating profusely, kneeling down with a hand resting on his sword pommel and his breath coming hard. He wore a comfortable jerkin and pants that gave no nod to his rank. She caught the glint of the chain around his neck showing the prizes he had won. He saw her approaching him from the bailey doors.

"I didn't think you liked getting up early," she said, hands clasped behind her back.

He rose and flourished with the sword. "I don't. I hate it, in fact. But I do it because I am determined. All the best swordsmen in the realm train early. Strange, but true. I'd hoped to find Staeli here this morning. I'm disappointed in the man."

Trynne blinked innocently at him. "He usually *is* here," she said, glancing around as if trying to spy him in the shadows.

"Well, as long as you're up, my lady," he said, walking over to the weapons rack. "I suppose I could give you a lesson this morning." He grabbed another sword from the rack and then walked over and handed it to her.

Was he testing her to see if she was the woad-faced boy who had saved him in Brugia? She stared at the blade.

"*Here*," he insisted, wagging the blade at her. She took it. "Remember when we were younger? You wanted to train as a knight?"

"I remember," she said, squeezing the weapon's cool, leather-bound grip. He'd chosen a lighter blade for her. "So you're going to teach me?"

"I've never understood the prejudice against women learning to fight," he said, positioning himself a few steps away from her. "I heard you argued for it at court." He raised his sword in an overhanging guard. "Come on. Follow what I do."

Trynne stifled a smile. With her magic, she reached out to him, just a little test. He had been trained and was no novice. But he was accustomed to his opponents holding back because he was a prince. Despite his urging them to work him hard, too many had flattered him.

"Like this?" Trynne asked, bringing up her blade to mirror his, but she let her elbow droop.

"Yes, exactly. Your elbow, a little higher."

Good for him.

"There was a young man at the Gauntlet in Marq," he continued, moving to his left by crossing his legs in front of him. Instinctively, she began to rotate with him to keep him from flanking her. Her skirts concealed her movement. "Had half his face painted in woad."

"In woad, you say?" she replied, trying to sound interested.

Fallon was giving her a knowing look. He *did* suspect her. She sensed what he was going to do just before he did it. He was going to try to trick her into revealing herself by attacking in a startling way. Someone trained in the sword would respond by instinct, thus falling into the trap.

He had no idea what she really could do.

Suddenly he double-stepped forward and swept the sword around toward her neck. It would have terrified a normal person, but she sensed his intention was not to harm her. It would have been all too easy to block, counter, and leave him on the ground weaponless.

Trynne gasped in surprise and flung down her blade. It clattered loudly on the stone.

"Fallon Llewellyn, are you trying to kill me?" she said in mock surprise, backing away from him.

He looked confused and chagrined at how his plan had backfired.

"I'm sorry! Please, I'm sorry! Forgive me!" he babbled, holding up his other hand while lowering his sword arm.

"I thought you were supposed to teach me," she said, trying to sound rattled.

"I'm very sorry. It was part of the lesson. I should have warned you." He was still reeling from her unexpected reaction. "You see, you never know when someone is going to really attack you. The overhanging guard, like the one I showed you, helps to counter a blow like that."

Trynne knew all this, but she enjoyed seeing him so discomfited. "Well, what was I supposed to do?"

He transformed into a patient and gentle teacher and spent the next hour with her in the training yard, going over the basics of sword strategy. She pretended it was her very first lesson and asked many questions.

After the sun rose, he dismissed himself to change clothes for their journey to Pree. Trynne also said she was going to change and would meet him for breakfast later. As she left the yard, she found Captain Staeli in the shadows of the corridor, leaning against it with a smug look on his face.

"Well done, lass," he said.

CHAPTER TWENTY-THREE

The Sanctuary at St. Denys

Trynne had visited Pree twice before with her father. The name Kiskaddon was not a cherished one in Occitania, but it was no longer hated. Her father had defeated King Chatriyon multiple times, leading to an alliance between the countries, consummated after the king died of natural causes and his son, also named Chatriyon, succeeded to the throne as a child. Truly, his mother, once an Argentine princess, was the de facto ruler of the kingdom. Elyse Vertus had been on good terms with Owen since his childhood at Kingfountain.

Because King Drew allowed Occitania to remain self-governing, there had been multiple years of peace and prosperity. Pree was flourishing and was known throughout the realms as a center of fashion, art, and music. For the visit, Trynne had chosen a beautiful Occitanian gown of silver and lavender.

"It suits you," Fallon told her with an impish smile when he saw her. They had arranged to meet outside the chapel in the castle of Averanche, from where Trynne would transport them over the ley lines.

Dressed in the garb of a knight of Ceredigion, he was leaning against a pillar, his thumbs hooked in his sword belt.

She inclined her head at the compliment. "Do you know where in Pree the Gauntlet will be? There are many sanctuaries in the city, and I can save us some walking."

He was admiring her openly, with a roguish look that made her uncomfortable. His unruly hair was certainly not in the Occitanian fashion, but there would be outsiders from multiple realms visiting for the occasion.

"They built the Gauntlet track outside the city," he said. "South side of town. The burg of St. Denys. There is a sanctuary there, I believe."

"There is," Trynne said. She knew of it. "Are you ready to go?"

He gestured behind him at the lapping fountain.

She turned to Captain Staeli, who was, as ever, close behind. "I'll see you this evening, Captain."

"As you will, my lady," he said, giving the young prince a wary look. She could see a hint of disapproval in the older man's frown. She touched Staeli's arm, drawing his eyes to hers, and gave him a look that said, *You can trust me not to be foolish.* Pursing his lips, he gave her a curt nod.

Fallon offered his arm, which she took before stepping over the rail into the fountain. The waters receded from her immediately, leaving little spots on the tiles. Fallon stepped over next.

"We're supposed to hold hands, aren't we?" he asked her slyly.

"This will do," she said, patting his arm with her free hand while trying to quell the sudden nervousness twisting her insides. She trusted herself; she trusted her instincts and her convictions. She kept a cool demeanor with Fallon because he was flirting with her deliberately. After the Gauntlet of Occitania, they were going to have a more frank talk.

Fallon looked disappointed, but didn't object. Trynne invoked the word of power and felt the world start to lurch and spin. It was still jarring but she was more used to it, and they emerged from the fountain at St. Denys. Before leaving the mist, she reached out with her magic.

Immediately, she sensed the pull of the Fountain. The mist collapsed around them, and they both exited the small fountain in a side room of the sanctuary.

"What's wrong?" he asked, noticing the look on her face.

The sensation tugged at her viscerally, an awareness of another magic, a hidden tether that bound her. She had never been to St. Denys before, and yet she knew it. A strange certainty settled in her that she had been there before. There was a brooding feeling in the air, like that of a stormy sky before the rain starts. Without answering Fallon, she began to walk toward the inner sanctum.

The sanctuary was full of visitors, which wasn't surprising since it was the epicenter of the Gauntlet. Families were gathered around the main fountain, and some children were offering their prayers and tossing coins into the waters. Trynne surveyed the crowd, trying to understand what she was feeling. She recognized the archways, the vaulted ceiling, the multifaceted stained-glass windows. All of it was familiar.

Had she been there as a child?

No, it was not that. It was a borrowed memory that came from the wellspring, a shared remembrance from another age. Another Oath Maiden had been there.

"Trynne, what is it?" Fallon asked, pitching his voice lower as they walked.

She gazed at the beautiful architecture, feeling the old stones thrum inside her bones like lute strings. There was a tall young man standing by the fountain, pressing a coin to his lips. She recognized him as one of the contestants she had met in Brugia. He was the young man who had tried to trip her. Now he had come to the sanctuary to seek strength from a ritual he had done as a child.

Trynne walked slowly to the main fountain, which was lapping loudly and forcefully, drowning out the conversation around them. The people spoke in Occitanian, but she had grown up hearing the tongue and knew what they were saying without invoking her word of power. There was excitement in the air for the upcoming test.

Trynne reached the barrier of the fountain and gazed into the water. Dark coins crowded on the bottom of the fountain, a shiny mess of them. Fallon stood at her shoulder, looking worriedly at her and then gazing up at the high arch above.

Suddenly the waters quieted. Trynne still saw them lapping and spurting, but she could no longer hear them. It felt as if her head were submerged. She sensed the magic of the Fountain opening up inside her. The mask of reality peeled back, replaced by an unexpected vision: The sanctuary was empty, save for a single person and her. There was a young woman with close-cropped dark hair kneeling at the edge of the fountain before her, facing her. The woman looked battered and weary, and there was fire in her eyes. She wore a soldier's garb, much like what Fallon was wearing. There was a sword strapped to her waist, the tip resting on the stone tiles. The girl's gloved hands were clasped together.

"By your will, I leave this here," the girl said, speaking Occitanian. Trynne heard the words in her own tongue. "Until the day comes when a new maid is chosen by you."

The kneeling girl looked up and stared right at Trynne. They were joined together for an instant, and in that instant, Trynne could feel the girl's thoughts, her worries, her anguish. She was going to be captured by her enemies. And then she was going to be chained to a rock in the mountains behind Dundrennan.

"*I leave this gift to you,*" the girl said to Trynne. Reaching down, she pulled a breastplate, silver and dented, out of the sack at her feet and set it into the fountain water. Then she put in arm bracers, greaves, the entire mix required of a knight—entrusting them to the Fountain until some future day when they were needed.

The Maid of Donremy. Trynne stared at her in astonishment. The Maid had left her own armor at the sanctuary of St. Denys. She had left it for Trynne to find nearly a century later.

A roaring sound filled her ears, as if she were suddenly in the midst of a violent waterfall, and she was jarred back to her own body again. Fallon caught her shoulders to keep her from tumbling face-first into the water.

Gone was the roar, replaced by the tepid splashing of the beautiful fountain. Trynne's knees buckled and she extended her arm to catch herself on the stone, but Fallon was already holding her upright—one hand on her arm, the other encircling her waist.

"Did you faint?" Fallon asked her worriedly.

Trynne glanced down at the water. The armor was still there, hidden just beneath the surface, but the people gathered around the fountain seemed oblivious to it. Only someone who was Fountain-blessed could see it.

"A little dizzy," Trynne said, feeling the strength return to her legs.

"Here, sit down at the edge," Fallon said, helping her. She was afraid her dress would get wet, but sitting did help calm her. The vision had been so powerful it had stolen all of her senses. The Fountain had wanted her to come to Pree. It had meant to show her where the Maid had hidden her armor.

"I will be fine, Fallon," she said, shaking her head, trembling with the memory.

The look of worry on his face was endearing. He knelt by her side, pressing his fist against his mouth. There was no sign of teasing in his expression.

"Should I fetch a healer?" he asked.

"No, I will be well in a trice. I just felt dizzy for a moment."

Trynne heard the sound of boots approaching.

"Not *now*," Fallon muttered under his breath, his eyes darkening with anger. Then he hissed abruptly and stood, his manner and bearing changing in an instant. His shoulders flared back and he dropped a hand to his sword hilt. Trynne quickly turned and saw Prince Elwis approaching with two lackeys.

That explained the sudden change in mood. Trynne almost gasped aloud when she caught sight of Elwis's face. He was riddled with the pox and had splotches of discolored red skin on one cheek, one brow, and over half his jaw. Even his nose had crusted over like a moldy potato.

This was no rare disease; it was magic. Trynne remembered how Elwis had taken Fallon's ring during the last Gauntlet.

The two young lords looked as if they were about to murder each other.

"Well met, Prince Elwick," Fallon said disdainfully. "That looks like a terrible rash. Did you forget to bathe?"

Elwis grabbed a fistful of Fallon's tunic, his teeth bared like a wolf's. "It won't come off," the prince said in a choking voice. "The ring is cursed. If I must slice off a finger to get rid of it, believe me, you will lose one as well." His other hand tightened around a dagger on his belt.

Trynne shot up, the motion making her head spin with dizziness. "This is a sanctuary of Our Lady. Calm yourselves."

Elwis looked at her and then did a double take in recognition.

"Prince Elwis, please," she pressed. "Let him go. Let's find another way."

"It is *his* fault," Elwis said. He was wearing a hooded cloak to partially conceal the disfigurement. "You better have a cure, Atabyrion braggart, or so help me I will spill blood in this sanctuary. I don't care about the superstitions."

"It's *my* fault?" Fallon said with a bark-like chuckle. "Actually, my absentminded lordling, you started this when you insulted Trynne in the first place. I've had my revenge. If you want me to remove that ring safely, then you will apologize to Lady Tryneowy for your ill conduct, your pompous attitude, and your foul breath."

Elwis's eyes flashed hot at the insults and he clenched his fist even harder. Trynne could sense the magic coming from Elwis's hand once he was so close. The ring was probably uncomfortable to the point of distraction. Based on the fatigue in his eyes, the Prince of Brugia hadn't slept much since their last encounter a fortnight earlier.

"Apologize?" Elwis spat.

Trynne wanted to punch Fallon in the stomach. That was one of the reasons he had wanted to bring her with him to Occitania. He had been plotting his revenge for years and was determined to humiliate Elwis. Why did he have to be so thickheaded? She shot Fallon a frustrated look as she tried to think of the best way out of their dilemma. She could make Elwis release Fallon. His little finger was right in front of her, and if she grabbed it, she could have him groveling on his knees in a moment, but it would only humiliate him, fomenting the need for more revenge. People were staring at them, whispering and pointing. Perhaps the deconeus or the sexton would intervene.

Trynne put her hand over Elwis's wrist—gently, not angrily. "Please, can we not be civilized?" she asked. "We're causing a scene. Unhand him. You are peers."

"He is *not* my peer," Elwis snorted, his face flushed with anger. "What is Dundrennan compared with the might and power of Brugia? You'd be no more than an earl in my realm."

Fallon quirked an eyebrow. "Is that your best insult? I had hoped for better. Now let go of my jacket, or I will make you."

"Fallon," Trynne warned.

He held up his hands, trying to show her that he wasn't the aggressor at the moment. "All I require is an apology. You insulted a woman and my dear friend. You called her ugly, which she is not. But now you bear the stain of your own remark. How does it feel?"

Elwis's eyes glowered with hatred.

"I won't ask for an apology on my own account," Fallon continued with contempt. "Despite the way you and your gormless friends beset me during the last Gauntlet. You are knaves, the lot of you, but I don't fear you, Elwis. If you want my blood, you'll have to earn it."

"Fallon!" Trynne snapped. She was furious at him for making things even worse, and at a time when the realm needed to be united. "This is unseemly. We have enemies enough that we cannot afford such childishness. Prince Elwis, let him go. I implore you."

Elwis's lip sneered and he released his tight grip. His other hand still held his dagger. "You are lucky to have a woman to intercede for you."

"I imagine you are finding it difficult to have women in *your* company at present."

Trynne shut her eyes, trying to summon the shards of her shattered patience. "You are both behaving like training-yard bullies," she said crossly. She turned to the prince. "Take off your glove. Let me see the ring."

His eyes were still smoldering, but he obeyed and tugged loose the glove. The skin of his hand was a vibrant red and looked very painful. It was a debilitating curse, one that would only grow more serious with time. She felt the strains of magic coming from it, brimming with dark purpose. The ring had powers of disguise and concealment, yes, but a curse had been overlaid atop it. She sensed the binding that prevented Elwis from removing it.

She took hold of the prince's hand, studying the markings on the ring. They were written in the ancient tongue. The word of release would be etched into the inner band, but she already knew the word of power that would dispel the charm.

"*Ekluo,*" Trynne said. It was a stronger form of the word that would have released the ring from the prince's finger. It unmade the charm that had cursed it. The taint of the magic vanished, and Trynne slid the ring off Elwis's hand.

A look of relief flooded the prince's face. He was about to pull his hand away from her, but she held on and murmured another word. The marks on his face were gone, his nose restored. The curse of the ring was to make the wearer ugly in his own sight. No salve or mixture would have changed the condition because it was only an illusion.

"You are restored," Trynne said, clenching the ring in her fist. She glared at Fallon, who looked at once angry and disappointed.

Prince Elwis looked at his hand. The only sign the ring had been there was an indentation in his skin where it had clung. He let out a sigh, but he still looked full of wrath. He glowered at Fallon, his eyes and twitching cheek promising the game of revenge would continue.

Then, without a word, he turned and started to walk away.

Fallon chuffed. "He didn't even thank you?" he said with disbelief.

"That was very misguided, Fallon Llewellyn," Trynne said, rounding on him.

"Please, you're not going to lecture me right now, are you?" he said. "You won. You were cleverer than either of us. A born peacemaker. No need to rub it in."

"Do you realize how angry he was?" Trynne said, her voice rising.

"I don't care how angry he was," Fallon countered. "Do you really think he was going to draw his dagger and stab me here in front of all of these witnesses?"

Trynne blinked. "Yes. Yes, I do think he would have. This rivalry with him must end, Fallon. That road has no good destination. Turn around."

He looked displeased by her rebuke. "I did it for you. For what he said to you."

She threw up her hands. "Strange how I stopped caring about the whole thing long ago. Why do you keep shoveling fuel into the brazier?"

"How wonderful it is for you to forgive such a slight, but I'll not have people speaking ill of you." His face was livid with emotion. He was deeply bothered by something. She could see him wrestling inside with some dark emotion.

She wanted to be away from the sanctuary, away from Pree. She was going to best them both during the competition. With the ring in *her* possession, she would be able to deceive them all even better.

217

Suddenly Fallon's expression changed, his eyes bulging. When Trynne turned around, she saw Morwenna striding toward them, a flushed look on her face.

"What is it?" Trynne gasped, running forward and taking the other girl's arms. "What has happened?"

Morwenna blinked when she saw Fallon. Her eyes went from one of them to the other. Then she shook her head. "There's little time. We must get to Kingfountain, straightaway. The king sent me to find you."

The sound of boots came again, and then Elwis was there, his eyes narrowing with concern. "Lady Morwenna, what brings you here?"

"We must all go to Kingfountain," the poisoner said. "The whole council of the Ring Table has been summoned by the king. The invasion has begun. Gahalatine has attacked Brugia."

"Where!" Elwis nearly shouted with shock. His eyes were wide with desperation.

"The eastern fortress of Guilme. They attacked by sea."

CHAPTER
TWENTY-FOUR

Troubled Waters

The feeling inside the main hall of Kingfountain was as turbulent as the fountain waters in the chapel. Within the span of a few brief hours, the king's council had assembled in chairs around the ancient Ring Table. Guards had barred the doors, and no servants were admitted. Trynne had helped bring Fallon's parents from Edonburick, while her mother and Morwenna had assembled the other nobles of the combined realms.

Trynne did not have a seat at the table, but her eyes kept returning to the one Myrddin had named the Siege Perilous. It was empty at the moment because her parents were standing off to one side, conferring with the king and queen in low tones while the rest of the assembled lords and ladies were discussing the news of the invasion with great agitation. Trynne stood aloof, feeling out of place. Her insides squirmed with worry at the thought of losing her father. There could not be much time left. She knew that she would be asked to stay behind to defend the homeland, but she equally knew that it was the Fountain's will that she accompany and protect the king. How could she accomplish both?

To drive away her frantic thoughts, she cast her eyes over those assembled. Not since the royal wedding and coronation had so many nobles gathered together. But this was not a festive occasion. The absence of Myrddin was conspicuous.

There, at one end of the table, were Prince Elwis and his taciturn father, heads bent low in conversation. Elwis knelt alongside his father's chair, speaking to him quietly but urgently. The father kept stroking his lip nervously as Elwis whispered to him, occasionally earning a cross brow or a curt shake of the head.

Fallon paced like an animal in a cage. He longed for conflict, and Trynne could judge from his bearing that he was spoiling for a confrontation with Gahalatine's hosts. His mother, Elysabeth, could be heard even over the tumult.

"Well yes, Iago, but if we hire Genevese merchant ships, we can triple the number of vessels and transport the soldiers faster."

"But can we *trust* the Genevese?" asked Iago Llewellyn disdainfully, shaking his head. "Perhaps they are in league with our enemies."

Trynne saw the embassy from Occitania, the Queen Dowager Elyse and her son, the child king looking about as out of place as a young man could in such an environment. His eyes were wide and terrified. His mother looked unflustered, but she had the steel of the Argentines in her blood. Standing behind her chair was the aging herald Anjers, who had a keen eye and a wary expression.

Near them sat the Grand Duke of Legault, a vassal of the crown of Ceredigion. Lord Amrein, who was both lord chancellor and head of the Espion, looked pale and troubled as he spoke about the numbers they had been preparing for the invasion. He wondered aloud if it would be enough.

Duke Severn caught her eye next. Although he was not a member of the king's council, he had commandeered one of the vacant chairs and sat there stiffly, as if the wood bothered his back, a discontented frown contorting his mouth. Morwenna stood at his side, her hand on his shoulder. Seated next to him at the table was his wife, Lady Kathryn, and Trynne saw them holding hands under the table. Severn's other hand was gripping his dagger, which he slowly drew from the scabbard, then slammed back down. Trynne thought it curious that Morwenna stood by her father's side, not between him and her mother.

The dukes of East Stowe and Southport were also present, and Lord Ramey tossed up his hands and, patting the table, asked rather vocally when they could begin discussing the threat.

"My lords and ladies, if you'd take your seats," King Drew said, his voice cutting through the noise. It quelled in an instant.

Most leaned forward, eager to learn more than the scraps they'd been given before the summons.

The noise of chairs scooting finally ceased as everyone took their places. The king remained standing, his knuckles on the table, his handsome face drawn with concern. He was a young man still, a father-to-be, though most in the room didn't know it. Trynne could feel the palpable worry emanating from him. He wore the hollow crown and it fit him well, but it was a burden at such a moment.

King Drew waited until everyone was seated in the extra chairs brought in for the occasion before lowering himself into his own chair. His voice was firm and controlled when he spoke. "Thank you all for answering the summons. I received word last night that the invasion has begun. Gahalatine's fleet left Chandigarl weeks ago. I was told"—here he glanced at Trynne's mother—"that the fleet has attacked Brugia and will besiege the fortress of Guilme. A ship arrived today from Lord Maxwell confirming it and asking for relief. Rucrius's warning has been fulfilled. He declared war, and Gahalatine has struck." The king paused then, raking his eyes across those assembled. "It would be tempting to consider that Gahalatine might be satisfied by conquering Brugia alone, but I do not think he will. It is not only your dominions he seeks to conquer, Lord Maxwell, but Kingfountain itself. He is threatened by us. Like any man driven by ambition, he will not rest until he's succeeded in his aim. If we do not stand all together, we will topple like so many tiles." He offered Owen a knowing smile. Stacking tiles in intricate designs had been Trynne's father's way of filling his well of Fountain magic when he was a young man.

Drew leaned back in the wooden chair, smoothing his hand across the polished table. "After the Wizr Rucrius appeared, uninvited, in this very room and threatened our city, I sent my sister to learn more about our enemy. She returned with dire news." He looked at Morwenna and then nodded for her to speak.

Morwenna stepped away from her father's chair and all eyes went to her. Despite her best intentions, Trynne could not help but compare herself with the other girl. Morwenna was a more impressive figure, tall and athletic and striking. Her raven hair and gray eyes marked her as her father's daughter, but she was still a mix of her parents.

"My lords and ladies," Morwenna said with an air of confidence. "I have been to Chandigarl. The threat we face is indeed very real. That kingdom is spilling over with riches from Gahalatine's conquests. His city shines like a jewel. I've never seen the like in my life. There are no poor, no slums. The people conduct business with ferocity until noontide, and then they retreat to public forums to discuss and debate with one another. There is much wisdom in Chandigarl. It is an ancient city." She shook her head. "There is nothing in our realms to compare it to. The city of Marq is no more than a pebble next to a boulder. Pree? A street." She shrugged. "What I was most keen on learning is what power this ruler possesses. He is Fountain-blessed and highly respected by his people. They say he is quick to laugh and of a kindly disposition. But I also learned he is utterly ambitious, to the point of being ruthless."

She began pacing around the Ring Table as she spoke. "I was able to insinuate myself into the royal palace. I have seen him use his Fountain magic. He did it in the great hall, which is the size of an amphitheater. One of his generals had captured the kingdom of Neffar at his behest and brought its ruler to bend the knee before him. The man was an ancient enemy of Gahalatine's. One of his distant cousins. You could see the fury and humiliation in his eyes as he cowered before him. He looked as if he wanted to stab Gahalatine, but he had no weapons. I was disguised as a servant. There are *many*, too many to keep track of. Gahalatine rose and started to speak. He spoke about his vision of uniting Neffar with his dominion. He praised the ruler for having done the best he could, the best his traditions would allow, but said that he had failed as a leader because his people were suffering. For their sake, Gahalatine could no longer allow him to rule, but he would bring him and his concubines to Chandigarl so he could be taught the proper way to rule. Perhaps, in the future, he would once more be granted dominion of his lands. As Gahalatine spoke, the magic of the Fountain worked on the ruler. His hatred and animosity melted away. He suddenly became . . . servile. He thanked Gahalatine ardently, to the point of tears. I've never seen such a transformation. The man had literally lost his kingdom and he was thanking the man who'd wrested it from him. He was given a position in court. There are many such people in Chandigarl, living in the city's royal mansions. It is a prison, to be sure. But they have the appearance of wealth and power." She paused, considering her words. "It is my conviction that Gahalatine is blessed not with the power of speech, but with the power to inspire other men. As I heard him speak, I felt his power wash over me. If I had not trained my mind for many years, I would have fallen sway to him and betrayed this council. I think only someone Fountain-blessed can withstand such a force of will."

Morwenna turned and faced the king. "As I told Your Majesty earlier today, Gahalatine is equipped with a fleet of treasure ships. I did not see them because the boats had already sailed from Chandigarl when I arrived. Gahalatine also has at least sixteen Wizrs serving him."

There was an audible gasp when she said this.

Morwenna nodded, her eyebrows raised. "Rucrius is not even his chief Wizr. The pattern, so far as I have discerned, is that one of the Wizrs is sent with a warning to the court Gahalatine plans to attack. Not an ultimatum to surrender." She shook her head decisively. "Gahalatine *wants* to defeat other rulers. He wants to prove he is the more able leader. They say a hundred kings have already sworn homage to him. I'm sure some of them have petty domains, but his conquests are still boasted about throughout court. He has fixed his eye on Kingfountain. I heard him announce that he was going to conquer our kingdom personally. His Wizrs reported that the fleet had landed at the fortress of Guilme, and he announced his intention to travel there this very day. The cheer in his hall was deafening. As soon as he vanished out of sight, I returned to bring my grim news."

Morwenna clasped her hands behind her back, her cheeks a little flushed, and walked back to stand behind her father's chair. Severn had a scowl on his face. His eyes were fixed on the king.

King Drew spoke next. "I'm sure you all have questions. But this is not the time or the season for being indecisive. The issue at hand, as I see it, is how to protect our borders. Gahalatine struck at the heart of our kingdom first. He sent Rucrius to demonstrate his might and power and the insignificance of our traditions. He stopped the river from flowing for a moment. He meant to break our spirit." The king's voice grew more steady and forceful. "But instead, he strengthened our resolve. He will not claim one city or plow one field uncontested," he said, striking the table with his finger. He chuffed to himself. "We have been a fractious realm. We have fought against one another as squabbling brothers do. Well, that discord has taught us one thing. We know how to fight. My counselors have advised me that if we do not wield the hammer of war with *all* of our strength, then *we* will be shattered and not the stone."

He paused, looking across the table at the variety of faces. Trynne was impressed by his cool demeanor, but also the throb of passion in his voice. She could feel the magic of the hollow crown wafting from him like vapors of mist.

"I have entrusted Queen Genevieve with the defense of Kingfountain. She has already chosen warriors to defend the homeland.

The rest of you must gather every capable man and arm him with whatever is available—sword, spear, arrow, or pitchfork. From the reckoning we received from Grand Duke Maxwell, Gahalatine has brought over a hundred thousand trained warriors to conquer us. We do not have as many. But what we lack in training, we will make up in courage. We are fighting to protect our homeland, our wives and daughters. We will break the siege of Guilme and throw back those who would chain us into servitude. Do not provide for the defense of your own lands. If we fall in Brugia, we will all fall. Suffer no illusion that Gahalatine will make you lord of your own dominion. He will take it all. And I, for one, have no desire to sip his wine in bondage or pay him tribute from our coffers for the privilege."

The king looked decisive and very regal in that moment. He then turned to Owen. "My lord duke, give the orders."

Trynne's eyes were fixed on her father. This was the prophecy her mother had given them so many years ago. This was the battle from which he would not return home.

Owen looked haggard but determined. He rose from his chair. "I've given this some thought previously, but I won't bore you with the permutations. Legault, Atabyrion, North Cumbria, and East Stowe will sail to the city of Aosta. That is north of Guilme, and your attack will come from the north. Southport and Occitania, you will be shuttled and join forces with the King of Pisan to attack from the south. Do not worry about supply lines. Pisan and Brythonica will help provide support. Lastly, the king's forces will join with Westmarch and my lord of Glosstyr. We will cross to Callait and hasten to join the three segments together. We will attack as one at Guilme. Loyalty binds us together."

As he said those words, Owen stared across the table at his previous master.

Trynne knew she needed to tell her father about Severn's secret visitors before he departed. Or maybe he already knew and that was why he had determined to keep the former king close to him?

♦ ♦ ♦

We are always wanting. We crave another man's hat or his shoes. Women are jealous of other women for the color of their hair. He who is not contented with what he has would not be contented with what he would like to have.

Myrddin

♦ ♦ ♦

CHAPTER
TWENTY-FIVE

The Ring of the Grove

It was nearly impossible for Trynne to find time to speak to her father alone. Sinia had returned back to Brythonica, and Trynne would join her there after she made her orders to Captain Staeli. He was to bring the soldiers of Averanche to Tatton Hall to join her father's host. Then they would march to Kingfountain to combine with the king's host before crossing the river.

She had never seen her father so worried. Reports came in almost constantly, which he reviewed with Lord Amrein. The two men had not slept in a while, and it seemed unlikely they'd have an opportunity anytime soon. Trynne knew she had to go, but she couldn't leave without first warning her father. When she realized there was little chance he would leave the room called the Star Chamber that evening, she braced herself and knocked on the door. Lord Amrein opened it, his worried eyes softening when he saw her.

"Good evening, my lady. Owen, it's your daughter."

Her father stood over the table that was overflowing with messages. He glanced up, his brow furrowed with stress. When he saw her, there was almost an involuntary wince of pain on his face.

"I thought you had gone already," he said, straightening. "I was hoping you hadn't." He rubbed his hands along his whiskers. He hadn't shaved in days.

"Papa," she said, feeling her throat suddenly seize with emotion. He was her rock, her pillar. She rushed to him, hugging him hard, and she felt tears squeeze from her own lashes. The thought of losing her father was unbearable. *It can't be the Fountain's will! It mustn't be!* She remembered again the promise she'd made herself all those years ago. If there was anything she could do to save him, she would. The oath of obedience she'd made to follow the Fountain's will chafed her mercilessly. Would she defy it if she could?

She felt his lips brush against her hair. He hugged her back, leaving the table of his troubles behind, and held her close.

"I won't leave for Guilme without saying good-bye," he said softly. "Your mother will bring me to Ploemeur before we go to Tatton Hall to join the soldiers."

"I know," she said, feeling her chest tremble with suppressed sobs. "Forgive me. It's just that I needed to tell you something. I didn't want to forget."

He pulled away and then sat at the edge of the sturdy wooden table, bringing himself down to her height. There was so much he needed to do . . . She hated that she was robbing sleep from him, but he didn't seem concerned about it. "What?"

Trynne licked her lips. She was *going* to the battlefield. Neither of her parents knew it. The Fountain had asked her to keep it secret.

"I learned something from Fallon," she said. "I wasn't sure if you knew." She glanced at Lord Amrein, uncertain of how to proceed. Had the Espion master told her father yet? Would it put him in a bad light if she was the one who revealed it? She didn't want to say anything to offend Lord Amrein, but the news was too important for her to withhold it.

"Tell me," her father said simply, clasping his hands against his front.

"There have been men visiting Glosstyr. Riders wearing black with silver masks. Fallon thinks it's a conspiracy. You are going to be riding with Severn. I wanted to be absolutely sure that you knew this."

Her father betrayed no look of surprise. He glanced at Kevan and then arched his eyebrows.

Lord Amrein chuckled. "Lord Fallon is better informed than I suspected," he said in a lighthearted way. "If he wants this job, he's welcome to it."

Owen smiled. "Anyone who *wants* it deserves the curse. It is a position of great trust. I like Fallon very much, but I also worry about him. He wants too much to prove himself. And he's a little rash. Like his father."

"So you already knew?" Trynne said, judging the answer by the look on her father's face.

He nodded.

"Then who are these men in silver masks?" she asked.

He glanced at Lord Amrein again and gestured for him to speak.

"We don't know," he answered simply, folding his arms. "They started coming rather recently. No pattern in their arrival or departure. As you know, we've always had trouble maintaining Espion in Glosstyr. We've asked Lady Kathryn, and she was completely ignorant. We've asked Morwenna, and she claims to be equally baffled. We've kept her rather busy these last months, so she's rarely in Glosstyr for long. I concur with Fallon's reasoning—it does feel like a rebellion is brewing."

"And what are we doing about it?" Trynne demanded. She felt a bit presumptuous, but it would be unthinkable to walk away without asking.

"Lord Severn is riding with me," Owen said. "I plan to ask him."

Trynne's eyes widened with surprise.

Owen shrugged. "It could be many things. It could be nothing. I'd rather have him away from his duchy, surrounded by the king's army and mine. Has he made a secret alliance with Chandigarl? We don't know. Does he intend to betray me as my father betrayed him at Ambion Hill? I hope not. If he doesn't give a satisfactory answer to my questions, then he'll be arrested prior to the battle." He sighed. "I wish we still had that Wizr board," he continued. "I especially miss how you could tell when someone changed sides because the pieces changed color."

"Another reason Rucrius visited us, no doubt," Lord Amrein said.

Owen nodded and then shrugged. "Does that ease your concerns, Trynne?"

She smiled and nodded. "I should have trusted Lord Amrein more. I'm sorry, my lord."

"Your father *likes* to worry," Lord Amrein teased. "We may be outnumbered by a sizable force. But we were outnumbered in Azinkeep as well. That turned out to be a rather crucial battle, did it not, between Occitania and Ceredigion? These foreigners haven't tested our mettle yet."

"True," Owen said wryly. "That doesn't mean we have to like it."

"I worried needlessly. I'm sorry for interrupting you both," Trynne said, coming forward and kissing her father's prickly cheek. He caught her hand.

"There is something I would tell you."

She paused, giving him her attention.

"When the battle is over, whatever happens, your mother will start training Morwenna as a Wizr." He looked in her eyes. "She's displayed an aptitude and interest for it, and we can use more Wizrs, especially if we need to retreat and fight a holding action against Gahalatine as he crosses to Kingfountain. This castle would be very difficult to siege. But with Wizrs who can control water . . . well, that changes things."

Trynne felt the stab of regret in her heart, but she wasn't disappointed. Being the Lady of Averanche was more to her liking. And she was determined to train other young women to defend the castle in different ways.

"I think she's a good choice," Trynne said resolutely.

Owen looked relieved. "There is something, however, that we are not going to teach her," he continued, his voice very low. She felt his Fountain magic start to rise up and bubble. He cocked his head, as if he were listening. Then the magic subsided.

"No one is eavesdropping," he said with a wink. "I wanted to be sure. Your mother and I have kept this secret. Lord Amrein knows, because he's proven himself over many years."

Her father held out his left hand, palm up. He took her hand and placed it on top of his. "You see the wedding ring. You can feel it, can't you? But there is another ring on my finger. One that you cannot see."

She touched his hand and examined his ring finger. She felt the metal edge, wrapped in magic that was so subtle it gave off no trace. It had to be a powerful relic to be able to disguise itself thus.

"What is this ring?" she asked.

"Remember the story I told you about the grove in the woods near Ploemeur? How your mother and I told you to keep it secret and never go there without us?"

"Yes. I've only been there a few times. There is strong magic there."

Owen nodded. "That is where a past duchess of Brythonica entrapped Myrddin. King Drew, your mother, and I freed him. You've seen the silver bowl fastened to the chain."

"Yes, and the little waterfall by the ancient oak tree." She smiled eagerly.

"We showed you what happens. It is one of Brythonica's greatest defenses. Whenever you pour water from that bowl, it summons a huge storm. Your mother used it during the battle of Averanche to help me defeat Chatriyon's army. The father, not the son," he added, wrinkling his nose. "I am the champion of the grove because of this ring. Marshal Roux was the previous champion. I took the ring from him." His voice dropped lower still. "Trynne, if I fall in this battle, I've instructed Lord Amrein to bring the ring to your mother or to you. You must pick someone to become the new champion of Brythonica. I've had my eye on Captain Staeli for many years. I think he's the one. I just wanted to tell you in case anything happens."

She felt humbled by his trust and the secret he was confiding in her.

He put his hand on her shoulder. "Trynne, it was this ring that helped me save Genevieve when she fell into the river all those years ago. Dragan knows about it."

Trynne's eyes widened with shock. "How?"

Owen shook his head. "I don't know. It was many years ago. Kevan, remember when Severn had me arrested for treason?"

A sickened look came onto the Espion master's face. "How could I forget?"

"That was a bad day," Owen said, chuckling. "I was locked in the tower and Dragan followed the guards, invisible like the cockroach that he is. He wanted revenge on me for his daughter's death. Revenge that he's already taken out on you, but I don't think he's satisfied with the injury he caused you. He also said he would be paid an enormous sum to bring my left hand to Chatriyon. I knew he was after the ring, even if he didn't. That means Chatriyon knew of it somehow." Owen turned and looked at Kevan. "If I fall in the battle, someone may try and take it."

"Shouldn't you leave it here before you go?" Kevan said worriedly.

Owen shook his head. "I cannot. It is my responsibility until I die. I cannot just give it to someone else. Roux gave it to me only as he was spitting up blood. I don't think I could even take it off unless I was passing the responsibility on to someone else. Dragan is still after this ring, Trynne. He hasn't forgotten nor forgiven. I wanted both of you to know that." He paused. "I think one of the reasons we can't find Dragan is because he's hiding out in Glosstyr. He'll probably be disguised as one of the soldiers who comes with us. I plan to set a trap for him. That is one worry I'd like taken care of permanently. I owe Etayne that much," he added, a hint of grief lingering in his voice.

◆　◆　◆

The rush of magic rippled through Trynne's body. When the mist faded, she and Captain Staeli were standing in the shallow pool of a dormant fountain. Moonlight streamed in from the high arched windows of the sanctuary. The room was empty and still, except for the tiny sounds of lapping water. Trynne listened for noises. Down one of the corridors, she saw the glow of a lantern as someone, probably the sexton, patrolled the grounds.

"And where are we now?" Staeli asked gruffly, screwing up his nose and glancing around. "Occitania?"

"Pree, the sanctuary of St. Denys," Trynne whispered, releasing his hand. "This is where the Maid left her armor."

"We're here to find armor?" he asked in confusion, looking around at the empty room. The wall sconces had extinguished torches. Staeli was still rubbing sleep from his eyes.

"Yes, the Maid left it here for me. I need you to help me carry it and teach me how to put it on. You're leaving at first light for Tatton Hall. I'll be joining the army along the way. Have a tent ready for me, but it needs to be apart from the rest."

"If you say so," Staeli said with a yawn. "Where is this armor? I don't see any."

Trynne heard the sound of approaching footsteps and saw the bob of the lantern light on the wall moving toward them.

"It's here in the water with us," she said. "Quiet, they'll hear!"

She reached out and summoned the armor with her magic. As with all treasures hidden in the Deep Fathoms, only a Fountain-blessed could draw it out. The armor materialized once again within the ripples, and Trynne reached into the water and hefted the breastplate. As she drew it from the water, the weight of it surprised her, and she nearly stumbled forward. Captain Staeli caught her and then grabbed the top of it with his hand and hoisted it over his shoulder like a sack of grain.

"Is someone there? Who is there?" called a voice in Occitanian. The light from the lantern was going to reach them in moments.

Trynne quickly assembled the other pieces, handing some to the captain and gathering others to herself. The sounds of the footsteps were nearly upon them when she grabbed Staeli's hand again and summoned the Fountain magic to conceal them and whisk them back to Averanche.

◆　◆　◆

Back inside her private chamber, racing to beat the brightening sky, Tryneowy Kiskaddon stood before a tall mirror, adjusting the arm bracer and flexing at her elbow. The armor was sturdy, but it was surprisingly light once she had it on, and it fit her perfectly. Was it a coincidence that the Maid of Donremy was her own height and build?

The armor was dented and scuffed, even though it was polished. It had seen battles.

"Now for the breastplate," Staeli said, standing behind her. "The rivets tighten here and here. You won't be able to arm yourself in this, you realize? It takes two to put on a full suit."

"I'll find a way," Trynne said, unconcerned. She was usually loath to look at herself in the mirror, but seeing herself in a suit of armor made her feel giddy with excitement. Two overlapping pieces of metal met at the apex of the breastplate and were sculpted and shaped into a decorative design.

She twisted her torso as Staeli encased her in the breastplate like a crab shell.

"I don't like this part," he said, pointing to the small gap between the breastplate and the shoulder guard. "A broadhead arrow could pierce right here." He clucked his tongue and shook his head in wonderment.

At his words, Trynne felt a momentary dizziness as the wellspring surged up inside her, filling her with the screams and groans of a long-ago battle. For a moment, she was the Maid of Donremy, feeling the pain of the arrow piercing her as she was carried off the field. The smell of blood overwhelmed her, as did the noise and confusion. The terror of the field was real.

She snapped back to her own time, her body starting to tremble with the emotions the vision had released. Trynne would soon be going to a battlefield of her own.

"And now for the sword belt," Staeli said, wrapping the leather belt around her waist. There was a ring in the back and two rings on the front, which held scabbard straps. In lieu of a shield, Trynne would use two swords at once as she had trained to do.

She saw Staeli in the mirror over her shoulder, appraising the armor. He frowned and tightened some of the straps.

"How does it feel in the shoulders?" he asked her, looking at the reflection.

"Well enough," she answered, bringing her elbows and arms together. The pieces of metal slid with her motion, providing for movement. The hilts of the twin swords protruded from her hips. She stared at herself again.

"Am I ready for this?" she breathed out loud to herself as her hands dropped down to the hilts. They felt comfortable, ordinary. She had trained for years. She had sworn the five oaths and could feel the magic rippling inside her, waiting to be called on.

"Aye, lass," Staeli said, his grim expression turning into one of approval. He gave her a fierce grin.

Trynne smiled.

CHAPTER
TWENTY-SIX

Siege of Guilme

Trynne wondered if her brother, Gannon, understood what was really happening as he hugged Owen good-bye. It had been several years since their father had defeated Brugia in battle. Papa knelt on the flagstones in his chain hauberk and new tunic bearing the badge of his house. The raven-marked scabbard was belted to his waist, but it didn't offer Trynne much comfort. Her mother was never wrong. Owen pressed a kiss to his son's flaxen hair and rose, his mouth tight.

"You're to be the man in my absence," Owen said to his son, putting his hand on the lad's shoulder. "I was made a duke when I was your age," he added in an undertone, his voice throbbing. Owen's parents were gathered in the small assembly, along with his siblings and their children, all of whom lived in Ploemeur. Owen hugged his parents next.

"However many men this foreign king has brought against us, Son," said Owen's father grimly, "you show him our mettle."

His mother embraced him next, pressing a kiss to his clean-shaven cheek. Her skin was pale and wrinkled, and her dark hair was losing its battle against the gray. "Bless you, my boy. You are still my miracle."

Owen smiled sadly at the comment, then kissed her in return. Owen's parents and siblings were still unaware of Sinia's prophecy. Owen had confided to Trynne that he felt it best, since they had already suffered so much guilt over the years he'd spent as a boy hostage to King Severn.

Trynne felt her heart aching with sorrow, but she was determined to be brave. She had to show her father that she was equal to the task. He finished embracing the rest of his family and then turned to her. There was a smile he gave her, one that was unique to her alone. Trynne favored him with one of her crooked smiles in return and then gave him a subdued hug, even though she felt like sobbing into his tunic. She wished she could tell him that she was an Oath Maiden; she wished she could tell him everything. He took her hands and kissed her knuckles.

"I will miss you," he whispered right before kissing the hair at her ear.

That nearly undid her, but she blinked rapidly and summoned her courage once more. "I love you," she said simply, squeezing his hand in return. "Ankarette is my namesake, so I know she'd want me to remind you of the advice you've always given me." Her voice was a little choked, but she mastered it. "The most important gift is discernment. To know the heart of your foe. I think you've always had it. But I ask the Fountain to give you an extra portion."

Owen smiled with gratitude. Then he sighed. "Into the cistern?" She had always loved listening to the stories of his childhood. Lady Evie was the one who had taught him to be brave and to jump into the unknown.

"I would jump in with you. If I could."

He tousled her hair. "I wouldn't let you. But thank you, Trynne. I love you. I didn't know the full meaning of that sentiment until I held you for the first time." He pinched her chin. Then he turned and hooked arms with Sinia.

Trynne saw her mother was also struggling to maintain her composure, but she did so with grace and determination.

Owen cast his gaze around the chamber once more, staring at the faces of those he loved best. His eyes were shining, close to tears, and it wrenched Trynne's heart to see him that way. It looked as if he might break apart at any moment, but the Fountain must have been giving him strength to turn his emotions into purpose.

"Farewell, my children," Sinia bid them, her voice betraying the ache in her heart.

A moment later they were gone.

♦   ♦   ♦

It would take a fortnight for her father's army to reach Guilme. Sinia, who had remained at Kingfountain to advise Queen Genevieve, informed her of the progress through messages left in the fountain. Each morning, Trynne returned to Averanche to train the ladies the queen had sent to her. She practiced in her new armor, getting used to the heft and feel of it. She had also sewn a war banner for herself—a horse's head painted blue. Because of her many duties in Averanche and Brythonica, her grandparents had assumed the primary responsibility for her brother's care, and he enjoyed the time spent with his cousins. But he missed his mother deeply, and Trynne found herself consoling him at the end of each day. She spent time reading him stories from *The Vulgate*. He liked the adventures and the names of the heroes from the past, especially the Fountain-blessed ones. Often he'd fall asleep while she read, his face a picture of peace that melted her heart. She imagined that her father might have looked like Gannon as a child, except for the dark hair with the tuft of white. Seeing her brother in that way filled her with tenderness.

It was an agonizingly long fortnight. Gahalatine's army was encamped outside the city of Guilme. Strangely, it had not yet begun to test the city's defenses. The fleet of treasure ships blockaded the harbor, preventing aid from reaching the city by water. Grand Duke Maxwell and Prince Elwis had set up camp within a league of Guilme to keep an eye on the hostile army. Reinforcements arrived every day as King Drew's army began to build. Despite the detailed reports, Trynne longed to be at the camp herself.

She spent time studying the charts with the ley lines to determine the course of her arrival. She could disembark from the ley line anywhere along the strand, although it would be easier to arrive at a fountain. There was a village west of Guilme along the same line where she could purchase a horse, though she imagined they would be costly during a time when the army would need them.

And then the word she had been patiently awaiting finally arrived. Owen's forces had reached Maxwell's camp with the king.

◆　◆　◆

Trynne rode toward the encampment atop a blue roan with a dark mane and speckled hide. She wore the ring on her finger that would enable her to disguise her appearance, but she didn't want to attract attention from Morwenna or her father or any other Fountain-blessed by using it yet. She'd painted half her face with woad, just as she had at the Gauntlet in Marq. Most of the soldiers were decorated somewhat in mud and dirt from the long march across the kingdom. Smoke from cook fires choked the hazy sky. She'd arrived later in the day than she'd expected, but her mother had told her that was common when traveling on the east–west ley lines.

No one tried to stop Trynne or ask her questions. Everywhere she looked, soldiers were setting up small tents. Many were just sleeping on blankets on the ground. Her father had chosen to camp with his army, separated from Gahalatine's host by a river and a single stone bridge. It was on higher ground and overlooked the plains where the enemy was camped. Trynne hoped that their position afforded them some advantages.

When Trynne reached the hub and summit of the camp, a hilltop thick with shaggy eucalyptus, twisted pine, spear-like cypress, and a strange fernlike plant with purple flowers, she could finally see the coast and the city down below. It was immediately clear why her father had chosen the hillside for his camp. It gave an unparalleled view of the battlefield, plus it was far enough from the enemy—and the city—to be defensive, but not steep enough to make communications difficult. Soldiers had been tromping up and down the hill all day to share the view of the enemy and to prepare for the coming conflict.

From atop her roan, she stared down in awe and fear.

Guilme was a sizable city built on a bay fed by the main river that formed a protection for the king's army. The walls were formidable and full of towers and spires that bore the flag of Brugia. It was a hilly city full of elegant manors and crowded streets that were arranged in orderly rows. From her vantage point, Trynne could see the streets were deserted. Most of the inhabitants were skulking indoors, no doubt.

It was not the size of Gahalatine's fleet that had made Trynne gasp, but the bulk of the ships that had transported them. She had never seen such waterborne monstrosities in her life. They had been called treasure ships, but that did not do them justice at all. She had often visited the harbor at Ploemeur and seen the Genevese trading vessels docked there. One of these treasure ships would have occupied the entire wharf. Each had nine masts with sails that looked large enough to capture the wind and hold it fast. The ships of Kingfountain looked like rowboats in comparison. The ocean surrounding Guilme was teeming with similar ships, more than she could easily count, and each had a cortege of smaller vessels hunkering near it like barnacles.

"By the Fountain," Trynne whispered aloud, shaking her head. She no longer wondered how Gahalatine moved such massive numbers of men.

"Impressive sight, isn't it?" said a soldier nearby, seeing her gawk. She collected herself and nodded.

"The king's spies are still tryin' to count the size of the army camped below us down there." The soldier grimaced and shook his head. "Don't think a man can count that high. Thank the Fountain that Lord Owen is on *our* side."

"You from Westmarch?" Trynne asked the young man.

"Aye," he said proudly.

"Do you know Captain Staeli?"

"Sullen Staeli? Course!"

"Where are his men camped?"

"Yonder, midway down the hill," he said, pointing in that direction. Trynne squinted and saw the banner of Averanche.

She tapped the flank of her roan and started down through the brush. As she went around, she saw that fortifications had been erected, mostly pickets topped with sharpened stakes. Soldiers were hard at work digging trenches and clearing ground. They looked confident and stubborn as Trynne passed them. Their morale was high even in the face of such a host. That was promising.

The color of the ocean was dazzling, reminding her of Ploemeur. She had told her grandparents that she would be traveling for the next few days. Everyone at Kingfountain would be waiting for news of the battle, news that would travel by bird and rider. Or be delivered by the king's poisoner. Trynne tried to sense the presence of Fountain magic but could not.

She rode down the hill to the camp of Averanche and her forces. Again, she found herself ignored. It was no surprise seeing a mounted knight in such a camp. Men were sharpening swords and spears with whetstones. A few were sparring in the gathering darkness.

Trynne arrived at the captain's pavilion and dismounted. One of the guards approached her.

"Orders?" he asked her, holding out his hand.

"Is Captain Staeli here?" she asked in a husky voice.

She was their lady, and yet no one recognized her. Just as her father had taught her, people were fooled by what they were conditioned to believe.

"Inside," the guard said.

Trynne nodded and then followed him into the pavilion, not needing to duck her head at the flap because she was so short.

Staeli's hauberk was dusty and travel-stained beneath his tunic. He wore a chain hood, as did she, and his beard was unkempt and scraggly. When he saw her, there was a little start of surprise, and then he dismissed the other soldiers in the tent.

After they were gone, he said, "I had a feeling I might see you today."

"You know I couldn't miss this," she answered with a look of determination.

"It's decent ground," he agreed, smiling wryly. "They know we're here, of course. They've waited *patiently* for us to arrive." His emphasis on the word "patiently" made Trynne look at him warily. "Yes, they are waiting for us."

"What do we know so far?" she asked. "Their ships are massive."

"Aye. The cut of the sails is strange. I can't imagine the speed they must get with so many masts. How they must ride the sea."

"What else?"

Staeli folded his arms and started to pace. "Gahalatine surrounded his army with wagons. They put up the nets each evening while it's still light."

"Nets?" Trynne asked in confusion.

Staeli nodded. "Their army drags these spiked nets between the wagons and fastens them to the ground to impale anyone who tries to climb over. Gives them protection, you see. From a night raid. They've heard of Lord Owen. Their camp is disciplined. They've brought enough food to feed such an army. They've even brought docks with them! The ships come back and forth every day, rotating soldiers and bringing provisions. It's highly organized. We've not seen anything like it."

Trynne rubbed her mouth. "What about Gahalatine? Has he been seen?"

"Lady Morwenna is the only one who knows what he looks like. She's been down in the camp and back. She says he's there, not on the ships, but they haven't started besieging the city yet either. After they set up camp, they've simply waited for us to arrive."

That didn't make any sense to her. "Besieging a city is no easy matter. They've blockaded the harbor, which prevents reinforcements from arriving by sea. I thought they would have tried to take the city before we arrived to have some defense against us."

Staeli tapped his nose. "Lord Owen thinks they do this deliberately as a show of skill and cunning. They plan on sieging the city and attacking our army at the same *time*."

The news filled her with apprehension.

"They're going to attack us on a *hill* while starting a siege on Guilme?"

Staeli raised his hands. "It sounds foolhardy and a trifle overconfident, don't you think? But it's the only thing that makes sense. We don't see any siege engines down in camp. No battering rams."

"They have Wizrs," Trynne reminded him grimly. "Many Wizrs."

"Exactly," Staeli said. "In other words . . . we don't know what they are capable of. Lord Owen wants to test them, to attack them where they are instead of waiting for them to attack us. There is some secret strategy he's betting on. He's not telling anyone, even the king. All companies have been told to make ready at a moment's notice. It may even happen tonight."

Trynne squeezed her sword pommels tightly, her stomach bubbling with excitement.

Staeli continued, "I have a small tent ready for you, as you requested. I hope you're well rested, because you probably won't be getting much sleep. It's up the hill but not all the way to the king's camp at the summit. I'll send a squire to bring you to your tent. He'll wait on you. The lad's name is Jerrison."

Trynne thanked him, then couldn't help but ask, "This hill is a really good vantage point. But why would Gahalatine have left it unprotected?"

Staeli shrugged. "We don't know. I suppose we'll find out soon."

♦   ♦   ♦

Dusk was falling as Trynne followed Jerrison up the path. The boy gripped the reins of her roan. He was about fourteen or fifteen, with sandy brown hair that was cropped close as a soldier's. A lanky young man with smudges of dirt on his face, he chattered with her about Averanche and how much the city below reminded him of his home. He asked where she was from, but she evaded the question.

"There is the tent," Jerrison said, pointing to a small tent pitched up the windy trail amidst a copse of eucalyptus. Trynne wondered if Staeli had chosen that place because it resembled a piece of hillside in Brythonica. "I'll brush down the horse and then fetch you some dinner. What was your name again?"

"Sir Ellis," Trynne said huskily.

The hillside was still full of soldiers coming in and out with orders from the command pavilion. It was a cool evening. In the distance, a bank of fog was starting to roll in. Trynne frowned, wondering if it would come ashore, and if it did, how it could impact her father's plans.

She saw a tall, dark-cloaked man striding along the main road just below her. But it was the silver mask he wore that made her eyes fix on him.

CHAPTER TWENTY-SEVEN

Fog of War

When she saw the silver mask, she felt a strong urge to follow the man. The squire Jerrison was handling the reins of her roan as he led it farther up the hill.

She patted the animal's withers and then said firmly, "I'll return shortly for dinner. Thank you, Jerrison."

"It's my pleasure to serve," said the lad offhandedly, his eyes focused on his work. The roan snorted hungrily as Trynne angled her steps down the small scrub-choked path. The cowled figure was disappearing into the gloom, so Trynne hurried to catch up.

The foot traffic had lightened somewhat, and a few men carried torches against the gloom. Trynne noticed that the man in the mask averted his face when they approached. Not far down the path, around a bend in the neck of the road, the hooded figure slipped off the trail into the woods and started mounting the hill toward King Drew's encampment. Trynne gritted her teeth and increased her stride. What nonsense was he planning?

The destination wasn't far from her own tent, she realized. There was another tent settled in the copse of eucalyptus, without a banner or watchmen guarding it. The fabric glowed from a light inside, but it was too thick for her to make out any shapes other than bulky shadows. The tent was tall and round, with an iron spike protruding from the apex. The hooded man ducked into the entrance of the pavilion and disappeared.

She was standing off the main road, perfectly visible to any passersby. Inside the tent, she thought she heard a muffled voice. What should she do next? Wait for the man to come out? Should she go inside and challenge him? Try to find a way to warn her father?

The sounds of the camp wafted in on the night breeze. The grinding of steel on stone. The shared laughter of comrades eating dinner. The rustling of the leaves. The wind also brought the smell of smoke and the briny scent of the sea. It reminded her of home. She didn't know what to do, and the hesitation only increased her trepidation.

Better to confront the trouble directly. Time was not an ally at the present.

Steeling her courage, she gripped the hilt of one of her twin swords and marched up to the tent. She tried to be quiet, but the cracking of twigs and hiss of the tall grasses announced her well before she got there.

The tent was still, no murmuring noise. She reached out with her magic probe for danger, letting it ripple from her. There was only one person inside who was armed, and he was standing to the side of the tent opening with a sword in a defensive posture, clearly expecting trouble.

She drew her sword and then barged into the tent. If the man attacked her, she was ready to defend herself. The Fountain magic whirled up in a cocoon around her. She would wait to be attacked. Her power was strongest then.

There was a small brazier and a lamp at the center of the tent, but her eyes immediately flew to the right side. Fallon stood by the entrance, sword held upright as if he were going to strike her on the head with the pommel.

Fallon.

But he hesitated when he saw her. Trynne walked deeper into the tent so she could turn to face him. She avoided the center pole that kept the tent from collapsing. Immediately, she invoked the ring on her finger and disguised her features, giving herself a slightly altered appearance of a soldier with a woad-painted face.

"Sir Ellis?" Fallon said in surprise, lowering the sword.

"Prince Fallon," Trynne said in her lower voice. Warily.

Fallon wore a boiled-leather tunic over his hauberk. Why did he not wear the badge of the Pierced Lion marking him as a man of Dundrennan?

"What are you doing here?" Fallon demanded in confusion. "You *are* the young man I met in Marq, are you not?"

"I am, my lord," Trynne replied, trying to understand what was going on. Where was the man with the silver mask? She realized instantly that Fallon was alone. *He* must have been wearing the disguise, and confusion and distrust began to swell inside her heart.

"And why are you here? Why did you come armed into my tent?"

"I didn't know it was yours, my lord," Trynne replied. "I was . . . following someone."

The wary look began to subside. "Ah. You were following someone, you say? Who? I'm quite alone, as you can see. Well, except for you."

Trynne felt the presence of another Fountain-blessed approaching the tent from higher up the hill. Was it her father? Morwenna? Was she close enough to their camp that they had felt her using her power? She needed to leave immediately.

"I'm sorry for the intrusion," she apologized and started for the tent door, but Fallon quickly stepped into her path.

"Why the rush?" he asked in a distrusting way. "I never did thank you properly for helping me during the Gauntlet. You've painted your face, but you're not from Atabyrion, are you? You said your name was *Fidelis*, but are you faithful to the *true* king?"

The presence was drawing closer. Trynne's nerves ached to knock Fallon down so she could run from the tent. Then she spied a rumpled black cloak on the floor where Fallon had discarded it.

"The *true* king?" Trynne asked suspiciously.

"Yes, the true king of Ceredigion," Fallon said. "You said you were following someone. What did he look like? You seem so familiar to me. Are you part of the Espion?"

"I am not," Trynne answered. "Stand aside, my lord."

"But we have so much to talk about still," Fallon said, giving her a meaningful smile while continuing to block the exit. He was stalling her. Deliberately. "I don't think your name is Ellis. It's a disguise. Who are you, truly? Maybe we can help each other."

Trynne's heart was sinking at the evidence before her. Had Fallon told her about the rebellion against King Drew to hide the fact that he was a part of it? Was this true king he spoke of Severn Argentine? His words were all buried beneath layers of nuance, but they hinted at treason. How could Fallon have gotten himself so mixed up in the intrigue? Because he wanted to be important. He wanted to be useful. If he could not be useful to Drew, perhaps he'd found a new master to serve who was willing to give him more power. Or it could be that he'd gotten so caught up in playing his game of Espion that he didn't realize the danger to himself.

His expression changed, twisting with something like guilt. He stared at her, unable to see through the magic, but his senses were screaming at him.

"You do remind me of someone," he said softly, almost tenderly. "Who are you?"

"Stand aside, my lord," Trynne warned for the last time, taking a step forward.

"I'm sorry, but I won't let you go this—"

His words were cut off when she suddenly kicked him in the stomach, knocking him backward out through the tent flap. She snatched up the cloak from the floor and felt something hard underneath it. Assuming it to be the mask, she tucked it all under her arm and stormed outside the flap. Fallon was standing again, gripping his stomach, and he leaped at her with a look of rage in his eyes. Below them there were shadows and trees and laughter and smoke, but no one was close enough to notice them. Trynne dropped into a front roll, and Fallon sailed over her, grunting as he smashed into the bark and earth. She spun and then whacked him upside the head with the bundle containing the silver mask.

He slumped to the ground again, groggy and stunned, but not unconscious.

Trynne sheathed her sword and marched partway down the hill, releasing both the magic of the ring and her own power, letting it dissipate into the wind. Then she cut another angle and hid in the brush, hoping to overhear what happened back in Fallon's tent.

She heard Morwenna's voice first, her tone full of worry and concern.

"Fallon? What happened? Who struck you?"

Trynne squeezed her eyes shut for a moment, trying to blot out the memories of everything they had shared for so many years. Memories that threatened to sting her eyes with tears. She felt betrayed. The possibilities jumbling inside her mind frightened her. Had Morwenna told Fallon about Trynne's feelings? Were they both trying to use and manipulate her somehow?

"It was that lad from the Gauntlet," Fallon said heatedly, stifling a groan. "The painted one. I told you about him."

"He's here?"

"Down the road yonder."

"I'll go after him."

"No!" Fallon said urgently. "My head is about to burst open. Tend to me first. Have the Espion search for him. It hurts, Morwenna!"

"Men cannot endure the slightest pains," she chided, her voice a little mocking. "I'm going to warn the king about this."

"Later. I'm so dizzy. Help me sit down."

"Come, my weak prince," Morwenna said soothingly.

Trynne couldn't stand to hear their banter. Tears streaked down her face as she melted into the night.

♦   ♦   ♦

The fog reached landfall after midnight.

Captain Staeli stood at her left elbow, arms folded, his finger stroking his mustache as he stared down at Gahalatine's forces. The moon was radiant and silver in the sky, but the ocean of fog down below masked everything. It was silver and purple and rippled with an otherworldly quality. Only the highest spires of Guilme pierced it. The lights of the city were all illuminated, creating an eerie mix of colors in the deep night. The hill of the king's camp was just barely above the fog. The fleet of treasure ships anchored off the coast had vanished in the haze.

"Real or magic?" Trynne whispered softly in awe. The air had a bite of chill to it. Her senses were searching for the presence of the Fountain. There was only silence.

"Grand Duke Maxwell said it's normal to have mist along this coast. Comes almost every night at certain seasons." He sniffed. "They can't see us and we can't see them."

Trynne looked up the hill at the king's camp. All the fires were out. The whole hillside seemed like it was slumbering. It was just as deceptive as the fog.

"Father is going to attack tonight," Trynne guessed. "He's waiting for the right moment."

"It'll be too loud," Staeli countered. "And what about the net?"

"That's why he'll do it," she said, smiling. "The mist evens the odds."

Their brief discussion was interrupted by a member of the Espion who jogged up to where they were standing.

"Captain Staeli?" the man asked, out of breath.

"Aye," he replied gruffly.

"Lord Owen wants you to make ready. He's given the order. We're going to attack tonight."

Staeli turned to Trynne in shocked admiration and then started chuckling.

The Espion continued. "Quietly rouse your men. Hauberks only. Blankets are being laid down to tread on. The watchword is 'Sinia.' Come to the command pavilion. Your force is going with Lord Owen himself."

Trynne felt her throat constrict.

Guard the king, the Fountain whispered to her.

◆　◆　◆

The Battle of Guilme started before the first cock crowed.

Trynne paced in suspense and agony, standing on the hillside overlooking an endless sea of fog. She waited for it to start, each hour that passed adding to her torture. The camp was roused and ready to fight. Soldiers stood along the road running the perimeter of the highest hill, where the king's camp was in darkness. There were no lights to provide a hint to the enemy that the forces of Kingfountain were on the move. Every night bird that shrieked made Trynne's heart race. She waited for the moment.

And then it came.

Thunder crashed down from the star-filled sky. The sound was a portent, startling the soldiers and drawing everyone's gaze skyward, where no storm clouds existed to cause such a ruckus. Trynne flinched as if a huge hammer had struck her soul. She felt the white-hot stab of magic emanating from the bank of fog down below. And then it snuffed out.

There was noise and shouting, the clash of arms. The battle had begun, but it was invisible within the shroud of fog. Trynne's heart thundered in her ears. She had felt the magic. She'd recognized it as the same magic of the silver bowl from the grove. Her father had recently reminded her of that place, and of the storm he'd summoned to show her how it worked. His magic had shielded them both from the hailstorm, but it had still frightened and thrilled her.

Suddenly she felt the ripples of Fountain magic and a keening wind began to blow and howl. The trees started to sway and groan. Hunks of bark from the mighty eucalyptus trees began to slough off and crash down. Cries of pain and panic joined the clash of steel and arms.

And then the enemy came out of the mist like grasshoppers.

It was the only way to describe it. Trynne watched in startled horror as armed warriors wearing armor that was green like palm fronds leaped out of the fog, arching into the sky as if they had been catapulted from below.

The warriors had helmets tipped with thorny spears, and each carried wood-handled glaives with blades that were sharpened on both sides. The warriors' momentum slowed before they reached the hillside, and instead of crashing like boulders, they unfolded like strange plants just before they struck.

Watching them mesmerized Trynne until one of them was suddenly uncoiling in front of her. She ducked to the side, two swords in her hands, and blocked a blow that had already skewered one of the knights standing near her. Her magic rose to her defense and she blocked his next five attacks before striking him down with a single blow. Another volley of enemy soldiers came up the hill, some landing even higher up the slope. Trynne knew they were going to attack the king, so she began to run up the slope to intercept them. One of the strange leaf-armored soldiers landed directly in front of her, swinging his glaive around in a circle. She dodged to the side, trapped his weapon between both of hers, and kicked him hard in the stomach. He flew backward and then suddenly he was floating in the air above her, like a puppet suddenly snatched up by its strings.

He plummeted down just as quickly, trying to slice her in half.

Trynne had never experienced such an enemy before. The knights of Ceredigion were collapsing all around as the warriors of death scythed through their ranks. Trynne caught that attack with both swords again, then reversed her move and sliced him in the side and neck with her blades. A look of surprise was frozen on his face as he died.

Trynne continued to charge up the hill, her breath coming in gasps as she watched more of the warriors fling over and around her. Running uphill put her at a disadvantage, so she muttered a word of power and lurched up a ley line to the top. The action drained her, but it brought her to the crest, where she found the king surrounded by Espion and his guards. There was a whirlwind of commotion. The fighting hadn't reached them yet, but it was imminent.

Archers were rushing up one of the hillsides to shoot at the flying warriors, but they dared not loose arrows uphill for risk of hitting their king. The battle raged across the hillside. Trynne stared in dread at the field below, exposed with the fog blasted apart. She saw tiny little specks in the distance, men leaping up to the walls of Guilme. Now it was apparent to all that the enemy didn't *need* siege engines. Gahalatine's army was attacking King Drew's army and the besieged city simultaneously.

Suddenly more of the leaf-armored soldiers dropped from the sky and the Espion were in hand-to-hand combat with them. King Drew freed his sword Firebos and joined the fray, trying to hold the hilltop against the invaders who had bypassed his entire army to reach him.

And then she saw the flag of the White Boar charging up the hill. It was Severn Argentine's sigil. He was leading about fifty men, all mounted, and they rode up through the ranks of fallen warriors.

They were heading straight for the king.

CHAPTER TWENTY-EIGHT

Lord Gahalatine

Trynne whipped around, slicing through another opponent while blocking his overhand attack with her second blade. The drain on her Fountain magic was palpable, but the leaching effect was tempered because she was acting in defense of the king. The soldiers of the White Boar were nearly at the hilltop when she heard Severn's voice ring out.

"To the king! Form a circle! No one gets past. Show these knaves our will is made of iron! Come, lads! To the last man standing, save the king!"

Trynne felt the first flush of relief. Perhaps Severn wasn't the enemy, but she still had to stay near the king to protect him. She ducked a glaive as it spun toward her head, then butted the warrior in the helm with the pommel of a sword and stabbed him through. The hillside was swarming with enemies, converging on the hill like fire sweeping through grass. The horsemen of Glosstyr barged in, the knights slashing and crowding their way to the hilltop. The leaf-armored warriors hoisted up into the air like poppet dolls on strings before slamming down on the knights and stabbing riders or steeds. The noise and commotion of the battle raged around Trynne as she closed up ranks.

"My lord, we're surrounded," Kevan Amrein said to the king in a tone of desperation. His sword was bloodied from the conflict. "Where is Morwenna? We need to get you out of here."

"I will not abandon my people!" Drew said fiercely, holding the blade Firebos in front of him. Trynne could feel the ripples of Fountain magic coming from it. Since their enemies could leap around like grasshoppers, many continued to drop down from above, and the king was courageous in his own defense. With each stroke of his blade, he knocked back several men, as if the sword brought the force of a waterfall with it.

Severn brought up his steed, its lips lathered with foam.

"What happened down there, Lord Severn?" the king demanded, not looking over his shoulder.

"I know not," Severn replied. "Owen suspected treachery and sent me back to guard you." Another warrior plummeted from the sky and Severn kicked his stallion forward to engage. The glaive clanged off Severn's shield before the old king took off the man's head in a counterstroke. Trynne's fears for her father bloomed. She hadn't known his strategy, but she did know that he had planned to test Severn's loyalty. Despite the strangeness of what had transpired between Fallon and Morwenna, it appeared the former king had passed the test.

"Here comes another wave," Lord Amrein warned.

They were hopelessly outnumbered. Like arrows shot from bows, the next phalanx of leaf-armored warriors dropped down on them. The knights of Kingfountain were falling at an alarming rate.

Trynne saw Fallon's father, Iago Llewellyn, emerge from the hillside, his face grimy with blood and dirt. There was Fallon at his side, shield in hand, sword drawn. Warriors from Atabyrion and Dundrennan came with them.

"To the king!" Iago shouted.

The sound of a hurricane ripped over the hilltop as their enemies continued to drop from the sky. Trynne couldn't make sense of the madness as she fought, moving from one foe to the next. Her heart beat wildly in her chest. The knights of Glosstyr were hewn down, man by man, their horses shrieking and writhing.

She caught a glimpse of Fallon in the midst of a desperate fight. He received a wound to his leg but continued to fight after he collapsed, his face wild with fury as he stabbed his enemy through the bowels and killed him. Iago was buffeted on the helm from behind, the glaive slicing into his back. When he arched and fell forward, his opponent spun the glaive around his head in a circle, clearly intent on impaling him from behind. Agony tore at Trynne—she was closer to the king, and though she could see what was happening, she would not be able to stop it.

"Halt!"

The voice speared through the air like a thunderclap. It shook the ground and drove all the leaf-armored warriors down on one knee. They stopped midmotion, stepping back from their foes, even though their eyes were full of anger and hate.

Trynne was stunned.

"Rucrius, take me to the hilltop."

The voice boomed again like thunder. Some of the soldiers covered their ears from the noise of it.

Trynne looked around. She was standing alone amidst a sea of enemies. All the men of Glosstyr around her had perished. There were maybe only six left from the fifty she had seen climbing the hill. Severn was panting for breath, his sword tip facing down but his shield still hunched up on his shoulder, braced for another blow.

The fog had totally cleared, and Trynne could see the battlefield down below. All fighting had ceased. Where was her father?

Then she felt the sizzle of Fountain magic and suddenly five additional men appeared on the hilltop. She recognized Rucrius instantly and was gratified to see his staff still bore the nick-mark from her father's blade. He looked proud and disdainful. Two of the others were clearly Wizrs and Fountain-blessed. Trynne could feel the waves of power emanating from them, but their magic slipped around her harmlessly. She reached out with her own magic and felt their weaknesses—all three were vulnerable around their necks.

The three Wizrs turned and looked at her as one, and Rucrius's proud look was replaced with bafflement.

The other two men who had been transported to the hilltop were not Wizrs. One was a warrior wearing different armor from the rest. It was gold rather than green, and he wore a forked helm that covered most of his face save a slit across the eyes and down the nose. The eyes that peered out were brooding and angry, and he held a greatsword instead of a glaive.

The final man wore a crown with a huge blue stone across the center of the forehead. His armor was very different from the others as well. It consisted of a chain hauberk and a fox-fur cloak covering a heavy leather jacket. Three leather thongs hung from around his neck, one with a claw or fang, another with a circular metal device she had never seen before, and the last was slung with a ring.

Trynne shuddered when she looked up at the man's brooding and handsome face. It was nicked with small scars from a lifetime of fighting. He had a short, close-cropped beard, and his dark hair was a little disheveled and tangled and cropped high on his neck. He had the bearing of a leader and eyes that were so blue they were almost purple. It surprised her how young he was, no more than twenty-five or so—around the same age as his opponent. She felt his Fountain-blessed power raging inside him like an ocean. This was Gahalatine. His presence was unmistakable. But she also sensed that his power did not exceed the combined strength of the Wizrs who were with him. Perhaps that would mean trouble for the young ruler.

"Where is your champion?" Gahalatine asked King Drew. "Where is Owen Kiskaddon?"

She recognized his voice, though it was no longer amplified by magic. He looked stern and serious, as if he expected some sort of duplicity. She was drawn to his face, his bearing. Her insides fluttered with peculiar emotions that rattled her deeply.

"I know not," King Drew said, lowering his blade. The two rulers faced each other on very unequal terms, but each radiated confidence. "He led a raid in the night."

Gahalatine pursed his lips. "I know that. But where is he now? I thought to capture him and win his allegiance. He is a great man, worthy of both respect and honor. He vanished from the midst of the raiding party before my Wizrs could capture him. I thought he must have come here to defend you, but here you are, defenseless. I've been holding my champion in reserve to face him." He gestured to the armored man next to him.

"You are Gahalatine?" King Drew asked.

The man nodded. "I am. I sent one of my advisors, Rucrius, to the palace of Kingfountain to issue my warning." He gestured to the Wizr they had met, but the look he gave Rucrius puzzled and surprised Trynne. Was it disapproval? "I seek to conquer your domain by right of conquest. But there is some trickery afoot." His eyes burned with anger. He raised a fist into the air and the blue stone on his crown glowed. His voice was broadcast across the fields again, but the thunderous words sounded more distant than before.

"Return to your posts. The battle is halted." The order was intended for his men, not for them.

Gahalatine lowered his arm. He looked sternly at King Drew. "If you did not summon Lord Kiskaddon to defend you, then I fear some mischief has befallen him. I had hoped to persuade him to serve me, for I hear that Fountain magic cannot work on him. He cannot be compelled against his will. His was your greatest piece on the Wizr board before I ordered it broken. Although I could defeat you at this moment, it would stain my triumph in dishonor. We will withdraw back to the city we have captured. I permit you to bury your dead. You have my oath that no harm will befall your people for the next twelve months. You were clearly not prepared for this conflict. That is not my fault, of course, but I grant you one year to prepare yourselves. Then we will come again, and I will take the hollow crown from you. Seek out your lost champion. Or find a new one. Until then, farewell, noble king."

♦　♦　♦

The shock of their defeat had permeated the army. Half of the army of Kingfountain lay dead on the field of battle. In contrast, it was one of the most beautiful days imaginable. The sun shone down from above, and a pleasant breeze cooled the air, but it spread the stench of death everywhere.

Trynne wandered listlessly, unable to comprehend the devastation that had befallen them. Never had such an army been so totally overwhelmed. Not since Azinkeep. The shame of the outcome was mirrored in every soldier's countenance. She overheard the soldiers talk as she moved around. Some said that Lord Owen had fled the fields a coward. Others growled angrily that he had been captured by the enemy king and made into a slave.

In the murk of despair, she spied Captain Staeli trudging up the hillside. His chain hood was askew, his face befouled from the battle. He held a glaive, taken from one of his enemies, the tail dragging in the grass.

"Captain," Trynne breathed out, seeing the look of devastation in the man's eyes. He caught sight of her and then sighed with relief.

"So many dead," he said with great sadness.

"What happened, Captain?" Trynne demanded. "You were there. What happened to my father? Did you see him fall?"

Staeli shook his head. "He didn't fall. He . . . vanished. We were riding toward the enemy's lines. All was perfectly quiet and still. It was to be a surprise attack. We waited at the river's edge for all the forces to arrive. He said he would part the river for us, and we could walk to the other side and attack. It happened at just that moment, as we were getting ready to cross. A clap of thunder came from above the fog. I looked up, surprised. When I turned back, his horse was there, but he was gone. He had vanished. That's when they attacked us." Staeli shook his head sorrowfully. "We were surrounded in moments and cut off from the rest of the army. Grand Duke Maxwell came to rescue us and he was cut down. He's dead, my lady. I saw his son fighting over the corpse, mad with rage. That lad . . . he's fearsome. We were all surrounded and fighting back-to-back. Then . . ." He stopped, shrugging. "Then we heard Gahalatine's voice halting the battle. They stopped killing us immediately. They are disciplined. Frightfully so. When a man's blood is up, it's hard to stop. They could have slaughtered us all, but they obeyed their king."

As Captain Staeli spoke, Trynne's eyes widened with horror.

"I might know where he is," she said, fighting a surge of worry. "You didn't see my father with a silver dish? He wasn't the one who poured the water?" It was a great secret, but she knew that storms could be summoned by pouring water from the silver bowl onto the plinth in the grove or anywhere else in the realm. Only the king, her parents, and Myrddin knew that, other than herself.

"Silver dish? I know naught of that," he said. "You told me to stay near him. To safeguard his ring. But he vanished from sight, my lady. He vanished before the battle started."

"Where is Morwenna?" Trynne demanded. "Didn't she go with you too?"

"Aye, she did. She fought alongside us. She kept calling out to your father. It was mayhem, my lady. Utter mayhem." His frown tightened, hard as a walnut shell. "Someone has betrayed us."

"Go find the king," Trynne said, feeling her stomach wrenching with agony. She put her hand on his armored shoulder. "Tell him what you told me. I must go back to Brythonica. Straightaway. I'll come back if I can. I don't think Gahalatine will attack us further. He's . . . he's strangely more honorable than that."

"Aye, my lady," Staeli said. He looked her seriously in the eye and then hefted the glaive. "I'd have been dead myself several times over if not for your training." He gave her a look full of tenderness and appreciation. "Thank ye."

She felt her throat catch at his expression of gratitude. Then she pulled inside herself, uttered the word of power, and clasped onto a series of ley lines that would bring her to the grove.

♦   ♦   ♦

The sun had just risen in Brythonica when Trynne arrived in the grove full of house-sized boulders, hidden deep inside one of the hunting forests. The oak tree with the stream trickling through its roots was full of leaves, acorns, and buds of mistletoe, and birds of all sizes perched in its branches, calling out heartbreakingly poignant melodies. The grove was winter-like, full of crushed hailstones. The magic of the silver bowl had been invoked, although it was still chained to the plinth.

Trynne could see her breath coming out in puffs of mist. The song of the birds was intensely beautiful, but she wished she could silence them. Her boots took a few crunching steps over the icy shards before she stopped, her eyes bulging.

There was blood everywhere. The ice was melting, but the stain stood vividly against the white.

Trynne covered her mouth, feeling light-headed from more than the magic. Her knees were shaking violently.

There, on the ground in the middle of the grove, lay a severed hand.

"No, no, no," she whimpered, dizziness threatening to make her faint.

Taking a few weary steps, she collapsed onto the wintry ground by the hand. It was as pallid as a lump of clay. Her skin crawled with dread as she reached out and touched it. So cold. The wedding band was missing from one of the splayed fingers.

She closed her eyes, unable to bear the sight of it. And then she groped the hand until she touched the press of metal on the ring finger. The invisible ring was still there.

Trynne slid it off the hand and the ring suddenly appeared in her palm. She felt a ripple of Fountain magic well up inside it.

"Papa," she choked, staring down at the ring through her wet lashes.

CHAPTER
TWENTY-NINE

Broken

There were tears in Trynne's eyes as she told the tale of what she had found in the hidden grove. She had not spoken a word about the Battle of Guilme. A hushed silence fell over the solar. King Drew took in a haggard breath, his cheekbone bruised from a buffet he'd taken on his helmet during the battle. Morwenna had brought him directly to the palace before returning to the battlefield to help tend the wounded. The king was stunned, his eyes betraying his despair, but also a spark of hope.

"Then Lord Owen may still be alive," he whispered faintly. He turned to Sinia, who bore her suffering with quiet dignity.

"I don't know," Sinia whispered. "I've seen Gahalatine's army attacking us again. My husband was not seated at the Ring Table. There was someone else in his stead. A knight with a painted face."

Trynne nearly flinched when her mother said the words. She glanced at Genevieve, who returned the look but also said nothing.

"The painted knight," the king said, nodding. "He was there at the battle." He rubbed his mouth, beginning to pace. "No one knows who he is. Some say he hails from Atabyrion." He shrugged. "Lord Iago cannot vouch for that."

Trynne, anxious to cut off that train of thought, interceded. "My lord, there were signs of a struggle in the grove. Muddy boot prints and redwood fronds smashed into the ice. I don't know how many were waiting there to ambush my father. Even with his Fountain magic, he would have been outnumbered and vulnerable. I didn't feel . . . *safe* trying to find a hunter to bring back to the grove. I left it in the condition in which I found it and came to the palace to tell my mother and the queen."

"That was wise," Genevieve said, nodding. "That grove must remain a secret. Even my husband did not tell me he had been there as a child until you shared the story." She looked pointedly at Sinia.

Trynne's mother sighed. "It has been protected by the Montforts for centuries. Owen was the champion of the grove. Marshal Roux was his predecessor. When the magic of the bowl is invoked inside the grove, the champion is summoned to defend it. This has been a great secret. There is only one copy of *The Vulgate* that contains the story of this grove. It is an ancient tale that I read as a child. It is there Myrddin was entrapped by his student, one of my ancestors."

Queen Genevieve arched her eyebrows. "Is Owen trapped there now?"

Sinia shook her head. "Myrddin was trapped when a boulder fell and blocked the entrance to a cave in the rocks. Your husband used the hollow crown to help break that rock after a thousand years. The cave is still there. Empty."

"I searched it myself," Trynne said. "There was evidence of a little camp there. The ashes from a recent fire. Men had hidden in the cave for protection from the hailstorm. My lord, there was a thunderclap . . . I've heard . . . during the battle. Was there not?"

King Drew nodded vigorously. "Indeed there was. It brought back the memories of my childhood. I suspected that it was your father's secret plan to attack his enemies with a storm, but the sleet and hail I expected never came."

"He shared no such plan with me," Sinia said. "Only someone who could use the ley lines could have done it."

"Morwenna?" the queen asked with a tone of suspicion.

The king shook his head. "According to Lord Amrein, she was with Owen the entire time and helped fight the attackers after he disappeared."

"Then it must have been one of the other Wizrs," Sinia said at last. "One who knew the story of the grove."

The pale-haired Rucrius came to Trynne's mind, and anger formed a white-hot ball in her chest.

"We must get to the council," King Drew said. "We must make plans to defend ourselves. Without the assistance of Lord Owen or Myrddin. What happened is a great mystery. Everyone seeks Owen in Brugia, but Trynne's knowledge leads us elsewhere." He tapped his bottom lip. "There's a Fountain-blessed hunter in Dundrennan. He was a lad when I first met him, but he's a man grown now. Carrick. He knew Lord Owen well and is loyal and discreet. He's the one who found my sword in the ice caves. Lady Sinia, I suggest we use him to examine the grove for additional clues. It is a singular place."

"Indeed, my lord," Sinia said with a grateful nod.

Trynne wrestled with her feelings of despair, grief, and hope. She was still perplexed as to why only her father's hand had been left behind. If he had been killed, surely they would have left the corpse behind. It was a sign that he had been taken, not murdered. She could imagine the pain he was suffering. At least he had the raven-marked scabbard on his person.

"Then we shall go to the council," the king said confidently. "Trynne—your assistance has been invaluable. You should be in attendance as well. I know Genny favors your advice." The king gave his wife an apologetic look. "And it seems, my dear, that you were right all along.

With so many losses, so many dead, we will need every able man and woman to defend this realm when Gahalatine's army rouses itself. We will need Oath Maidens. Would that I could snap my finger and summon them into existence." He gave Trynne a sorrowful look. "I wish I had heeded your counsel when you first suggested it."

Trynne felt a flush spread across her cheeks. She bowed her head. "Thank you, my lord."

"Having a man, a king at that, admit that he was wrong is compliment enough," the queen said wryly. "I would like to confer a moment with Trynne. We will join you for supper later. I have some ideas on this subject already."

"Very well," the king said. He proffered the crook of his arm to Trynne's mother in a gallant gesture. Sinia gave Trynne a forced smile that did not reach her sad eyes, then took the king's arm and followed him out of the solar.

Genevieve watched the door swing shut. Her expression changed into one of condolence, and she pulled Trynne into a fierce hug. "My poor dear," she said soothingly, sniffling. "You were at the battle yourself, yet could not speak of it. No one knows but we two and Captain Staeli." She pulled away and took Trynne's hands. "If you had been in Ploemeur, do you think you would have felt the magic of the grove? I could not ask this in front of your mother. She was with me at Kingfountain and did not feel the magic summoning your father. Nor did she have a vision about it. Isn't that strange?"

Trynne shook her head. "My mother cannot control her visions. They are glimpses into the future. But their purpose is to teach her the Fountain's will. If I had been in Ploemeur, I would have gone to the grove immediately. And if I had, I don't know what would have happened. Perhaps I would have been abducted. Two pieces lost instead of one from the Wizr board. The Fountain bade me to protect the king. I knew that's where I needed to be. I thought I could save my father as well, but . . ." She paused, shaking her head.

"Maybe you still *can*," Genevieve said firmly, squeezing Trynne's shoulder. "We will search for him, dearest. Believe that. But for now, we must prepare to defend Kingfountain. My husband told me that the invaders could practically fly. That their ships dwarf ours in size. How did they assemble such a fleet? How did they acquire such strange powers?"

Trynne shook her head. "I don't know. But I know this. It wasn't magic that made those warriors fly. I would have felt it. They are different from us, my lady. What manner of men these people are, I don't know. But I do know that Gahalatine is honorable . . . in the realm of warfare. He could have vanquished us easily. Once he suspected betrayal, he called off the attack. His reputation was more precious to him than a quick victory. He's not an evil man in the manner we supposed. Ambitious, to be sure! But there is so little we know about the Chandigarli. We have only Morwenna's interpretation of them."

Genevieve's eyes narrowed. "Indeed. I think it may be wise to learn more through a different source." She gave Trynne a knowing look. "Would you be willing to go there yourself?"

Trynne could not hold back her smile.

"Let's confer before you leave," Genevieve said. "The council will be convening in several days when the others return safely to Kingfountain. Walk with me." Arm in arm, they left the solar and started toward the council. "My husband plans to invest Prince Elwis as the new Grand Duke of Brugia. He says the man's countenance has changed. He's more subdued now. Less resentful. He's bearing the full brunt of leadership."

"How is your father?" Trynne asked.

"He was grievously wounded in the battle. Of course the surgeons want him to lie on his stomach and heal properly, but he chafes at being so idle. It seems hopeful he will recover."

"Thank the Fountain," Trynne breathed.

Genevieve patted her arm.

◆　◆　◆

A brooding cloud of defeat hung over the gathering of the king's council. There were bruised, puffy cheeks and dark scowls. Trynne spied Fallon slouching in a chair, his leg wrapped in bandages, his look dark and sullen. He waved away a servant offering a drink in annoyance. As Trynne approached the king with the queen, she attracted the gaze of many onlookers.

King Drew was conferring with Lord Amrein at the head of the table. The Espion master had a cut lip, a broken nose, and hadn't shaved in days, which was unusual for him.

"I have every available man searching for the painted knight, my lord," he said. "The first reports came from the Gauntlet of Brugia. No one minded them back then. It was an oddity. The Gauntlet of Occitania was canceled. But several witnesses, myself included, have reported that the painted knight was seen on the hill the eve of the battle. Near your camp, my lord."

"I wonder who it is," the king said with amazement. "We were fortunate he came."

"Indeed, my lord," said Lord Amrein. "Very few had the skills to combat the enemy's weapons. The glaive is not common in these parts. Yet I watched the painted knight fight the Chandigarli with ease. I've never seen the like—not even Lord Owen could fight like that. It's a mystery."

"See to it, Lord Amrein. Find the painted knight. We will need him in the days ahead."

The queen stood by the king's chair and gently touched his shoulder. When he looked up and saw her, he smiled with exhaustion and sadness. Together they both glanced toward the empty chair. The seat Trynne's father had been called to sit in. The chair of the king's defender.

You will sit in that chair, the Fountain whispered to Trynne. *But not yet.*

"My lady," said a voice near her, pulling her attention away from the seat of the Siege Perilous. She was startled to find Prince Elwis at her elbow. He was very tall, wearing the fashions of his realm. A small red slash on his cheek had been stitched shut by a surgeon. His eyes were full of pent-up emotion, a look of intense grief and pain.

She felt a small throb of compassion in her chest. She was about to speak, to offer her condolences, but he started speaking first.

"Please, if you'll allow me," he said in a low, regretful tone. "I am sorry, Lady Tryneowy." He looked down, abashed, then met her gaze again, and she could see that he was roiling with discomfort. "I am sorry about your father. I know the Espion will do their best to find him. But I wanted to personally assure you that if he is somewhere in Brugia, I will do everything in my power to restore him to his rightful place." He swallowed, and she could tell there was more he wished to say, so she remained quiet. "I resented him . . . I'm ashamed to admit it now. He was an honorable man. He came to the defense of Brugia when he was needed most. My kingdom has lost—" His throat seized up as he battled with tears. But he mastered himself, keeping his voice calm and steady. "It is no matter what we lost. We *all* lost much to our enemies. Some have whispered that your father betrayed us. I hold no credence to such tales and will punish any who besmirch his good name. I also apologize for my unkindness toward *you*." He grimaced. "I woefully regret my words to you. And I appreciate the undeserved kindness that you demonstrated to me in Occitania. I am in your debt, and humbly seek your pardon."

She could tell his little speech had been carefully thought over and possibly rehearsed, but it was obvious that it came from his heart. It left her speechless with wonder.

He bowed curtly to her and started to withdraw, but she caught his sleeve. When he winced and flinched with pain, she realized he was concealing a wound in his arm.

"I'm sorry," she apologized, but he waved off the attempt.

"It is nothing, truly," he said, waiting guardedly for her to speak.

"You lost your father, my lord," she said with sympathy. Over the years she had watched Prince Elwis with his father. Grand Duke Maxwell had often been exasperated by his son's vengeful attitude. Perhaps there were some unspoken regrets the young man harbored. "I grieve for your loss. He was a good man."

The young duke gave her a pained smile. "That is kind of you." He glanced around the room as the noise started to subside. "It seems the council is coming to order. I'd best find a place to sit down."

Trynne gave him a polite nod, still reeling with surprise at his humbled demeanor. She felt someone's eyes on her and looked over to see Fallon watching her with wide eyes. He had witnessed the entire exchange and looked chagrined. Trynne gave him a cool look in return and took her seat at the table.

The room settled into silence. Trynne had never had her own seat at the table before, and it felt both unfamiliar and uncomfortable. Silence hung in the air, along with a cloud of despair. So many things had happened in the chamber . . . She wanted to rub her hand along the polished wood of the Ring Table.

King Drew rose and leaned forward, resting his palms on the table. The hollow crown glinted in the torchlight. He cast his gaze around the table.

"My lords and ladies," he began. "I bid welcome to the new members of my council. I recognize Duke Elwis of Brugia, who sits in the seat of his father. I recognize the Lady of Averanche, Tryneowy Kiskaddon." His voice throbbed with emotion as he spoke her title. He hung his head a moment, mastering his own face. The empty seat, the Siege Perilous, sat there like an oversize Wizr piece. "On our wedding day, a few years ago, some of you remember that Lady Sinia arrived rather suddenly." He rubbed his chin, squinting at the memory. "She came bearing news of this terrible tragedy. She had a premonition, of sorts, that our kingdom would be invaded. That her husband would be lost to us. My pain cannot equal hers, but I feel it keenly still. I have known that I would lose my champion, my defender, my *friend*. Now that the bitter dregs are in the cup, I must name another. Gahalatine has given us but a brief reprieve before his engine of war rouses like a tempest. If we continue to fight and squabble amongst ourselves as we hitherto have"—his gaze raked Fallon's face, which went scarlet with mortification—"if we are proud and concerned only for ourselves and not the common well-being"—his next glance was for Elwis, who did not even flinch at the rebuke—"then we will lose all. We have already lost a goodly number of knights, archers, and stalwart soldiers. The number of wounded is nearly beyond counting. Gahalatine's army lost only a tithe in comparison. We cannot win this forthcoming contest unless we fight with all of our strength, all of our will, all of our ingenuity. In Ceredigion, we have a history of facing down larger forces than what we find ourselves up against now. I do not fear their numbers. I fear our own weakness more."

It was a powerful speech, and Trynne felt her soul moved at his words. It was a rebuke, but a loving one. He was vulnerable, for he stood to lose the most, but everyone sitting at that table would be supplanted by one of Gahalatine's governors if the Chandigarli won the day.

The king clenched his fists and planted his knuckles on the table. "I was given counsel by Lady Trynne and my queen that I was too hesitant to implement. It has long been the culture of our realms to forbid women the right to bear arms and to train to use them. In the distant past, according to Myrddin, there were times when men and women fought alongside each other when the need was dire. These warriors were called Oath Maidens. My queen has taken on the responsibility to arm and train any maiden who wishes to fight in defense of Kingfountain. She has the authority to call her own captains. With so many of our young men bruised and slain, we must use every resource to defend ourselves. And when the year is nearly expired, I will summon all the warriors of the realm to the Gauntlet of Kingfountain. There is no time left for local competitions. All will gain the chance to earn this seat—the Siege Perilous. From the victors, I will choose a new champion. Be they man *or* maid. I will brook no argument against this aim. This is my command. See that it is done."

After he had issued the command, the Ring Table began to thrum and vibrate. The sound of the Fountain began to murmur around the gathering, and the grooves of the table, the inner rings of the massive tree trunk, began to glow softly. A feeling of power radiated from the ancient wood.

King Drew appeared to be startled by the sudden manifestation. The looks on the faces of everyone in the room were full of astonishment. Fallon's mother and the queen beamed with triumph. Many looked more uncomfortable with the king's pronouncement. Some of the men were staring aghast at the suggestion. Severn looked disdainful, but Elwis was merely subdued. He stared from the table to Trynne with deep concentration, and it made her uncomfortable to be stared at so. Fallon, on the other hand, looked grave as he shook his head and muttered something under his breath to his mother, who swatted his arm in annoyance.

And then Trynne caught sight of Morwenna standing near the doors leading to the secret passageways. She was surprised the king's poisoner didn't look pleased. In fact, her look was unguarded for once, and she seemed furious.

CHAPTER THIRTY

Unrequited

The magnolia petals had all fallen, save only a few that still stubbornly hung on to the branches. As Trynne knelt in the grass, staring up at them, she clung to the silent hope that her father still lived. Visions of his severed hand haunted the shadows in her mind both day and night. It was time to return to Ploemeur with her mother—and then Averanche. Genevieve had promised the first girls would arrive soon for their training.

It was not possible to describe the feelings in her heart. What would have happened if she had not followed the Fountain's direction before the battle? Would it have made a difference for her father if she had appeared in the grove with her magic and two swords? She had to trust that the Fountain had used her for the best possible good, even if that good was devastating to her personally. She had kept the oath she had sworn before Myrddin; she had obeyed the Fountain's will. So why did it hurt so much?

A breeze teased through her hair and the branches of the magnolia trees, carrying the sweet scent of the blooms. She shut her eyes, trying to will away the pain and the longing to see her father. Part of her had been ripped away. It was a wound of the heart, and it would never fully heal. If only she knew what had become of him, whether she would ever see him again. Eyes pressed closed, she listened for the faint stirrings of the Fountain. She hoped for something, a message—a sign.

Nothing came except the sound of someone approaching in the grass.

Disappointment battered her. She had hoped to find solace in her favorite spot at the palace, but even that balm was being denied to her. Opening her eyes, she glanced over her shoulder and saw Fallon Llewellyn striding toward her.

He looked angry.

Not now, she thought in despair. *Not another burden.*

She brushed the strands of grass she'd plucked from her lap and then rose quickly. If she was on her knees when he arrived, he would tower over her.

There was no preamble of teasing from him this time. It came out as an accusation.

"You *knew*, didn't you? About your father. That was the secret you wouldn't tell me."

"I was forbidden to tell *anyone*," she answered in misery. She did not want to have that conversation with him. It was too painful, and the fierce and wounded look in his eyes only added to her agony.

She started to walk away, determined to reach the chapel fountain and return to her lands. There, she would have the slender comfort of grieving with her family. Fallon snatched at her sleeve and then gripped her arm. The warrior in her was tempted to heave him face-first onto the ground. She tensed, barely able to suppress the urge to humiliate him.

"Leaving already?" he challenged.

"I don't want to argue with you, Fallon. Please let me go."

"Not until I've said my piece."

It tortured her to know she held secrets from him still. He was ready to complain about the least of them. She pressed her eyes with her free hand—he still gripped her arm. The wind rustled the branches again, and one of the magnolia buds broke loose and spun in a circle on its way down to the lawn. It was painful to watch it and think of that long-ago day they'd played so carelessly in that very grove.

"Say your piece, then," she muttered darkly, and shook her arm free of his hold.

Fallon looked very unstable at that moment. He was too emotional. So was she. It was an ill omen.

"You should have told me," he said. "My parents kept me in the dark. So did my own sister. But you . . . I thought we could trust one another. I thought you would have shared the truth before it happened. I was there at Guilme, Trynne! I might have prevented it if I'd known!"

"How?" she snapped. "What could you have done that would have helped? My mother had a vision of this long ago. She's been carrying this grief for years. And so have I. I wasn't at liberty to tell you, Fallon. It would have broken the king's trust. It would have broken my father's."

His forehead was wrinkled with agitation. He pinched the bridge of his nose with his fingers, muttering to himself. "There is some treachery afoot in the kingdom, Trynne. I warned you of it before. The men in silver masks."

She had to grit her teeth to prevent herself from accusing him of being one. She still had the cloak and mask she had taken from his tent the eve of the battle. How could she fully trust his words? He was scheming and unreliable, cavorting with Morwenna while trying to win Trynne's trust. Or was he faithful to his sister, to King Drew, to *her*. He was like a glob of quicksilver, always darting away when poked.

"My father knew of them," she said passionately, resisting the urge to hit him. "Lord Amrein knows. If you have information that would help, say it! Stop tottering between sides, Fallon."

"I'm not tottering between sides!" he said, nearly shouting. "I am loyal to the king. To my sister. There is nothing I could be offered that would tempt me to break my allegiance. I want to be useful. I want to prove that I can do *more*." His voice throbbed with pent-up

275

disappointment and rancor. He stepped closer to her. "I loved your father. Maybe not as much as you do. But I always respected and admired him. I would wheedle my mother to tell stories of their child-hood adventures." He had a half smile as the memories came. Then he looked pointedly at her. "We grew up together, Trynne. I loved those years in Ploemeur. Walking on the beach of sea glass with you. Finding pies and other delights to share while we rode the lift up the mountain to the castle."

His voice dropped off suddenly, becoming husky. "I was there the night Dragan hurt you." He gently pressed his thumb to the edge of her mouth, and she saw tears dance in his eyes. His hand lingered there, his touch so soft and tender. It made her feel dizzy, and she realized he was about to say something, to commit himself in a way that would forever alter their relationship.

"I must go," she said, her voice shaking.

"You must hear me out," he insisted.

"I . . . I don't think—"

He stopped her words with a kiss that startled her. She did not reciprocate it, but she could not help but feel it burn all the way down to her toes.

His fingers had slid into the nest of her short hair, behind her neck. He pulled back, a devious smile on his mouth. "I've wanted to do that for a long time."

Part of her wanted to fling herself into his arms—to cry, sob, and kiss him back. She was stunned, off balance.

"You are too reckless," she said, shaking her head. She brushed her wrist against her mouth, but it could not remove the memory of the kiss that lingered there. Her blood raced, her heart was pounding in her ears, making her almost abandon all reason.

"I am," he said with a curt laugh. "Too much like my father, I sup-pose. He stole a kiss from my mother before she left Atabyrion the first time. It was his way of claiming her." He raised his eyebrows archly.

"Fallon," she said, shaking her head, her heart bursting with pain. He couldn't be hers, no matter how much she wanted him. No, she could never forget that her mother had seen her wed someone else in her vision. Trynne had made an oath to follow the Fountain's will.

"Trynne, I failed to protect you that night. I went off in search of pies! You don't know . . . you cannot know how much I have regretted that choice to leave you alone. If only I had been less selfish. If I had been with you, perhaps I could have thwarted his attack."

"I don't think so," she said.

"Would you be quiet a moment?" he said, growing a little exasperated. He took her hands in his warm, inviting grip, and the desire to let him hold her, to let him speak, warred with the certainty that this could not be. "Now your father is gone. Some whisper he is dead. Others say he betrayed us, which we both know is an utter falsehood. But he was the most powerful lord of Ceredigion. He was your chief protector. Your father. You are now the Lady of Averanche. With your father gone, you are an even more valuable heiress. There are many men, even those as dense as a brick like *Elwis*, who will overlook your childhood injury now and seek you out as a bride. Trynne, your smile has never bothered me. In fact, I think it makes you especially lovely. What I'm trying to say, and mussing up badly, is that I've always seen myself as your protector. I had thought to wait until we were both a little older and on my part, at least, more mature—you've already surpassed me there—but what happened to your father has hastened the intent I've always had."

His eyes burned into hers. "I want to be yours, Tryneowy Kiskaddon. And I want you always to be mine. Let there be no confusion between us. No more secrets. I hereby plight you my troth."

Her mouth was so dry she felt like choking. Her heart buzzed with a thousand giddy emotions. Yet her head felt doubt, insecurity, and worry. She closed her eyes, wishing briefly that perhaps this was only a vision, a dream—a nightmare to be awakened from. Part of her had instinctively felt that he was just rash enough to promise to marry her.

It flattered her immensely. There was a large part of her that still yearned to say yes. Her heart wanted her to. But her head prevailed. She knew she could not.

When she opened her eyes, she felt she was breathing too fast. It would hurt them both, but it needed to be said.

"I cannot marry you, Fallon Llewellyn," she said in a strong, clear voice.

His eyes, so eager and hopeful, blinked with shock. "What?" he asked with a confused chuckle.

She shook her head no resolutely, feeling the ripping tugs on her heart even more. "I should have left earlier," she said with a half-choking sigh. "I cannot marry you."

The transformation of his face showed she had caught him utterly off guard. That he had been expecting a positive response.

"Oh, Fallon . . . you have always been the most impetuous, exasperating young man I know! Why speak of love now, when the kingdom is so fragile? I cannot think about love yet. I don't *want* to think about love yet." She struggled to find the right words. "I just wanted to go on as we've always been, as dear, dear friends."

"And that is all I am to you? A *friend*?" His tone showed his disbelief.

"Fallon, this isn't the time—"

"This absolutely *is* the time! I love you, Trynne. Can I speak it any plainer? Do you not care for me as well?"

He had taken things too far, like a boat rushing down the current toward the falls. There was no going back now. She knew from her mother's vision that she wouldn't marry him. She wanted to stop the wreckage she knew was coming.

Her cheeks were so hot. "You have been a dear friend to me, but I cannot marry you."

He gripped both of her arms, not threateningly, but as if he were drowning in misery. "Do you *love* me . . . or not? Is there someone else you care for instead? Tell me the truth, Trynne. I must know, or I cannot bear it. Tell me!"

Trynne didn't want to tell him, knowing it would break not only her heart but his as well. But all his masks had been stripped away, at least in that moment. The cocoon began to rip and tear. The secret wriggled free.

She hung her head. "Yes," she whispered, her voice thick with tears. "Yes, I love you, Fallon. I always have. But please don't make me say that again. I love you so much it causes me pain because I can't be with you the way I desire to!" She looked into his eyes then, pleading with him to understand and believe her. "My mother had a vision about my marriage. And it was not with you. I have been tormented by that vision ever since she shared it with me. My heart has been breaking since then, and it has not stopped. Even now, my heart doesn't want to accept it, but I have seen time and time again the truth of my mother's visions. They come from the Fountain. And as hard as it has been for me personally, I *know* I must follow it."

His hands dropped from her arms as he stared at her in wild shock, the realization hitting him like a sledge.

She rallied her courage. "But, Fallon, that is not the only reason I must reject you. It gives me great pain to tell you this, but I do not trust you. Not fully. There are events happening underground, things that you yourself have hinted at. The secrets between us are not only mine. I want to trust you, but you've shaken my faith in you. For so long you've hungered for glory. Know you not that trust is earned instance by instance, moment by moment? And it can be broken so easily. You flirt with danger like it means nothing." She took a deep breath and let it out. "You are untrustworthy, Fallon. It pains me to say it, but I *couldn't* marry someone who treats his integrity so casually."

His look changed to one of outrage in an instant. "You have no ken what I have done to protect my brother-in-law the king. None at all. One day you'll regret saying that you did not trust me."

"Think on what I've told you," she pleaded miserably. "I did not mean any unkindness by it. Our parents once loved each other." Her voice throbbed with grief. "Perhaps we are doomed to repeat the same painful love. If so, we should both look to them as an example. Our lives, even if they must be spent apart, will turn out better than how it feels right now."

She tried to reach for his arm, to comfort him with her touch, but he brushed her hand aside as if it would burn him.

"I can never accept that!" he said in anguish. The look in his eyes showed the depth of how much she'd hurt him. He was pale, his humor slit open and spilled. "I can't believe that you and I are meant to repeat their story. We are different."

Without another word, he whirled and stormed away from her, trampling the grass with his stride. He stalked off quickly, vanishing from the garden in moments.

She watched him go, and once he was gone, she finally released the tears that were lingering on her lashes. The sobs hurt, but there was a feeling of profound relief too, like drawing a sharp splinter trapped beneath the skin. She might have lost Fallon's love and his friendship forever. It was possible his grief would drive him to someone else, someone like Morwenna, in retaliation. She had to prepare herself for such a possibility. But she believed she had done the right thing, despite how broken she felt.

She decided she could never go back into that garden again.

◆　◆　◆

Trynne and her mother stood on the beach full of sea glass, watching the sun set. Trynne held her own slippers as well as her mother's while Gannon knelt in the moist sand, sorting the different colors of pebbled glass as the breeze tousled his hair. The smell of the air was delicious and fragrant, a soothing balm. She had found her mother's slippers at the foot of the steps leading down from the rock wall. It was her mother's place of solitude and comfort. But it was also full of ghosts.

"Did I do the right thing in *how* I rejected him?" Trynne asked her mother, giving her a sidelong look.

Sinia smiled as she put her arm around Trynne's back and squeezed her shoulders. She kissed Trynne's hair. "Most people are afraid to tell others the truth about their foibles and weaknesses. We fear to offend, and for good reason. Most people are so easily offended. But you did the right thing, Tryneowy. And I'm proud of you. Fallon needed to hear it, even if he didn't want to."

Trynne put her arms around her mother's waist and pressed her cheek against her bosom. "Men prefer to be flattered, I think."

Sinia laughed softly. "'Tis true. But people generally despise where they flatter. And I don't think you despise Fallon."

"Not at all," Trynne said. "He probably despises me now. But someone needed to tell him the truth about himself."

"Indeed. Your father and I have had many discussions about this," she said as they enjoyed the sound of the crashing surf. "He was always thinking about discernment because of Ankarette, you know. How can you learn to trust someone? We all have weaknesses. Some we know about ourselves, and they are obvious to others too. Then we have faults that we are blind to ourselves, but are plain to everyone else. Some weaknesses we deliberately conceal from others. But the most rare are the ones that are both invisible to us *and* to others. Those we are *blind* to. They may be our greatest weakness of all."

Trynne turned her head and looked up at her mother. "But how can you find out about those, Mother? I've never thought of that before."

Sinia stared at the sea, her gaze a little distant. "Your father said these were the greatest threat to happiness. The blind weaknesses. We agreed when we first wed that we would be honest and helpful to each other. That we'd help each other learn to see our own weaknesses. Like me forgetting my shoes," she added with a tender smile. "But there is only one way we can ever discover the blind ones."

"How, then?" Trynne asked hopefully.

"Actually, it was Myrddin who helped us get to the answer. Long ago. Sometimes we can learn about them from the Fountain. Not in whispers. But by circumstances we face. Those circumstances reveal the weakness we never knew we had."

Sinia smiled once more, gazing at the gray-green horizon. "And then we are no longer blind to them."

◆　　◆　　◆

Trynne swung the glaive high, and Captain Staeli caught it, jammed it down, and followed through with a knife toward her ribs. She twisted, trapping his arm, but he levered her backward, nearly making her fall. His counter was perfectly timed.

She released his hold and stepped back, feeling the sweat streak down her cheeks. Her training clothes were sodden from their lengthy practice. She twirled the glaive around as he watched her movement, preparing himself for her attack.

"Well done, Captain. This weapon can strike from either end. Be ready."

"I've seen well enough what it can do," he grunted, his eyes intense and focused.

The door of the training yard creaked open and Farnes limped into the yard with the help of a walking staff. Trynne stilled her weapon and straightened, turning to face her herald as she saw he had come with news.

"My lady," Farnes said in his wheezy voice. "Several ladies have arrived at the castle. Some are young. Others are much older. The queen sent them. You mentioned, when you returned, that you were expecting some . . . visitors?"

Trynne gave him a broken smile. "I am. Let them come and see."

♦   ♦   ♦

Sometimes we put walls up not to keep people out, but to see who cares enough to break them down.

Myrddin

♦   ♦   ♦

EPILOGUE

The Hidden Vulgate

Morwenna Argentine smoothed her hand across the ancient page of the wrinkled vellum, staring at the marks and runes and feeling the overwhelming giddiness that always came when she read from it. The book was ancient, bound in fraying leather with sigils and wards on the cracked spine. Whoever had created it had been a master Wizr, one who had lived a very long life. It was a compendium of the words of power, what they did, and how they were invoked. It was a book of intrigue, of subtlety, of the machinations of power. It should never have been created. And yet it was hers.

She still remembered the day she had discovered it in the hidden vaults of the poisoner school in Pisan. It was the school's deepest secret, and no one had really understood its significance until Morwenna came along. Only the masters of the school knew of it. But she was good at ferreting out secrets. And with the book, she had discovered an entirely new world. The book had probably been stolen again and again over the ages. It was *The Hidden Vulgate*. The keeper of secrets. The lore of the Wizrs. Her mastery of the craft had seemed miraculous to everyone else, but with the book, she knew information it would have taken ten lifetimes to acquire piecemeal.

Her sly smile turned into an angry frown. Yet despite all her knowledge, all her skill at intrigue, events had wobbled out of control at Guilme. The wagon cart of her destiny had crashed. She was still furious about it. So close—she had come so close to achieving her aim!

She sensed Fountain magic coming up the stairs of the poisoner's tower. With a thought and a wave of her hand, the book vanished. It was still there, but it was invisible and insubstantial. She rose from the chair and walked to the window, gazing down at the autumn-shrouded grounds of Kingfountain from its lofty spire. It was the highest tower in the palace. If she willed it, she could cause storms to rage down on the inhabitants. The thought made her feel smug, but she silenced it. She was not invulnerable yet. Another threat loomed. Another person she had to destroy.

The door of the tower was locked, of course, but no lock was a match for Dragan.

The thief carefully opened it and stepped inside, then shut it quietly behind himself. The illusion of invisibility sloughed off him like hunks of snow. He stood at the doorway, eyeing her with satisfaction.

"Do you have the ring?" Morwenna asked, turning around and facing him.

"I do indeed, my lady," Dragan said slyly. "It wez worth fifty thousand before, but I'm sure it is worth more now. Interest, sez I."

"You know I despise your disguise as an illiterate," Morwenna said. "You play the role so often I think you've forgotten who you truly are. Or where you come from."

Dragan shrugged noncommittally. "How much is it worth to you, my dear?"

"A king's ransom, certainly," Morwenna said with a hint of mockery. "Let me see it."

"I knew you'd be anxious, my love," Dragan said. He made a wave of his hand, a parlor trick really, and a gold ring seemed to appear from behind his earlobe. "This is the wedding band," he said with a growl of disgust. "On the left hand."

"Useless, of course," Morwenna said, waiting in anticipation.

"Aye, and then here is the other," he continued with a flourish, producing another ring with his other hand. "This one I couldn't see until I tugged it off. This be the one you're truly wanting."

Morwenna gazed hungrily at it. "Oh yes, that's the one. You left the decoy back in the grove?"

"I did. A hand with it as . . . a treat."

"That's macabre."

"If it pleases my lady to think so," he said with a bow. Then he wrinkled his brow with a little show of ferocity. "I thought Kiskaddon's *treasure* was going to come. His daughter. I had hoped to murder her in front of him. I still owe him *that* pleasure."

"I thought she would as well," Morwenna said and then shrugged. "We often want things that do not happen. I had intended to be betrothed to Gahalatine by this point. Now I must wait a year because of foolish honor." She was still burning with anger because of it. "You'll get your chance, Dragan. As will I."

"So shall I hold on to this ring, then?" Dragan said with a mocking smile. "For a year? I be thinking you'll want it now regardless."

"Oh, I want it," Morwenna said with a dark smile. "And you will get what you were promised now or later. The ransom. The position. The honor."

Dragan's eyes narrowed with a look of cruelty and desire. "No laws. No rules."

"None at all. The kingdom you wish for already exists. You will be one of its lords. A mighty one."

Dragan's grin was horrifying. "I'll wait for it a bit longer," he said. "And I'll be keeping this until I get it." He waggled the ring at her. "I put the cursed ring on the hand instead. Who do you think will wear it?"

Morwenna shrugged. "I don't really care. I know you'll keep that safe until I come asking for it."

"Where *did* you hide Kiskaddon, my love?" Dragan grinned.

Morwenna raised her eyebrows mockingly. "You mean you don't remember?"

The thief blinked at her, startled. "Remember?"

In her mind's eye, she saw the oak tree thick with leaves and mistletoe with water trickling from its roots by the plinth and silver bowl. The original story was in her ancient copy of *The Hidden Vulgate*. She had learned of it in her first month at the poisoner school. She had learned so much after finding that vellum tome. Sometimes she fancied the book was alive.

Morwenna gave him a cunning look as she flexed her hand, feeling once again the invisible ring that was already around her finger.

AUTHOR'S NOTE

When I wrote in my note at the end of *The King's Traitor*, I mentioned that I thought the children of these main characters needed a turn on stage. I saw more light farther down the tunnel. I've really enjoyed respinning obscure Arthurian legends into this new world. The famous Round Table of Camelot is the inspiration behind the prominent Ring Table in this book. But the idea that really ignited my imagination had to do with the character of Sir Lancelot du Lac. He was the most famous and often mysterious of the knights of the Round Table. And the thought that struck me was, What if Lancelot were a girl?

Once you tip an idea over on its head, all sorts of offshoot ideas come into play. I needed a heroine, someone who was Owen and Sinia's daughter. She needed a weakness. She needed someone to love who couldn't or shouldn't love her back. The name of her character came to me as I was listening to Kate Rudd's narration of *The Queen's Poisoner* and it struck me how likely it was Owen would want to name his child after the woman who had saved his life. It all worked.

But Trynne's character is not based on a legend. She is based on a young woman whom my wife and I have known for many years. A young woman who, through a freak accident, developed Bell's palsy as a child. Her resiliency and courage through this trial has been a source of inspiration for me and many others. She is currently serving as a

Spanish-speaking missionary for my church in Washington, DC, and won't read this note until after she returns home again.

The world has many people who are examples and inspirations to me. And so I dedicated this book to one of them.

ACKNOWLEDGMENTS

My editor, Jason Kirk, always encourages me to raise the stakes. After sending him the pitch for this new series, he wrote me some very encouraging words and helped champion this idea to get it to you. There are many others who play a role in my process. I'd like to thank my sister Emily, who nearly had panic attacks each week waiting for the next installment to arrive. I'd also like to thank my wife, Gina, for helping me perfect the final scene between Trynne and Fallon. Her suggestions definitely improved it. Also, thanks to my wonderful early readers: Robin, Shannon, Karen, Travis, and Sunil. And to the amazing team at Amazon Publishing and my editors for their support: Jason Kirk, Courtney Miller, Britt Rodgers, Angela Polidoro, and Wanda Zimba. Thank you all!

ABOUT THE AUTHOR

Photo © 2016 by Mica Sloan

Wall Street Journal bestselling author Jeff Wheeler took an early retirement from his career at Intel in 2014 to write full-time. He is, most importantly, a husband and father, and a devout member of his church. He is occasionally spotted roaming among the oak trees and granite boulders in the hills of California or in any number of the state's majestic redwood groves. He is the founder of *Deep Magic: The E-zine of Clean Fantasy and Science Fiction* (www.deepmagic.co), a bimonthly e-zine featuring amazing short stories by established and new writers, as well as interviews and articles about the craft of writing.